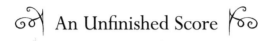 An Unfinished Score

An Unfinished Score

Elise Blackwell

UNBRIDLED BOOKS

BLACKWELL ELISE

This is a work of fiction. The names, characters, places and incidents are either the product of the author's imagination or are used fictitiously, and any resemblance to actual persons living or dead, business establishments, events, or locales is entirely coincidental.

Unbridled Books

Copyright © 2010 by Elise Blackwell

All rights reserved. This book, or parts thereof, may not be reproduced in any form without permission.

Library of Congress Cataloging-in-Publication Data

Blackwell, Elise, 1964–
An unfinished score / Elise Blackwell.
p. cm.
ISBN 978-1-936071-66-1
1. Musicians—Fiction.   2. Adultery—Fiction.   I. Title.
PS3602.L3257U55 2010
813'.6—dc22
2009053805

1   3   5   7   9   10   8   6   4   2

Book Design by SH ▪ CV

First Printing

For Meredith Blackwell

I. Doloroso

One

She hears the words on the radio. It is the radio that announces her lover's death. His is not a household name, not in most households, but he happens to be the most famous person on the plane that went down. The plane's wreckage, strewn across Indiana farmland, is being examined for clues. Crews search for the voice recorder, the black box that holds the secret of two hundred seventy-one deaths. *Two hundred seventy, plus one.*

Suzanne's rib cage shudders—a piano whose keys are struck all at once—yet she does not cry. She does not cry, but only closes her eyes and presses her palms flat on the cool counter. None of the facts of Alex's life suggests that it ends in a soybean field.

At the dining room table, playing a board game and separated from her by the counter on which she works, sit the other members of her household, a household in which Alex's name at least rings a bell. Her husband's dice clack against the wood; her best friend sighs as her game piece is sent back to start; Adele's hands clap three times.

"Starting over isn't all bad," Ben says, and Petra does not respond.

Suzanne lifts onto her toes to search the high cabinet for the olive oil, her hand grabbing only the air the bottle usually occupies. She spies it on the counter, where she obviously set it earlier. It has been right in front of her all along. She minces the cloves of garlic that she peeled before she knew her lover was dead, heats oil in a wide skillet, salts a pot of roiling water. The simple sounds of knife on wood, of water rising to slow boil, of onion sizzling become the distinct tones of grief.

If she lives, this will be how: moment to moment, task by task, left foot then right, breathing in then out. An eternal present in which every sound is loud. This is something she should be good at, if anyone can be. For four years she has practiced pretending that everything is fine, that she is what she seems to be.

Ben, who has been listening to the broadcast, who has heard the honey-voiced announcement, says from the table, "That's sad. Don't we have a couple of his recordings?"

"I think so. Chicago Symphony playing Brahms's Double Concerto and some other stuff." Suzanne presses her voice flat, passing for normal. "I played under him in St. Louis that time, right before I moved to the quartet."

"Why is death always sad?" Petra says. "I mean, wasn't he a total asshole, even for a conductor?"

"I kind of liked him." Suzanne shakes water loose from the greens, tries to dry her hands on the oily dishcloth. *Moment by moment, left foot, right foot, breathe.* "Can you clear the table after the next round of turns? Dinner's almost ready." She breathes in and out again, short on oxygen, lungs shallow and on the edge of panic. "Such as it is." A sputtered almost joke.

While Petra and Adele pack away the game, Ben sets out white plates. His form contradicts the domestic setting: his strong forearms bared by rolled-up sleeves, flexing as he folds the cheap paper napkins on the diagonal.

Adele signs something, and Petra interprets for Ben: "She says she's never seen you do that before—fold the napkins. Usually you just toss them out. She says they look like sails."

Ben spells *party* letter by letter, but he knows the sign for *hats*. Adele claps and makes one of her unconscious noises, a chirp of delight.

Suzanne watches them, grateful that they are safe on the ground yet also afraid of their emotional compasses, each tricky in its different way, each seeming to point at her all the time as though she is true north.

Ben's absorption with fact and music rarely extends to interest in the breathing world, and never outside their small, odd family. It is a distance that feels studied, as though he made a decision in some formative year not to be touched by other people. He shields his emotional barometer so well that even Suzanne and Petra often take it for an absence, for some hole in the fabric of his nature, and their surprise borders on fright when he names some human truth, extracting the insight from his emotional hollow like a magician pulls a ribbon from the thin air.

Petra's moods slide across her face all day—intense, shifting, and mostly short-lived. They rule her though she cannot name them, yet she easily measures the feelings of others, taking the pulse of one person or an entire room, if only so she'll know whom she can make angry and when to run the other way.

Yet it is Adele Suzanne most fears. Adele's emotional compass is keen because she is still a child—no one spots a liar faster than a smart child— and unrelenting because she must watch people closely or she will lose the world.

Suzanne turns to drain the pasta, hot streaks of steam pelting the side of her neck and face.

Ben does not set out wineglasses, so Suzanne does not uncork the bottle she picked up earlier, reading labels against price tags, the sun filtering through the store's filmy window warm on the back of her neck, the clerk watching her with slight interest. She does not open the wine she chose before she knew her lover was dead. Before he was dead, or at the moment he died? The radio has not said what time the plane dropped from the sky.

"Like a stone in water." The witness voices an accent so Midwestern that it sounds Southern. Suzanne turns the dial, clicks off the cheap radio. Without the word *survivor*, and there isn't one, the details can do her no good tonight.

Suzanne distributes water glasses, and they take their usual seats around the food. Adele lifts her glass, leaving behind a wet circle she traces with a fingertip. She looks at the food, at each of them. Had they been a household of three, which for a while it seemed they might be, family dinners would have been shaped by sound. Rising or falling or stalled, but always sound or its absence. But Ben and Suzanne's baby did not arrive, and after Petra and Adele made them a quartet, they worked to make a world defined by sight, touch, smell, taste rather than by sound and not-sound.

In their deep concern for Adele—the child who never turned to Petra's violin, who never winced at sudden noise, the child with wide eyes but only a small seal of a mouth—the three musicians do the best they can. Suzanne has trained her eyes and hands to move with some fluency. Now that Adele can follow the shapes and motions of lips, Suzanne speaks slowly and faces her squarely. Of course none of their hands are so nimble in language as Adele's. The swift precision of hers is that of a conductor who knows the music so well that he does not use a score.

Suzanne watches Adele's fingers through dinner, sometimes forgetting to answer, forgetting to mouth or sign, "Yes, I had a good day, too." She is thinking of Alex's hands at work, and that today feels like the worst day of her life.

Petra carries the conversation with Adele, chatting away like an older sister, asking Suzanne if Adele can have soda with dinner, as though it is Suzanne and not Petra who is the mother. Suzanne does what Petra wants her to do: she says no for her.

Away from her violin Petra's long fingers lack the speed and clean sweeps of her daughter's, but they share their exuberance, the beguiling lack of self-consciousness. They move without her watching them, like Suzanne's fingers when they press and release the strings of her viola but at no other time. Suzanne envies this fundamental honesty, this fluency in a speech not yet divorced from action and feeling by time and intent. For all her faults, Petra doesn't lie. She says she doesn't have to, an advantage of not giving a flying fuck what other people think. Suzanne wonders what it is to lie in gesture, whether it is easier to detect deception in a first or second language, in spoken or signed speech. *Hands caught in the act.* She folds hers in her lap, resting from eating the food she cannot quite taste.

She remembers to ask Ben about his work. He is collaborating on a composition with a man who is both a mathematics professor and on the adjunct music faculty, and they are arranging it for a small orchestra.

Ben nods, stabbing tubes of pasta. "We decided to cut the faux-scherzo."

"Too obscure? The joke that isn't?"

His hair, recently grown out from a self-inflicted haircut, flops side to side as he eats. He looks at Suzanne as though there is food on her face, more amused than annoyed but at least a little annoyed. "I argued that it pandered, and Kazuo agreed. The whole point of this staging, of using his contacts to get this performed for an audience, is to create an uncompromised piece."

"No such thing!" says Petra.

Ben ignores her. "I want the listener to have a distilled experience, something pure."

The listener. Suzanne pictures Richardson Auditorium one-third full: small clumps of math professors, music students, the odd mother taking a too-young child for a little culture after church, widows and widowers with the small hope of meeting one another and nothing better to do on a Sunday afternoon. Empty seats divide them.

She swipes her mouth with her napkin. "To experience the beauty of music intellectually, stripped of emotion," she says, a refrain from one of Ben's oft-spoken theorems.

Widows with nothing better to do. The thought recurs, means something new in its second iteration. Alex's wife—now a widow. Her carotid arteries tense, as though there is too much blood in her body, and her pulse is all she can feel.

Adele's eyes are fixed on Suzanne's mouth, trying to read her words. Petra's stare is about something else. In these faces she loves, Suzanne sees only danger. Her head feels heavy, engorged with grief beginning to swell.

Ben again shakes his head, hard, caring so obviously that his body discloses his passion. It is how they used to feel about the music—and each other—all the time, even back when they were students, when they were only posing as musicians and adults, rehearsing the people they wanted to be.

Now sarcasm sharpens his laugh. "Not stripped of emotion. Without emotional interference. No directions in the first place—no *agitato*, no *appassionato*, no *doloroso*—just the sublime."

"Isn't the sublime emotional?" Petra asks.

Suzanne closes her eyes and sees Alex. She opens them because if she thinks about Alex she will break like a glass shattered by perfect high pitch.

She concentrates on what is being said at the table, tries to close the distance fast opening between her and where she sits. Even her plate seems far away, Petra's voice oddly distant. When Ben launches into his long answer, his voice comes to Suzanne as if through a tunnel.

She knows his premiere will have three reviews. The local paper will send a cheerleader who knows nothing about music and will write up something sweet with the assistance of a music dictionary, a thesaurus, and the photocopied program. A more expensively educated and stealthy presence from the *Times* or the *Inquirer* will yield a scathing piece that neglects the composition itself in a jeremiad against the off-to-sea, out-to-lunch academy and its impenetrable, navel-gazing, masturbatory self-indulgences. The reviewer will use some of these very words.

The third review will be written by one of those several professors who knock between music and mathematics departments—a friend or admirer or enemy or former lover or teacher or student of Kazuo. It will appear, months later, in a journal carried by Princeton's Fireside Library but not by the libraries of universities with less funding and smaller collections. The review will be positive or negative or—most likely—mixed, but it will be dense and detailed, and Ben will pronounce that at least the reviewer understood what he and Kazuo were seeking, that the reviewer *got it*.

"You can call it Subliminal," Suzanne says.

Though he rarely joked himself, Alex always smiled at her silly puns, and the thought of his smile constricts her throat even to air. When it releases, she hears herself gasp, though only Adele looks up as though she has heard the sound of Suzanne desperate for oxygen.

"You know it can't be titled," Ben says, his voice like salt, the last of his amusement evaporated.

After dinner the evening pulls long like elastic, and Suzanne is relieved to cross the stretched time, moment by quivering moment, left foot then right. She volunteers to make Adele's school lunch while Adele and Petra withdraw to their part of the house—two bedrooms linked by a bath—for their nighttime rituals. She makes the sandwich, puts dried apple slices in a plastic bag, tucks a vitamin in a paper napkin, and stows the lunch in the refrigerator. She reminds herself, as she has promised herself she would, that Adele is not her child.

"I'm going to stay up and read a bit," she says when Ben turns in early. The lines traversing his forehead hold hurt, or maybe she imagines this. "We'll spend some time this weekend." She bends her mouth in a curve that is almost a smile.

Both times that he asked, once early in the affair and once two years in, Suzanne told Alex that she made love to her husband only rarely and when unavoidable. But that was not true. Sometimes *unavoidable* means preventing pain in another, or loneliness in yourself. Sometimes *unavoidable* means doing what someone else wants because you are the kind of person who does what others want you to do. Sometimes unavoidable means only your own generalized desire, that strong human need for touch.

"This weekend." Ben leans down, kisses her hairline.

"Don't forget the deadline this Friday." When he looks puzzled, she adds, "For the teaching position."

His face closes, his jaw tightening and his eyes cooling like water becoming ice. "I thought we already decided that commuting wasn't something I would do."

"It sounds like you've already decided, anyway."

While new to their marriage, they would argue late into the night. They did this less out of respect for the old adage against going to bed angry than out of their eagerness to engage with ideas and with each other. Now Suzanne knows the value of truncating a quarrel, if only in sleep gained, and her words are the last of their day. Tonight they do not even make eye contact again. As on many nights, they do not say good-night.

After the bathroom tap stops running and the bedroom light dims, Suzanne takes down the whiskey bottle from the high cabinet over the refrigerator. It's the only sure bottle in the house, not because Petra has never looked up there but because she will not drink bourbon, not even when the house is otherwise dry. Suzanne pours the whiskey heavily into a tumbler of ice cubes. Only after twenty minutes, after the last cough or toss can be heard from the bedroom or from Petra's part of the house, does she pull out Alex Elling's last CD.

Most recent and final. His latest and his last.

She sits with these two inanimate companions—cheap plastic case and highball glass—in the big blue armchair that has traveled with her and Ben from Philadelphia to Charleston, from Charleston to St. Louis, from St. Louis to Princeton. How hard they laughed when they stood in line at the DMV, coming to terms with the fact that they would have New Jersey drivers' licenses. "How did this happen to us?" they asked, pretending that they were still happy, that everything they had was good enough, Suzanne pretending that she wasn't in love with someone else. "What's next?" she said. "North Dakota? Alabama?"

A two-dimensional Alex looks out from the CD case, baton in his capable hand. As always, he looks as though he might have walked straight out of the Black Forest: dark hair going to curls only at the ends, unlikely green eyes, skin stained tan midwinter. Though he often wore a close beard, in this photo he is clean-shaven, the way Suzanne liked him best. His neck is slender, his jawline clean, and his nose so straight and strong that Suzanne can imagine him as someone who lived a long time ago. But not as someone who died a few hours ago. He stands still, prepared to conduct but not yet in motion.

She extracts the booklet inside the case, the one Alex signed, *Everything for you*. Ben, though a reader of liner notes, has never mentioned the inscription. Suzanne has turned this fact over, wondering whether Ben knew and decided to allow her the affair as the price of keeping her or merely from indifference—or whether the idea never occurred to him and he assumed this was how the great conductor signed albums for all his fans. Ben has never asked her what it was like to play under Alex, never asked whether they spoke of more than the music at hand, never asked, even, if he was a good conductor. Though this is just one of the many closed doors between them, she has always resented him for not noticing, or pretending not to, and hated herself for not knowing which and not being strong enough to ask.

It is the former, she tells herself now: he simply did not notice. And it is true that Ben has never held much interest in mainstream performance, even across the years it paid their bills, even though it is how Suzanne spends what time she spends away from him. He never asks. Of course he wouldn't notice.

When she confessed to Alex that she kept the CD among their others, in the living room, he laughed. "You are no Mata Hari," he said. "You obviously haven't done this before."

No, she told him, she had done nothing of the kind before. Afraid of igniting his easy anger, yet also afraid of the answer that might follow, she did not ask him how many times he had done something of the kind.

The night of her lover's death—already she thinks of it this way—Suzanne drinks harsh whiskey and cries and holds the CD in its case as though the plastic square holds the coded answer to life's hardest questions.

Her fatigue fights the clicking roll of the digital clock that sits atop a row of books in the bookcase as she tries to stay awake past midnight. She wants to feel every minute of this day. Alex was alive this morning, and that will never be true again.

It is three in the morning when she wakes in the chair, strangely bent and groggy but never forgetting, not for a sweet second, that Alex is dead, that this day does not begin with him alive. She finds her way to the bed she shares with Ben and presses herself down into sleep. She barely stirs when he slips from the room early, just as the grayest morning light seeps through the crooked slats in the blinds, leaving with gym bag and briefcase. She slides back into sleep, into a dreamy world that is beautiful because in it Alex breathes, touches her, tells her stories, and commands her to play the viola for him.

Two

When Suzanne does rise she has only shaky legs for support. As on most mornings, Adele is up but Petra is not. Through the blunt headache and the whiskey aftertaste that survives toothpaste and mouthwash, she fixes Adele's favorite breakfast of oatmeal with walnuts and too much brown sugar. She sits with her as she eats, a few quiet moments before Adele withdraws to dress for school.

Petra shuffles into the kitchen wearing flannel pajama pants and a tank top. She stands at the coffee maker, back to Suzanne, jumping up and down with her hands in the air, blond braid shimmying on her back like a fat, happy snake. Even in the morning Petra jangles. She pours herself coffee and spins around, revealing the kind of good looks that Suzanne grew up wanting: tall blondness, skin like a white peach, cheekbones giving structural elegance to small features. When Petra plays her violin, she bows long stretches with her eyes closed, and her lashes are so long and thick that they make fringed fans visible across the room despite their pale color. When the eyes fly open, always without warning, Suzanne is startled, every time, by their sea blue, by Petra's old-fashioned Swedish beauty. Yet when Petra stands to her full height, bends at the waist and not the knees to return her violin to its case, her look is thoroughly modern.

Sometimes when Suzanne looks at Petra, she wonders why she doesn't hate her on sight, as many women do. It helps that Petra thinks she looks common. Though perfectly posed when holding her violin, without her instrument she is no more coordinated than a cloth doll, and Suzanne loves her for her awkwardness. Many men look at Petra as if at cased jewelry, with appreciation for a beautiful thing they have no use for. When a man approaches the two of them at an after-concert reception, he speaks first to Suzanne, turns to Petra, and then, in a shift once surprising that now feels inevitable, refocuses his attention on Suzanne until she excuses herself to go home to her husband. There's something about Petra's blatant good looks that reveals Suzanne's more obscured beauty. But the real reason Suzanne doesn't hate or envy Petra is simple: Petra is her best friend.

"Hey," Petra says, "I thought today was supposed to mark your return to composition. Why aren't you composing?"

"Why aren't you?"

"I have a kid."

"Whose breakfast I just made." Suzanne hears something in her voice under the humor, feels the hangover pressing into her forehead.

Petra blows on her coffee, then looks up. "What's going on with you?"

"I'm sorry," Suzanne says carefully. "I'm just annoyed with you for being right. Not composing is just one more thing to feel guilty about."

Petra hugs her loosely, mug still in hand, and kisses her temple. "It's the only thing you have to feel guilty about. Thanks for getting Adele in gear."

Biographical histories of music include few nods to female composers, and it's something Petra and Suzanne have talked about since they met at the Curtis Institute. There are often chapters on Nadia Boulanger and her tragic sister Lili. And music historians like to praise the Italian nun Isabella Leonarda or weigh in on whether or not Cécile Chaminade's salon compositions—hugely popular in their day but mostly derided since—constitute a real contribution to music. Yet for the most part histories of the great composers are the stories of men's lives, the women cast as helpmates, muses, hindrances, nursemaids, business managers, performers, or lovers.

Petra always argues that this treatment stems from the same prejudice that led the music world to claim that women could never be great trumpet players due to the size of their lungs—a belief overcome only by hard evidence: anonymous auditions played behind opaque screens. But Suzanne knows, and Petra has admitted, that women have written far less music than men and, when they have composed, it has often been with less dedication.

Petra flops a hand on her shoulder. "Don't pull a Minna Keel on me."

It was Petra who told Suzanne the story of Minna Keel, who gave up composition—at the age of twenty and for forty-six years—to work in her mother's business, marry, raise a prominent son, become politically active over the Spanish Civil War, and work for years as a secretary in the dullest of offices. There was family pressure guiding her choice—her series of choices—and perhaps a lack of encouragement, though she had male teachers who supported her. Ultimately it was a man who convinced her to compose again: a musical examiner who'd come to test one of the third graders she gave piano lessons, after her retirement from office work. Her sixties is when she really began to write.

It was a story that sometimes depressed Suzanne and sometimes gave her hope. It's not too late for her to write music, not even close—that's the moral she wants to take away. The loss of Lili Boulanger's music is the responsibility of her time and place, of her own traitorous body, of bad luck or fate. But what about the loss of forty-six years of Minna Keel? Whose fault is that?

"Ben did a number on you, you know."

"I know your theory about that, but Ben always tells me to compose if I want to compose."

"Yeah, but he says other things, too. Just because what you were composing was different than his stuff doesn't mean his stuff is better."

"It was," Suzanne says, "And who's to say that anything Minna Keel would have written earlier would have been any good? Maybe she started at exactly the right time for her. Maybe she just waited until she knew what she wanted to make."

"Excuses, excuses!" Petra adds, "You look like shit today."

"Exactly how I feel."

"Maybe that'll be your creative fuel. You can compose because you feel like shit."

You can compose because you are riddled by grief and about to break.

"Yes, a lot of people will want to listen to that."

"That doesn't stop anyone else. It doesn't stop the complexity composers or the fucking sound poets." She pauses for a better example. "It doesn't stop Ben."

Yet it did stop someone. It stopped Alex. He told Suzanne that he didn't write music because there was nothing left to write and no one left to write it for. It was a pose, of course, but he at least half meant it. It was one of the reasons he didn't compose.

"Actually," said Suzanne, "I might sit down at the piano with a pen sooner than you think."

"But not now because I need to change my strings before practice. Please, please, please, I need you to drive Adele to school for me. Sugar on top. Cherry. Hot fudge. Whipped cream. The works. Know I should have done it last night, but big surprise, I didn't."

Adele's school is across town, but Suzanne knows they are lucky to have it anywhere. Suzanne has heard Petra field the stupid questions. "A musician with a deaf child? How ironic!" But at Adele's school they say mostly wise things. They say, "How beautiful Adele is. She's the best math student we've ever had."

Once when Suzanne picked Adele up from school, a teacher waved her over and asked her how Adele responds to Petra's playing, whether she ever touches the instruments at home or asks about reading a written score. Hard questions but good ones, and after that Suzanne watched Adele carefully, though she never mentioned the conversation to Petra because she did not want to cause her pain.

When they pull to the curb in front of the school, Adele climbs over the seat and nuzzles Suzanne's neck with her small face. Suzanne kisses both of her cheeks—surprised yet again by their softness, their cool smoothness— and nods, grateful for the affection. She watches Adele's thin form move down the sidewalk, up the stairs, and into the school's foyer. She watches until the heavy front door falls shut behind the little girl she sometimes imagines carries the spark of her own, though of course she knows that her child would be two years older now. Almost exactly, she thinks, making the calculations again, though she's already locked them in memory.

She drives back to her posh town's shabbiest neighborhood, to the house she and Ben could afford because they pooled their money with Petra, to the house they could afford because so many of their neighbors are black or speak Spanish, to the house they could afford because it needed—still needs—so much work. The one-way street, which runs only the few blocks from the hospital to the small freeway, is at its prettiest in spring. The wildly prolific callery pear blossoms lace a canopy over the road and infuse the air with a pungent sweetness. Their petals drop confetti-like over the cans and candy wrappers littering the curbs.

Suzanne idles while the next-door neighbor—a man who has avoided speaking to them since he returned their lawn mower broken—backs out of the shared driveway. She returns the car to its parking space against the wire fence that separates their neighborhood from married-student duplexes. *Left foot, right foot, breathe.* She cranks up the window, arrives at the back door with the keys in her hand, suspecting that every little thing will be hard from now on, that every move will hurt in the marrow of her arms and legs, that she will be undone by a simple doorknob and shatter.

Petra does not answer her shout. In the kitchen Suzanne finds a note: "Will restring in the practice room. See you there later." Predictable unpredictability. Suzanne knows that Petra takes advantage of her, that she could have driven Adele to school herself, but she doesn't mind.

At the desk in the bedroom she shares with Ben, the computer screen fills with headlines. "Two hundred seventy-one people killed in plane crash," she reads. "Human error among possible causes."

She opens her email, knowing there will be no new message from Alex and cursing herself for those few times—the last two months ago—when out of anger or panic of discovery she deleted every note from him or to him. She will have only the most recent of their correspondence. Most of their four years is gone. She doesn't know what happens to deleted emails, whether they exist anywhere or leave some trace, the electronic equivalent of ashes from a love letter set on fire. She wonders why she does not know this crucial fact of modern life.

The phone. She sees her cell phone on the floor, where she left it charging yesterday, knowing Alex would not call because he was flying home, because his wife was picking him up at the airport as she always did. "It's nice of her, don't you think?" he said casually, more than once, and Suzanne had murmured yes. Because Princeton was nearly an hour's drive from the Philadelphia or Newark airports, Suzanne usually flew into Newark and rode the train home, calling for a ride from the station only if the small connector wasn't running or she had more than the single carry-on bag she usually traveled with.

She grabs the phone, yanks it free of the charger, presses its power button with a too-strong thumb, her breathing rapid, uneven. There are no messages at all, and she shudders a long exhalation, wondering whether Alex was unable to place a last call or whether he did place a final call but not to her. She feels bloodless, her head drained, her fingers tingling.

She turns back to her email, scans the dozen new messages, most of them spam in some form. In the list she sees a name that registers though she cannot place it. Steven Levertov has confirmed her as a Facebook friend. The name clicks. She and the other members of the quartet signed up for Facebook and LinkedIn because Anthony insisted, sending them links to articles on how to self-promote without seeming to self-promote, telling them it was part of their job to be "out there."

"If you want to hide in your house and play, that's fine, but you've chosen to perform for a living, and this is now part of that."

Yet she'd made the friend request to Levertov not for herself but for Ben, who made an ugly face the one time she suggested that he might try using social media himself. Levertov is one of the few composers in the United States who has had work performed by multiple full symphonies here and abroad. Though Ben doesn't think much of Levertov's self-conscious cleverness, others do, and his work has been buried in time capsules and fired into space. "I guess one way to stand the test of time,"

Ben said when he heard that a Levertov composition was being shuttled to the space station, "is simply to have your scores physically survive. To be outlasted by paper."

She closes her email and searches for Alex's name, finding several notices of his death and two lengthy obituaries praising his accomplishments. The writer in Chicago mourns the promise, now broken, of even more. "This tragic loss to the music world," Suzanne reads aloud, but her voice narrows into something porous. Like the other obituary, it quotes Alex as saying, "Music is a universal gift that unites people, repairs ruptures, and heals our pain." Reading it again, she registers the strangeness of the words: they sound like something Alex would sneer at, not like something he ever said. Perhaps it was a comment he made when very young, or—more likely—some journalist recorded a moment of sarcasm as literal.

She scrolls down to the bottom of the story, which mentions a future public memorial and private funeral arrangements. With a shock that feels like abandonment, she recognizes that she cannot attend the funeral. His wife and son belong there; she does not. Only the most private and hidden forms of grief are open to her, and this is her own fault. *Human error.*

She reaches for the object she always reaches for—out of habit and love and discipline and commitment and self-loathing and simply because it is, more than anything else in the world, more than anything else her mind holds, what she does and who she is. She begins the only piece that seems possible: her part in *Harold in Italy*.

It was what she played in her last St. Louis performance, in one of those end-of-season concerts that allow a local principal to show off. Suzanne had already resigned her position after holding it for only three years, admitting that her perfect job was a burden if her husband was miserable and she would never have enough time for a child. But at the end of that night she wanted to stay, to play before large audiences forever, to live within a five-hour drive of the man she already loved. Vibrating with *Harold*, she grinned before the entire hall, miserable.

She remembers every day of the week of rehearsals, Alex's stern instructions to the orchestra. *Clarity, clarity, clarity. The timbres are separate. Stop that damn blending.* But for her there was no scolding, only the one time when he added direction to her copy of Berlioz's score. *Doloroso*, he wrote over the beginning of the andante, saying, "Play it like your heart is being squeezed of its blood, so great is your pain. Play it like you are mourning for the beautiful life you might have led but were denied."

His accent fluctuated between a thud that fell with his words and a faint whisper underneath them, depending on whom he'd been talking to, how much he had been drinking, and—she learned—what effect he wanted to have. When he spoke to her that day his inflections were at their oddest, as though he and not his parents had fled small-town Bavarian poverty.

After those words, there were no instructions for her, only the watching like burning and then nodding, recognition. He saw her. Early on she wondered whether he thought she played perfectly because he already loved her or whether he loved her because she played perfectly. "There may be better violists in the world," he said later, "but no one plays *Harold* as beautifully as you do."

The applause approached wildness and the stage shook with it when Alex, again staring at her, both of them already consumed, turned his open hand for her to stand as St. Louis bid her farewell. Because she wanted to halt time but could not, she experienced the coiled happiness and remorse as though the moment had already passed, as though she was looking back on an earlier self.

Now she plays the thirty bars of the theme without error, but she is quaking and bails out before striking the 6/8 of the allegro.

Even Ben, who finds Berlioz's *Symphonie Fantastique* gaudy, admires *Harold*. He likes the story of Paganini commissioning a viola concerto and then being disappointed in the piece because his Stradivarius would not be a technical superstar but a quiet, melancholic voice. Then, after its triumphant premiere, Paganini allowed Berlioz to believe he'd paid him for the composition when really the money had been merely funneled through him—a ruse that allowed the composer's friends to keep him fed.

Yet Ben loves the music as well as the story, comprehending that the flamboyant, large-handed Romantic struck an ore of the sublime despite himself. So many musicians accomplish what they do in spite of themselves; it is dangerous to read the biography of a composer you love. *More dangerous still to marry one.*

In love Berlioz was passionate, misguided, faithful only in his way. Love inspired his music and often drove him feral. The *Fantastique* swelled from his obsession with the Irish actress Harriet Smithson. Over this object of his desire he wept in public and scrawled pages describing his immense anguish. Once Liszt, Mendelssohn, and Chopin searched the suburbs of Paris for their love-struck friend, convinced that he might kill himself over a woman he had never met and to whom he wrote frightening letters, bitterly jealous of her stage lovers as well as of the men who actually saw her chambers. In the final movement of his symphony, he represented her as a whore at the witches' Sabbath.

"And so it was," Alex once told her, taking the pedagogical tone he sometimes used with her, perhaps intentionally calling attention to the difference in their ages, "that sexual obsession resulted in one of Romantic music's innovations: the wedding of music and story." In the flawed, brilliant, highly autobiographical *Fantastique*, the hero thinks of his beloved always in association with a musical theme. Without words, the music tells a story.

After six years of bizarre courtship, occasionally broken by brief fixations on other women, Berlioz convinced Harriet Smithson to marry him. She proved shrewish and hard-drinking. They bickered for more than two decades until her death freed him to marry the mistress he'd taken almost immediately after his wedding, at about the time he composed *Harold in Italy*: a singer of no real talent.

About two and half years after the St. Louis performance—two and a half years into the four years of her affair with Alex—Suzanne offered herself to a recital series at Saint-Julien-le-Pauvre because Alex would be in Paris. He told her she was too good for the series—*Chopin butchers all of them*—but when she told him the date, his voice lifted, as close as he ever came to happy.

The church was domed but built to a more human scale than a cathedral. It still smelled of wet stone, as it must have in the twelfth century, when its presence tempted French peasants fresh from the countryside to choose faith amid squalor. She played well to several dozen people, a small audience but one appreciative of the music and a place to sit for two hours on a frozen January night.

The next day she and Alex walked the city, mile after shivering mile, and finally stood in front of Sacré-Coeur, all of Paris spread yellow-gray below them. "Is this why we fought the tourists to come up here?" she asked. He shook his head, and they ambled down through Montmartre, a walk that seemed aimless until they entered the cemetery squashed into the bottom of the hill. As they walked its narrow pedestrian avenues, Suzanne read aloud the names of the families interred in the idiosyncratic mausoleums, some of which looked shiny-new though they were centuries old. She was reciting one such name when Alex hushed her, pointing to a simple black crypt, an oversized coffin sitting on the pale dirt. Suzanne stepped toward it and saw the beaked face of Hector Berlioz etched into the dark marble, his name, the dates of his birth and death.

"This is why we came out to Montmartre," Alex said.

That night he surprised her again, producing tickets to a concert at the Théatre des Champs-Elysées. As she sat in the art deco cylinder she could feel its history, imagine the rioting audience at the 1913 premiere of *The Rites of Spring*.

That night's program was less scandalous and more appreciatively received: a Russian pianist with horrible hair who so delighted the French concertgoers with Schumann, Chopin, and an unusually human Prokofiev that they stamped their feet until he played four encores. Even Alex, who believed the encore destroyed a program's integrity, clapped loudly, stamped his foot, laughed with Suzanne. "They're going to have to turn up the houselights," she said, "before the French ruin this poor guy's wrists." But she knew the pianist didn't mind; what musician doesn't want to be adored? "Promise me we'll come back to Paris together," Alex said, his tone stern and a little alarmed. "I promise," she said, but it was a lie. It was made a lie by a plane crash in the American Midwest.

Again Suzanne raises her viola, tucks its familiar hard cradle under her chin. She swipes the bow across the strings. Without planning to, she begins again the theme from *Harold*. The sound is sweet—always it has been sweet. The vibrating strings feel abnormally thick, as though they have been submerged, bloated by water. Despite their thick feel under her callused fingerprints, and though she grips her bow harder than usual, the run-through is clean. Her right tricep is sore when she finishes.

She will never perform the piece again. Perhaps she will play it, probably she will, if not for a long time, but she will never again play it when she is not alone. Its performance belongs to the past, when her lover breathed air in and out of his lungs, told her ear that he loved her as if it were a secret between him and it. This is the present and not the past, when she was certain that she and Alex would return to the Théatre des Champs-Elysées after again paying homage to Berlioz in a Montmartre cemetery.

She pictures Hector Berlioz alone, seeking refuge from the Italian heat in the cool chambers of Saint Peter's, his volume of Byron heavy on his lap. Suzanne has never been to Saint Peter's, but she imagines it as Notre Dame, as Saint Paul's, as the Cathedral de San Juan and the one in Seville—all the cathedrals Alex ever pulled her into. Alex shared Berlioz's love of them, though less for their cool sanctuary than for the ambition they represent—that human desire for height and beauty and something better. When they entered a cathedral he would stand at its center, put his hands to his hips, nod satisfaction, as if to say, *This is good enough.*

Once Alex drove Suzanne through the neighborhood where he'd grown up, past the cheap house where his father had hit him with too many fists to count and more than once with a full bottle of beer. Down the street from the house swelled a large church, made huge by the stinginess of its surroundings. "You could see it from every street. It was like a cathedral to us, and it saved me." But Suzanne knew that the building had not saved him. Alex had escaped his childhood with his brilliance intact through music and through pure will. He built his own invisible cathedral and rose from the ground.

Suzanne was born to parents afraid of height. She remembers her mother, pinned against the panel between two elevator banks, unable to take one step toward the glass walls of the Empire State Building's observation floor while Suzanne walked its circumference, looking to the ground for her father, who had been unable even to enter the building, who has been unable to do many things in his life.

Yet Suzanne sighted in Alex something beyond her own absence of fear—a passion for altitude, a desire to ascend from the filth and stupidity that hulked over his childhood. He had a friend who took him up in a small plane. It scared her when he told her, and she understood why he had been so alarmed when she'd told him about a high school boyfriend who'd taken her on fast motorcycle rides.

"I don't even want to think about your having died before I met you," he said.

Flirting more than anything, not really thinking, she said, "But you wouldn't have known what you were missing."

He turned toward her, staring hard, voice angry. "Don't say that. Don't ever say that."

When he told her about the friend with the small plane, she said, "That's the kind that goes down. But it's back-page and not front-page news because only four people die at a time."

"I'm not afraid of dying in that sort of plane crash," he explained. "It's not like being hit by a bus. How awful that would be, everything just smashed and over before you knew what hit you. Going down in a small plane would be visceral. Falling and thinking, *This really isn't happening, except it is. This is a great thrill, and now I am dying. Look how high we are, how far we have to fall.*"

Suzanne despised the image, but she understood and told him so.

"But I would hate to die in a big plane," he said. "No view. Dying know-ing that the last thing you'd see in life is some Tom Cruise movie or a fat woman in a pink track suit."

It was a full-sized jet, the one he'd gone down in.

After dialing the 800 numbers advertised for family members, Suzanne spends the hour she is on hold cleaning the house with one arm, a crick in her neck. The phone is uncomfortable in the hollow of her chin. Unlike her viola, it is small and easily dropped. Its hardness feels cheap.

Using lemon oil, she polishes the single piece of furniture she has from her mother: a heavy cypress buffet, plain except for its three drawers en-graved with intricate leaves. She spends a long time in the depression of each leaf and accesses her clearest memories of the woman who hid birth-day presents in the drawers. Avoiding the overwhelming new grief by re-turning to the old, Suzanne clicks through the mental pictures like a slideshow. Her mother, about a year after the Empire State Building visit, hair disheveled, fending off Suzanne's father with a skillet as they back out the porch door for the last time. Her mother through a fogged passenger-side window, standing in the front yard of a tract house she desperately wants to sell so she can pay the rent on their apartment and continue Suzanne's private lessons. Her mother, beauty evaporated by difficulty and illness, dying at home like Suzanne promised. But there are as many images of her mother not there: concert-hall seats filled by people who aren't her mother. The vacant front-row seat at Suzanne's graduation recital at the Curtis Institute, the empty seats in Charleston, the seated strangers at all her performances in St. Louis. Her mother didn't live to see her succeed, though it was a future she always believed in, even when Suzanne did not.

A young woman's voice comes though the line, startling Suzanne from her crooked housework.

"What was the movie on the plane, on the plane that dropped like a stone from the sky?" Suzanne's words tumble into one another as she rushes them. "Do you know who the actor was?"

"You're horrible," the high voice answers. "People died. Their wives and children are trying to find out information, and you're playing pranks."

Suzanne thinks of Alex unwrapping his tray of food, struggling with the cellophane to extract the disposable fork, fumbling with the paper salt packet that might make the portions edible. "Wait," she says, trying to suppress the crazed tone she hears. "This is more important. Was there a meal or a snack box? Was there a choice?"

"You're either a bad journalist or a bad person," the young woman on the other end of the line says, her voice lifting and tight. "You're a sick woman. You need help."

She hangs up before Suzanne can explain that it isn't a prank, that it matters to her what her lover saw and tasted in the last minutes of his life. She hangs up before Suzanne can tell her that, yes, she is a bad person, that she is not Alex's wife, but that she mattered to him and needs to know. She wants to say that Alex should have gone down in his friend's plane, toward a screen of greenery, holding a perfectly crisp apple missing one sweet bite, every foot of lost altitude a measure of how far he had risen.

Three

There is no black on the right side of her closet, the side of her days. The clothes there are gray, white, blue, green, and tan. On hangers are a purple blouse, a red tee-shirt, and a pair of maroon pants—a gift from Petra she has worn only once.

The left side of her closet is monotonous night: solid black, the attire of performance. Like a widow in eternal mourning, Suzanne has pairs of black trousers, black skirts, black jackets, and black shirts. She has a black sweater, long- and short-sleeved black dresses, the formal black dresses of the soloist and plain orchestra dresses, black dresses designed to be seen from the opera boxes and those seen to best advantage from the floor. They seem extravagant in quantity, but each piece has been with her for years, worn many times, a fact once mentioned—a gratuitous cruelty—in a Charleston weekly whose music reviews were penned by a wealthy man's wife who fancied herself a critic and likely had no idea what she cost Suzanne, a young woman born poor, pressed to pass among those who assume that people who wear the same outfit twice in a season lack self-respect.

Though Suzanne never wears black offstage, not since she was twenty, today only the left side of her closet feels possible. She finds black pants that are not too dressy and a black silk tee usually worn under a shimmering sweater at a winter concert. She knows Petra will ask her what the hell is going on, but she cannot help herself. She tries to dress the clothes down with boots, with dangling silver earrings, with a face scrubbed clean.

When the phone rings, she answers it. A woman's voice says her name, more statement than question.

Suzanne repeats her own name. "Yes, this is Suzanne."

"Suzanne, you owe me a great deal." This is said so softly that Suzanne can hardly hear it. The woman hangs up, or maybe they are disconnected. Suzanne stands with the phone in her trembling hand, mouth growing dry until she breaks the frozen moment.

She knows a phone call can change your life. It was a ringing phone that brought her into the quartet. When Petra called with the invitation, Suzanne had been mulling over the possibility of resigning her seat in St. Louis and moving to a place where Ben would be happier and perhaps have more opportunity. Without first identifying herself, Petra greeted Suzanne, as usual, with a viola joke: "How do I keep my violin from being stolen?"

Suzanne delivered the tired punch line for her: "Put it in a viola case."

"But this time, I actually need a viola," Petra said. "I told them we'd probably have to get someone else now that you're rich and famous, but I have to ask." She told Suzanne that Anthony, a classmate from Curtis, was starting a quartet in Princeton, that he'd married a woman with family money willing to float the ensemble for two years, that he had a serious business plan, that their friend Daniel had already committed. "Not that you'd be interested, not with your job, but there's no one Daniel and I would rather have. Anthony's still such an asshole, but we'd have him out-numbered. Plus there'd be more stuff for Ben to do—an hour from New York and Philadelphia."

"That already crossed my mind," Suzanne answered.

"Your dad still lives in Philly, right?" Petra paused. "Or maybe I shouldn't have reminded you of that."

"It's okay," Suzanne said and asked if Petra thought working with Daniel would be all right, given his propensity to fall in love with whomever he played with.

"Suz?" Petra paused again—a long silence. "I really need you. With Adele. I'm failing as a single mother. There are problems. I need help."

For four days, Suzanne kept Petra's call to herself, knowing Ben would make the decision if she told him while she was still undecided. If it wasn't her decision, she might hate him forever. So she decided on her own, and then she told him. She resigned her chair, with apologies, helping to ar-range the auditions for the lucky player who would replace her, trying not to care who it was. She, Ben, and Petra emptied their penny jars and made an offer on the cheapest house for sale in Princeton. By the time Alex con-ducted her in *Harold in Italy*, it was too late to stop, and Suzanne's life changed again.

Anthony did indeed have money, and he had a solid plan. Suzanne, Petra, and Daniel committed to stay with the quartet for at least two years and to accept no other work that would interfere with the quartet's schedule—no playing in other ensembles, no session work in season, no solo perfor-mances without an okay. The contract each signed was so fastidiously crafted as to include practice schedules. In exchange, each would receive a modest but reliable salary. At the end of two years, the salaries would stop. If the quartet was not yet solvent through a combination of grant money, donations, CD sales, and performance income, it would dissolve. "It's a business," Anthony said when they gathered to sign the papers in the presence of his wife's family lawyer.

"It's a job," said Daniel.

Anthony watched him. "No drinking before practice or performance. I put it in the contract, so make sure you read what you're signing."

Petra put a long arm around Suzanne's shoulders. "Don't worry," she whispered. "It's music, too."

At the end of two years, the quartet was solvent, if barely, and after four, its members' earnings are just about what they were when they received salaries—sometimes a little more.

Now Suzanne risks arriving late, and they all promised never to be late. She walks fast to stop her shaking, but she thinks about the voice coming through the receiver, the voice entering her ear without permission: *Suzanne, you owe me a great deal.*

The practice room of the Princeton Quartet is almost subterranean, its only natural light coming from the long horizontal windows just below the ceiling, the rectangles that show only the moving shoes of passing students, often shoes of a kind and quality that Suzanne still never splurges on and could never have owned while in school. When she notes this, she recognizes the old bitterness of want and reminds herself that she does not have to work in an office or, like her mother, try to sell starter homes on the side in an effort to make something better. Suzanne plies her art for a living. She is a musician, which is what she has always wanted to be.

She drops the last step both feet at once and stands in the open doorway. Petra faces a far corner, jumping up and down with her hands in the air, still getting her jangles out. Daniel hunches his six feet three inches over his cello, his glossy head sagging. To someone who doesn't know him, he might look relaxed, but Suzanne knows before she looks that his right hand is tense with his bow, his pinky finger rigid. He looks up at her, his face softening as though he is seeing her for the first time after a long absence. Suzanne worries that the crush that has wavered from her to Petra to her to Petra to her and most recently back to Petra is about to alternate again.

Though they joke about it, it really isn't funny, and Suzanne feels too tired for it, for the delicacy and compassion it requires of her. Yet sometimes she wishes that she had fallen in love with Daniel, who lets his passion guide his choices and who lucked into the best halves of his Manchurian father and Canadian mother. He's dark and tall, made sensual by large eyes and curving lips. With Daniel, she never feels as though she has said the wrong thing and is being judged for it. With Daniel, she almost always knows what he's thinking and how he's feeling. With Daniel, she never feels as though she is alone in the room and he is far away.

Suzanne is staring at him when Petra, without looking around from the corner she faces, asks why the viola players were found standing outside the party. She spins around to deliver the punch line before Suzanne can. Instead she freezes and says, "You're wearing black. What the hell is going on?"

Daniel meets Suzanne's eyes. "You look beautiful in black."

"We're almost late," Anthony says, closing the door. "Two minutes."

Handsome but effete, with a flourish of freckles high on his cheeks and forehead, Anthony is, as ever, well-dressed above the ugly tasseled loafers he was partial to even as a student. His pants hike as he sits, exposing two inches of extravagantly thin sock—an effect Suzanne suspects is planned.

Suzanne takes her seat. Now there is nothing but the familiar smell of wood and rosin, the sound of string being slackened and tightened, the asymmetrical weight of the bow in her right hand, the familiar plate of the chin rest, still cool under her jaw.

Playing chamber music involves an intimacy between people that is no weaker than the closeness of love or sex. To play with others is to be bound by and respond to their rhythms and desires without sacrificing your own. Like sex, great music can be made with someone you know well or not at all—and with someone you loathe so long as there is passion in your hatred. Yet, unlike sex, great music can be made even with someone you merely dislike. This explains why Petra, Daniel, and Suzanne play well with Anthony, even when they find his arrangements too facile. There is some other, unnamable sensibility they share.

Having married a domineering woman from a rich family whose wealth has been diluted but not drained by generational expansion, Anthony thinks always of the books and of appearances. He is a man who subtracts tax and wine before figuring a tip, who divides a four-way bill not into quarters but by calculating the exact cost of each person's meal. The sole time Suzanne saw him pick up a whole check—at a luncheon with his father-in-law and a potential donor—he figured the tip in odd cents to make the total charge an even number, leaving the poor server to count out from the till her too-few dollars and sixty-seven cents. "Makes the ledger much cleaner," he announced as he produced the loops of his elaborate signature.

"Cherubini," Petra whispered, not softly, making Suzanne smile though she tried not to.

Maria Luigi Cherubini. As *directeur du conservatoire* he was dictatorial, demanding separate entrances for men and women and once chasing Berlioz around the library tables for using the wrong one. *Cherubini*. Timid in his harmonies, known to history as a textbook composer of white-key music of no great significance, now a man seen but not heard: the Louvre's millions of visitors see his face, as painted by Ingres, but few hear his music. Yet in his day he was considered by Beethoven to be one of the immortals. He was admired by musicians for his technique and was financially successful during a time when the Parisian scene was all about money.

Cherubini. A way for the quartet to think about Anthony, who plays his violin with a rare and sturdy clarity and is capable of originality of interpretation—particularly of Debussy—that baffles those who know him away from his instrument. His tastes, when he steps away from questions of money, when he considers the Princeton quartet's critical as well as monetary success, are fine if a bit cold. His choices for the quartet have been mostly wise, including bringing in Andres Flanders to perform Bocherinni's fifth guitar quintet as part of last year's February program. He's also made a name as a reviewer, his exertions toward fairness giving decency to his fastidious judgments. Ben should hate him, yet does not, which Suzanne supposes suggests something good about them both. And because Anthony functions by reason and not by feeling, he is easy enough to work with. He holds no grudges. Suzanne arrives on time, works hard, and knows what to expect.

Too often, though, Anthony stays near safe musical shores. The quartet plays Beethoven and Bach, of course, and sometimes Brahms or Ravel. Never Janáček and never the Shostakovich string music that Suzanne loves. Anthony is cautious about including contemporary composers, keeping them occasional and unassailable. All too often the quartet's programs include some piece of pretty-headed, many-noted brunch music by Haydn or Telemann—music written at the behest of someone who could pay for it. Suzanne fears that one day the quartet will wind up playing "Happy

Birthday" for some snarling old woman or unctuous child before she realizes what is happening in time to stop it.

"At least you play for a living," Ben said when Suzanne complained about a Vivaldi quartet, a piece of music she knew Ben despised. So many times at Curtis she had heard him say, "Vivaldi is the enemy of music's future—and its past."

Alex always called Vivaldi supermarket cake frosting—pretty if you don't know better, unpalatable if you've eaten freshly whipped cream on real pastry. Like Suzanne, he loved Fauré, that undervalued treasure, the musician's composer. Though they broke on new music, she and Alex shared some peculiarities of taste, including an adoration of Janáček, his seemingly reckless juxtapositions, his refusal to comfort with transitions of either melody or silence, his controlled anger, his generosity, his respectful demands on the musicians who would play him, their finger pads be damned. And they shared an unlikely soft spot for Schubert, poor drowned boy who should have been stronger but whose music is so bright it sparkles. Suzanne understands that weakness is a fact of her art but knows it is not true that Schubert and the great composers wrote out of their insanity and indulgence. They wrote around it, despite it, as best as they could in the midst of it.

Today the quartet works on a piece surprising from Anthony: Bartók's sonorous but disturbing final quartet, written while the composer was changing publishers after refusing to answer a Nazi-authored questionnaire about his race. He was contemplating the larger decision of changing countries, though he would wait to move until the death of his mother, whom he supported. No doubt Anthony—who might well have filled out that paperwork to protect his position—chose the Bartók as a show-off piece.

He hopes they will impress the audience with their glissandos, with the *ponticello* and *con legno* bowings, with the acrobatic stoppings and the notorious Bartók pizzicato. They will play the piece first, to a still fresh audience, or perhaps sandwich it between intermission and some problem-free piece that will let the people leave happy.

They repeat brief and long segments, hammer a few measures at a time, begin anew. They finish with a full run-through, playing through their small errors of timing as though they have to, as though they are on stage. This reminds Suzanne of the funniest thing Rachmaninoff ever said. Playing with the famous composer in music's most famous venue, violinist Fritz Kreisler lost his place and whispered, "Do you know where we are?" Rachmaninoff, the story goes, didn't wait a beat before saying, at a volume audible to several rows of the audience, "Carnegie Hall."

The quartet works hard today, but the music's difficulty brings pleasure and absorbs the hours, even for Suzanne. Like most musicians, they turn into children when they play pizzicato. Daniel grins, bobs his head, exaggerates the movements of his hands and the tapping of his big foot. Just as Suzanne realizes she, too, is smiling, the piece is over and she returns to herself. Grief floods her, her smile now just a strange shape on her face.

The grief is for Alex, mostly, but it bleeds into the sadness she feels every time music is made and then gone—something real and loud in the air that disappears from all but memory. Sometimes Suzanne strains to imagine the music still living, playing on in some version of reality not organized by time, all its notes together like colors in black paint or white light. It might be a place, she thinks now, in which you can love two people without diminishing either.

As they pack their instruments, Petra's whisper is a hiss: "Coffee."

"Don't you have to pick up Adele?" Suzanne says, folding a flannel swathe around the viola's neck, careful with eye contact.

"You know the schedule. We have over an hour."

They agree to walk the short diagonal to the edge of campus and then the half block to the coffeehouse on Witherspoon, which they both like even though the coffee is as thick as syrup. Daniel lingers, watching them leave, but they do not invite him to join them. Though the breeze is cool, under it sits a hot day—the summer to come—and Suzanne's back feels slick by the time they climb the three stone steps into the shop.

Exiting as they enter is her friend Elizabeth. "It's a small world," she says, making an easy pun of the coffeehouse's name.

She embraces Suzanne, pressing her into the large breasts that can only be called a bosom. Elizabeth's maternal exuberance is how they met, at the public library, where Elizabeth spotted her as new in town and invited her to the first of many potlucks, warmly adopting her and Ben into Princeton community life despite their oddities, despite Ben's cool reserve, despite their lack of children.

"I haven't seen you in too long, Suzanne. Call me," she says, certainly knowing as well as Suzanne does that she'll have to make the call, understanding that Suzanne usually accepts but rarely initiates social interaction.

Petra and Suzanne take their coffee to a back table. The hour is odd, so they have a bit more privacy than is usual in their small town. Still, the place is noisy with coffee grinder, espresso machine, multiple conversations, someone humming, street sounds.

"Why the hell are you wearing black and not looking anyone in the eye? And your playing . . ." Petra trails off.

"Something wrong with my playing?" The viscous coffee tightens Suzanne's hungover stomach as she sips through its heat.

Petra shakes her head. "You played beautiful but different."

Suzanne shrugs, tells her that she isn't sleeping well. "Besides, you know, Bartók."

"You love late Bartók. You lobbied for that piece."

"It's the same as Prokofiev. I love it, but it puts me on edge."

"That doesn't explain the black clothes. Or you. You were very weird at dinner last night. You are weird today." Petra's accent thickens as she speaks, and then her words halt.

Suzanne watches the young men and women behind the counter steaming drinks and manipulating tongs to select pastries for the people in line. She scans the tables of professors—dressed as awfully in Princeton, land of the knee-socked laureate, as in any town—and the klatches of students and friends and mothers. She feels her cell phone buzz in her pocket, extracts it, and reads the caller's number. The Chicago area code flips her stomach again. Chicago has always meant Alex, but it is not Alex's number and the caller does not leave a message. Her throat constricts, and it feels like minutes before she can speak again.

When she does, her voice is half of itself. "Don't you sometimes miss the anonymity of living in a city? Sometimes I think I need to live in a city again."

Petra clenches Suzanne's forearms with cool fingers and forces eye contact. "I tell you everything, and now you won't tell me what the hell is going on with you."

It's true, what she says. Petra has always told Suzanne everything since the day they met, both new students at the Curtis Institute. Suzanne had deferred entry for a year so that she could nurse her mother through the final months of her illness while trying to cobble together a bank account with part-time jobs. No student pays tuition at Curtis, but she didn't know how she was going to live and was contemplating the drastic step of offering to care for her crazy father in exchange for a cot in his South Philly flat. She was granted a reprieve in the form of a need-based fellowship for expenses and the phone number of a new violin student wanting a roommate.

Suzanne sold the only thing her mother had left behind that had worth to anyone else (an eight-year-old Pontiac) and moved in with Petra sight unseen.

The first thing Petra said to her was, "Are you a tramp?"

Suzanne shook her head. "Practically a virgin."

"Then I'll take the bedroom and you can have the sofa bed. I don't mind paying extra, and that will spare you from seeing the naked men." She laughed. "It's worse than that, even, because I mostly date ugly guys. Really nothing you'd want to see." She paused, maybe looking to see if she'd shocked her new roommate. "And sometimes it's not a man, but the women are always good-looking. I don't sleep with ugly women."

Suzanne unpacked her suitcase of clothes into the dresser Petra had already moved into the living room. Later, over the first bottle of wine that Suzanne had ever partaken in, Petra shamelessly recounted her adventures and become the best friend Suzanne had ever had.

When Petra arrived in the country, a man offered her a free place to live in exchange for letting him photograph her legs spread. "He promised me anonymity," Petra laughed, "because he was going to take very close-ups." She'd turned him down, but kept a version of the idea. She called a company selling "adult services" and told them no intercourse. A lot of girls probably try that—getting paid as a call girl without having sex—but Petra had long legs, blond hair, and a real Swedish accent. They hired her on her terms. "When I have sex, it's always for free. Because I want to."

41

Growing warm and bold with the wine, Suzanne asked her for details about the work. Petra told her the stories: the young man who wanted her to teach him how to give oral sex, the tiny woman who wanted to spank her in old-fashioned underwear, the guy who wanted to be whipped. The one who wanted her only from the ankle down, the one who masturbated while she crawled around the room and talked like a baby, the one who wanted her to dance in dim light wearing a red dress he had hanging in his closet. "It was his wife's dress," she told Suzanne, her eyes glazing wet. "She had died and he missed her. That was too much, the last time. After that I got a job making cocktails."

"Mixing." Suzanne put her arm around her, almost a hug. "It's called mixing drinks."

Petra wiped her tears with her forefinger until the streaks on her face were dry, laughing. "Crazy, no? Diapers, sure, no problem, but not a dead woman's dress to make a widower feel better."

Now, after years of Petra's confidences, Suzanne feels guilty for not reciprocating, for separating herself from her best friend with deceit. She's used to it, though, used to feeling distant from others because she has a secret. For four years she hasn't been able to tell anyone why she is so happy when she is happy or why so sad or worried when she is sad or worried. For four years she's been lying to her best friend, to her husband, to everyone she meets.

Now she shrugs. "I'm expecting my period."

Petra surprises her by saying, "So you're sure you're not pregnant again?"

The lightbulb above their table flickers, and Suzanne looks toward the front of the shop, watching people pass the plate-glass window. She grips her drink. "Petra, we're not even trying anymore. You know that."

"I never believed that, you know, and I understand you don't want me asking every month. I do, but I wish you could tell me. I tell you everything."

Suzanne finds her eyes. "Petra, I swear. We aren't trying anymore. We hardly even were, and then Ben changed his mind altogether."

"What about your mind?"

"I decided it was for the best, too. My sister-in-law was right, I guess. You can't replace a lost baby with another one."

"Your sister-in-law is a bitch." Petra lifts her cup and drains it with surprising speed. "So then that answer about your period is a total bullshit answer."

"And you don't really tell me everything." Suzanne pauses, hating herself for using Adele to deflect Petra's inquest.

"There's nothing to tell there. I've told you. He was just a guy I slept with—nobody that matters."

"He's going to matter to Adele. She's going to want to know. At least you should get the guy's medical records, family history, that kind of thing."

"Then I'd have to tell him about her. If I could remember his last name, if I could even find him. And what if he's an asshole? What if he's some horrible person and wants to share custody and make decisions about her life?" Petra is glaring now. "But you're just changing the subject to avoid telling me what the hell is going on. Which is mean. And you're not mean, so something must really be going on."

"I'm so sorry, Petra. I'm having a hard time today. I guess I'm in mourning." She speaks this truth gingerly, eyes cast down. "For the life I didn't lead. For the baby I didn't have. It's my age, maybe, and my birthday coming around again. Lately I think a lot about my choices and how my life might have been different." She wants to tell her everything, but she stops herself.

43

Petra strokes Suzanne's hair, causing a table of male professors to stare at them without even disguising their leers. Performing for them, Petra kisses her cheek and holds her hand on the tabletop. "You say it like it's already over. Anyway, you have a great life. Musician married to a musician— how often does that work out? And the quartet is actually succeeding, and Adele likes you a lot more than she likes me. And she loves you just as much."

Suzanne lifts a smile. "If you and I make out right now, those men will die of heart attacks."

"Almost reason enough," Petra says, pulling back, dropping the physical contact altogether. "So, what do you call *Harold in Italy?*"

This is one Suzanne hasn't heard, so she waits for Petra to deliver the punch line.

"The longest joke ever written."

Suzanne bursts out laughing, but there are tears, too, and Petra looks stricken.

"I'm sorry," Suzanne says. "That's the last piece I played in St. Louis. It makes me think of one of those lives I didn't get to live."

Her cell phone vibrates again. This time there is no number to read, only the word *unknown*.

"Is it important?" Petra asks.

"I hope not." Suzanne returns the still buzzing phone to her pocket and lifts her viola case. Though she holds it on her hip with both arms, like a young child, she feels as though her arms are flailing, as though she has just stepped off a cliff and is plummeting, waiting for the ground to rise up and stop her fall. The sensation is as real as in a dream.

Four

By Saturday, Suzanne's phone has vibrated with another call from Chicago and two more *unknowns*. She knows that it has to be about Alex and that she should answer it, but she also knows that the woman who called her home is probably Olivia Elling. She cannot swallow when she even thinks the name, so she turns off her phone for long stretches. It's not denial, she promises herself, but a necessary postponement. It feels like time has stopped, just for a bit, right in the middle of her life flying apart. Soon enough some god will hit the start button, her universe will expand at the speed of light, and everything she has will be taken from her.

It is her turn to make the trip into the city, bringing the bows to the only person she and Petra trust to rehair them. Ben is at the dining-room table with blank score pages and a pencil. His neck curves, and his hair falls into his eyes. On a whim, she asks him to go with her. "We could get lunch," she says, but what she is thinking is that they can walk in the park and she can tell him everything. She can tell him everything before someone else does.

"No thanks," he says. "I need the work time."

So she makes her way to the back of the house and finds Adele alone in her room, arranging stuffed animals in circles on the floor. She waves for Adele's attention and asks if she wants to come to New York. "We have to bring the bows to Doug, but we can do fun stuff, too."

Adele smiles and signs, "I like the train!"

"Brush your hair and teeth and we'll go."

The trolley-style car that runs back and forth between Princeton and the train station at Princeton Junction—called the Dinky by everyone in town—is less than a mile away. Suzanne and Adele turn up John Street, walking across the neighborhood facetiously named Downtown Deluxe by the black families pushed there to make room for the upscale retail development of Palmer Square. Most of the original inhabitants—some of them descendants of valets and footmen granted their own freedom after accompanying young Southern gentlemen to Princeton—are elderly now, their children and grandchildren moved into suburban neighborhoods. Downtown Deluxe has turned partly Latino, attracting Princeton's new workforce, mostly young men and a few families from central Mexico, some from Guatemala.

Increasingly, though, as the rest of the town is grabbed by millionaires, the neighborhood is sprinkled with young white families. Suzanne's is one of these: she is part of the neighborhood's problem of rising property taxes that may push its poorer residents outside borough limits. Sometimes at one of Elizabeth's parties, someone reminds her of this, as though she could have afforded to live anywhere in town and is slumming for fun. Yet her neighbors are kind to her. They do not hold her responsible for wider demographic shifts, and, like people everywhere, they are sympathetic to a house with a young child, even if they can't figure out whether the blond or the brunette is her mother. It helps that Adele is a charmer, She waves and presses the word *hello* from her mouth as they pass Percy, a thin, elderly man who shuffles through the neighborhood, smoking cigarettes and striking up conversations with whoever walks by.

The handful of people on the Dinky are aggressively underdressed in a way that calls attention to their university affiliation. There are just a few more people—these in business clothes—on the breezy platform at Princeton Junction as they wait for the off-hours local. When the Amtrak train rushes through, Adele squeezes Suzanne's hand hard, a laugh monopolizing her small face.

On their train, people boarding and exiting smile at Suzanne as she signs with Adele as best she can with the bow cases tucked under her arm. Their expressions are a cross between the amused looks given to mothers of identical twins and the pitying looks laid on mothers of children in wheelchairs. Half adorable novelty, half handicapped. There are men in the world, Suzanne knows, who go out of their way to date deaf women. She reminds herself, again, that she is not Adele's mother. That she is not a mother.

The music in Pennsylvania Station—it is Brahms today—always makes Suzanne feel as though she is in a movie, the camera taking a long-scene shot of its troubled heroine, a woman about to find a suitcase that does not belong to her and will entangle her in mystery and adventure, in danger that she will narrowly avert by using her wits. As always, she is embarrassed when she catches herself with this thought. She focuses on the floor, made grimy by the day's thousand shoes, and holds Adele's hand as they press through the crowd's main current and rise by escalator to the street, one of Manhattan's least attractive stretches.

She tightens her arm over the bows, having heard the stories of musicians leaving instruments in cars or on street corners. The violist who left his four-million-dollar Stradivarius in a taxi and celebrated its recovery by playing a concert for the Newark airport cabdrivers. The most famous missing American viola left on a Chicago curb as its owner climbed into a limo, an instrument that reappeared years later in a murder-for-hire scheme. The Italian virtuoso who lost two separate Amati violins—a decade being time enough, it seems, to forget a hard-learned lesson.

She cannot imagine New York without sound—the city *is* sound—but she tries to give Adele a day for her senses. They start with taste at an outdoor café across from Lincoln Center. Crunchy granola parfaited with creamy yogurt and fruit. Suzanne closes her eyes, feels the textures in her mouth, notices which part of her tongue tastes sour, which sweet.

The café is next door to an Italian restaurant where she once ate with Alex after a Friday morning Philharmonic performance. Joshua Felder was the soloist that day, playing Bartók's unalloyed violin concerto. Afterward Alex told her that Felder would be the world's top violinist within a year and that once he was he would give them a private performance. "Not really going out on a limb with that first claim," she answered as they sat facing the street, autumn sun on their faces.

"But the second?" Alex asked.

"Far-fetched."

"Maybe I have the goods on him."

They laughed, and Suzanne forgot the remark until it came true, about a year later, when she entered Alex's hotel room in San Francisco and the blindfolded Felder began to play.

Her throat trembles and her hand is shaking. Adele looks up at her, her alarm visible, and Suzanne closes the memory and throws away their almost empty parfait cups.

They walk west through Central Park. At the small zoo, they breathe in the musky smell of mammals and dirty-straw avian smells of the bird pens. At the Met they see the jeweled colors of the Asian tapestries, the intense pastels of the Impressionist paintings, the dark shadings of the German Expressionists, the panoramic view from the rooftop sculpture garden, where Alex once bought her a glass of good champagne served in a plastic flute. Up the street, Suzanne lets Adele choose from the case of pastries at the café in the Neue Gallery: a forest-fruit torte that feasts first their eyes and then their mouths. They stop next to ride the carousel. The air swirls as the carousel spins faster and faster and their animals rotate up and down amid the turning. Suzanne tries to imagine how the ride would feel if she couldn't hear the calliope music, the cries and gasps of delighted children. She closes her eyes, shutting down one sense, but she knows that's not the same thing at all.

When it's time for the appointment, they make their way back down the city, to one of the few neighborhoods that still offers such ordinary goods and services as sewing-machine repair, pet supplies, and hardware. Doug's shop is unmarked save for a simple name plate; he does not advertise, and he does not need to. There is an old-fashioned bell apparatus, and Adele pulls the cord, smiling when she sees the movement of the bells that she cannot hear. Suzanne once saw a catalog with a baby monitor for deaf parents; a light shines over their pillows when their baby cries at night.

Doug ushers them down the tight hallway and into his small, stuffed shop. He's tall and muscled like a swimmer, noticeably handsome though his face sags a little, hound-like as if from gravity, and his skin has gone gray from two decades of nicotine. "I can't quit now," he always says in his bass speaking voice. "I'm no good to anyone with shaking hands. But I never smoke around the instruments. It alters the humidity."

"The dangers of secondhand smoke," Suzanne says before introducing him to Adele, saying, as she always says, "She's a pretty good lip reader if you look her square on."

He faces Adele, kneels, kisses her hand, says hello. Adele looks away and then back, uncomfortably pleased by the attention.

Doug straightens, stands again. "I'm checking out the condition of a stolen violin. Someone came in to have it appraised, and I recognized it from the registry. Told the guy I'd give him two hundred dollars and had him write down his name and address. I figured it would wind up being a donation, or maybe the musician would pay me back, but the guy actually wrote down his real address, and the police found him there."

"An idiot?'

"He bought it online and said he didn't know it was stolen. The owner plays for the Pittsburgh Symphony. I told her I'd check it out for her."

"She leave it in the car?" Suzanne asks.

"Don't know, but the guy who stole it had no idea how much it was worth. Banged it around a little and sold it cheap. But I think it's all right—lucky violin." Doug taps the instrument, front and back, with a rubber ball held by two stiff wires, a crude tool but his favorite for detecting open seams. "I really don't get people who steal instruments. It's not like taking money. It's like stealing someone's wife or husband. You just don't do it. I like women—you know me—but when I hear the words *I'm married* or *my husband*, then it's all off the table." He looks up to wink. "Lucky for you."

"I guess some people are just wired differently." Suzanne watches his work, feels Adele's thin arm twine into hers. "Something for your biographical theories."

Across two years, Doug has expounded and refined a theory that all music is autobiographical, even for performers and certainly for composers.

"As autobiographical as memoir," he says, "though much harder to tease out." Once he showed Suzanne a sketch of his ideas about the relationship among a composer's life, basic temperament, historical period, and influences. He'd been trying to refine his thoughts into a formula, accounting for the fact that some life events are more overpowering than others, that some musical periods particularly reward conformity, that certain personality traits are most likely to influence a composer's music. "Can you be a brilliant composer and an asshole?" he asked her once, and was surprised by the speed of her "Of course."

Occasionally Suzanne tests Doug, playing a piece he's unlikely to know and asking him to tell her about its composer. He's accurate in broad strokes. It's not hard to tell if a composer is generally intelligent or a musical savant, cool or expressive, happy or sad. It's the fortune-teller's art, and Suzanne's never been tricked by a good palm reader. But lately Doug has been peculiarly right, spooking Suzanne like the time a state-fair psychic told her that her mother was dead and her father was a conspiracy theorist.

Suzanne and Adele watch as Doug rehairs Petra's bow and then Suzanne's. "They don't kill the horses to get their tails," Suzanne says as Adele fingers the two black tails hanging among the many white ones—a stable with no bodies—explaining the difference in sound between black and white, answering that yes, everyone in the quartet uses white hair, but a lot of bassists use black for a rougher sound.

"I say it every time, but this is a beautiful bow."

Suzanne nods, slowly. "I'm very lucky with bow and viola."

"Almost as good as being lucky in love. Which would you trade if you had to, Ben or the Klimke?"

A few years ago, Suzanne would have said *Ben* to make the quick joke, but now she thinks of the other choice, her stomach a heavy ball. She'll never know whether she would have left Ben for Alex. She went back and forth so many times, and now she'll never know what she would have done had she been forced to decide. What she says is about her viola: "I was lucky to get in on a Klimke early. Got one just before they went through the roof."

Suzanne signs the story of Marcus Klimke, tells Adele how he models his violas not on Stradivarius dimensions but on Amati: just a bit smaller yet wider across the base. A darker, deeper sound. "Perfect for playing *Harold in Italy*."

"Will I ever go to Italy?" asks Adele, who has been reading about the Venetian canals.

Suzanne answers in both sign and speech. "I think you'll go everywhere you want to go, but be careful because everyone says Venice smells bad."

"Done!" Doug rosins the bow, holding it by the ebony frog. "And now you must play, even though I don't have a Klimke on hand for you. Let's see. . . ." He peruses the instruments lying on his work table, hanging from the walls and ceiling, in cases on the floor. "Just a minute."

Suzanne hears his steps climb the other side of the wall and then move overhead, in the apartment above his shop. He returns in a few minutes, handing a viola to Suzanne as casually as he would pass an umbrella. The instrument's most unusual feature is its scroll, which is carved to resemble a young woman with large, almond-shaped eyes and a slim waist. But she sees the viola is also notable for the quality of its finish and color—a strangely bright amber.

"A Stainer replica?" she whispers, her pulse quickening.

"The real thing. Your hand already knows it. So play us something pretty and don't tell anyone I let you touch it."

"Whose is it?"

Doug grins. "Lola Viola's."

It was only a week or so ago that Suzanne heard Lola Viola interviewed on the radio, saying, "I traded my real name for real fame" and talking about her new record and her million Twitter followers.

Doug's eyes tilt, just barely, toward Adele. He tips his chin at her, looks down, his smile winning against the gravity always dragging at his face. "It's tuned and everything."

Suzanne holds the viola to her chin, the bow to the strings, and opens Mieczyslaw Weinberg's Second Sonata for Solo Violin. A test for Doug, who listens with head cocked. When she finishes she tells him what a beautiful thing he has let her play.

"You know the story, right?" he asks. "About Jascha Heifetz? Someone walked up to him and said, 'What a beautiful violin you have.' He held it to his ear and said, 'I don't hear anything.'"

"Sometimes it is the player, but the instrument sure helps. I'd never let anyone but you near my viola with a mallet, that's for certain." Suzanne tucks her hair behind her ear, bow still in hand. "But you're stalling. Tell me about the composer."

"Let's see. A deep sadness tempered by innate buoyancy, though some of the sadness was coming from you, I think. So hard to subtract out the performer." He pauses to make eye contact before continuing. "A man— definitely a man, which makes it easier of course. A man with a deep desire for repair. A taste for the programmatic, possibly because of his time but also maybe because he likes stories or comes from a storytelling culture. Or he uses stories to make sense of his life. A Jew? Definitely listened to Shostakovich, maybe even in person."

"Bingo," Suzanne says. "Family members killed in pogroms and then most of the rest in the Holocaust. Emigrated to Russia, proved remarkably resilient, found some happiness in life and marriage, and mostly avoided trouble for a while."

"And Shostakovich?"

"Loved Shostakovich, who later tried to get him out of jail, but what saved Weinberg was Stalin's death. He was out in a month. You already knew that stuff, right? You recognized the piece?"

Doug is already reaching for the Stainer. "Nope. You know me, I don't know my music history hardly at all. I'm just a technician."

"No *just* about that, but, Doug, you're all theory these days anyway. Seriously, did you really glean all that from the music itself?"

"It's as good a way as any. I'm not always right, of course, and the women composers are much harder, more complicated, but I'm getting better and better. I think I'm going to write a book on it."

"Just don't start writing letters to the editor." Suzanne smiles. "Anyway, it's a game composers would hate, don't you think?"

"Not to mention music critics."

It feels good to be talking to someone she knows but not too well, to share some banter, to be thinking about something other than her own life. Yet she cannot help herself and says, "Up for one more?"

He hands the viola back to her, and she plays a stretch of the music she continues to think of as *Subliminal*, mimicking its thrust as best she can with a single instrument. The viola is suited to the task. She understands now how Lola Viola can sound like an entire ensemble all by herself, which, combined with her beauty, is the secret to her enormous commercial success—a rarity in their line of work.

"Wow." Doug stares when she finishes. "Feels like a trick question, but okay. I'll try. Contemporary, obviously. Innovative but with a strange conservatism. A streak of traditionalism, but not reactionary."

"You're describing the music itself."

"I'm working my way to the composer through the music. Very well-trained, especially in composition theory. Fair-minded but incredibly stubborn and sometimes blinded by it. Emotionally restrained—incredibly so—but not without some emotion. The emotion is there but suppressed, consciously maybe, but not uniformly. Someone who uses intellect to translate emotion because the emotion frightens him. I'm guessing a comfortable childhood but with a tragedy of some kind. A deep point of pain."

"Disappointment?"

Doug shakes his head. "Someone not unhappy with how his life has turned out, though maybe only because he didn't expect more." He shakes his head. "It's not that simple. The music pulls in more than one direction, even more than usual. I'm starting to think the composer is a woman, which throws everything off."

"You're a sexist, Doug."

"I guess, if you mean that I think men and women are different, and that women are more nuanced and complex." He combs his hair with his fingers, slightly clumsily, as though he has a new haircut and his fingers expect longer hair. "I'm stumped, I guess. Dedicated is the best I can come up with, yet also detached. An oxymoron, I guess. I'm sorry." He looks as though he really is.

"No, I'm sorry," Suzanne says. "It was a trick question. It's a collaboration: not a woman but two men."

Doug laughs in his deep bass. "I'm relieved. I was about to toss my book proposal in the trash."

Suzanne turns to case her bow and sees Adele, her teary line of sight following the beautifully carved Stainer across the room as Doug leaves with it. Suzanne cups Adele's face, presses her palm into the soft skin of her cheek, reassured by its softness and warmth.

Adele speaks, forcing out the awkward syllables, something she almost never does when her hands are free. "I want to hear you play. I want to hear my mom play. I want to hear Ben."

Now they are both nodding, Suzanne whispering, "I know, I know."

Doug returns and takes the check Suzanne signs for him. He shakes her hand, then bows low to Adele, pops up, smiles. "What's this?" he mouths soundlessly as he reaches behind Adele's ear and produces a quarter, which he places in her palm.

Five

Suzanne and Adele arrive home to find Petra and Ben watching baseball. Lounging on either side of the sofa, separated by a bowl of popcorn, they could be college roommates. Petra wears flannel pajama bottoms and a tank top ringed with condensation from the bottle of beer she steadies on her stomach. Her feet, stretched out to rest on the coffee table, turn out from her early ballet training, but she is otherwise boyish.

It is a rare moment: Ben and Petra fully at ease with each other.

"Who's winning?" Adele signs.

"Suzanne's team," Petra answers, grinning her support for the city where they met.

Petra pushes the popcorn toward Ben and pats the open cushion next to her. Adele fits herself onto the sofa, leaning into her mother, no longer Suzanne's ward.

With popcorn in her mouth and her eyes on the television, Petra says, "Oh, did you hear about that Wikipedia thing with Alex Elling?"

Suzanne, who was poised to leave the room, settles her weight evenly across both feet, holding still, swallowing away the catch in her throat.

"A bunch of his obituaries had this sappy line about music being a healing force, right?"

"I hate that kind of thinking," Ben says, his eyes also on the baseball. "Music is notes on paper, value-neutral."

"Yeah, yeah," says Petra, "and apparently the dead guy agreed with you. Turns out two Canadian journalists were proving a point. They were waiting for someone to die who was famous enough to have obituaries written but not superfamous. When Elling died, they planted that line in the Wikipedia entry on purpose because they thought journalists would go for the schmaltz and they wanted to see how many would pick it up. Trying to prove a point about sloppy reporting, I guess. Turned up in something like ten obits. Brilliant."

"That's a pretty mean thing to do." Suzanne's voice sounds weak, but at least it does not quaver.

"Journalists should know better, right? Check their facts."

"I mean a mean thing to do to Alex Elling."

"He's dead, what the hell. I know you kind of liked him, but he was famously a jerk, right? I think it's funny that someone put feel-good words in his mouth."

Suzanne walks to the bathroom to shower away the city and to be alone, noting that she wasn't interested in her favorite Phillies even before Petra told her about the false line in Alex's obituaries. Things that mattered last week no longer matter, and she does not even know whom her team is playing.

One of her several fights with Alex was about sports, though only on the surface; it was really an extension of a disagreement about music.

They only fought in the first year or so and most often in Chicago, in the city where he lived and worked, where his wife lived, where he could never fully relax the way he did when they were together elsewhere. On an early-summer walk along the boulevard that passes the aquarium, Suzanne mentioned Luciano Berio. It had rained earlier, just enough to raise the smell of wet concrete and leave the air humid.

"He enabled John Cage, so that's one strike," Alex said, his voice louder than it had been all day. "Then he wrote a bassoon piece that requires fifteen minutes of circular breathing. That's strikes two *and* three. Pretentious. Good music should not try to be physically impossible to play. You know how I feel about virtuosity."

At Curtis, Suzanne had had a bassoonist friend who had worked on his circular breathing, his goal to play the Berio piece. It had inspired her to think of her own practice as a form of training, as a physical discipline. Yet insecure about Alex's greater knowledge and experience, still desperate to please him always, Suzanne changed the subject, suggesting they catch an inning of the Phillies game at a bar, check in on the score.

"I might watch sports if time were unlimited," Alex said, not looking at her, "but really it's just false news—teams up one year or not, and nobody from the city they play in anyway. How many of your Phillies were born in Philadelphia?"

"*I* was born there," Suzanne answered, her hurt shifting to anger, adding, "It's not like most people on the Chicago Symphony are from Chicago."

He looked down the slope of his nose, eyelids half lowered—his look of disapproval. "Don't do that."

He let her change the subject again, but throughout the afternoon he seemed removed. He walked a little farther from her than usual, sometimes even pulling ahead a step or two, leaving her to feel as though she were trailing him. As though she wanted him more than he wanted her. Finally, on a park bench where they stopped to watch a pair of inept windsurfers in the bay, she said, "I can get disapproval at home. I can't stand yours. I don't want to watch every word that leaves my mouth. I don't want to worry all the time that I'll say the wrong thing."

"I know." He patted her knee but rose to walk more, again outpacing her just enough that she felt as though she were following.

Though his direction seemed aimless, she soon realized he had a destination in mind: a cab stand. He directed their cab to a small record store in Hyde Park. The clerk there knew him, chatting him up about rare recordings, mentioning a German import, a new recording of Grieg lyric pieces played on Grieg's piano.

Alex walked to a back corner, knowing the location of the music he sought. He paid while she poked around the store, checking to see if the Princeton Quartet CD was there, risking the disappointment that it would not be and finding herself cheered that it was.

She forgot, at times, that some of her dreams had come wildly true.

Outside Alex handed her the small bag that held his purchase, and she extracted a disc of Piotr Anderszewski playing the Bach partitas.

"Remember?" Alex asked.

"Of course I do. He played Chopin and Sibelius before intermission."

Alex stood looking at her, shifting his weight between his feet perceptibly. This was something she had never seen in him before—the impression that he was uncomfortable in his own body.

"I'm a bastard. You know that." He shifted his weight to the balls of his feet, moving that small amount closer. He raised his hands to cup her cheeks and grinned suddenly. "I don't care for Berio, but I actually like baseball."

She nodded. "So let's go back to the hotel and watch the end of the game."

He put an arm around her. "Somehow I don't think we'll ever have so much time together that we'll spend even a minute watching a television. Maybe if we live together for twenty years we'll feel like going to a game. Hell, maybe we'll even go to a movie."

The shower beats warm water down on her. She tilts her head sideways to let a stream trickle into one ear and then the other. She doesn't remember if her team won that day in Chicago, and she doesn't care if they win today. Alex was right, even in his annoyed posturing. She has no need of false news when the real news has ruined her life.

But then she smiles, just a little at the corners of her mouth. She'd been right about the quotation about music's healing quality, right that Alex would never say something like that. He'd been hard to get to know, but she had done it. He had loved her, and let her inside his mind.

Six

Weeks of torn sleep follow the trip into New York. Suzanne's nights shred like newspaper. In the middle of the night she bolts awake from dreams of her cell phone vibrating with Chicago's area code.

Her morning dreams, though, are mostly pleasant, and at dawn when she is half asleep she sees them rippling over the real bedroom like layers of mist. Alex's whispers slip between Ben's deep breaths, curling like vapor. She tries to roll herself back into the sweet fog, but always it dissipates quickly, abandoning her awake, too early, in a warm room, again facing a day that will feel too long.

One week bleeds into the next while another seems to flow backward, but each day's time is slow, its demarcations concrete. *Minute by minute, left foot, then right.* Seconds click by in painful increments, a metronome set on largo. *Breathe*, she reminds herself, coaxing her lungs to expand and then empty.

She does the things that have to be done. She attends rehearsals. She practices. She brings food home from the grocery store, helps with Adele, tidies the house, writes checks to the water company and the phone company, buys stamps. She tries to keep up with her online life, answering emails, accepting Facebook friend requests, hunting for an interesting link to post. Yet she notices things slipping through the cracks in her concentration. She cleans the bathroom but forgets the shower or the mirror. An email from a music blog requesting an annotated list of her five favorite pieces in the viola repertoire goes unanswered; when the reminder comes, a day before the deadline, she types out a paragraph from the top of her head and hits *send* without proofreading. She fails to answer questions posed directly to her in the Twitter feed. One day she sees an online ad with a woman's face, the caption reading, "This is what depression looks like." She recognizes the sad expression from the mirror and remembers what she said to an acquaintance worried about her after her mother died: "Being sad about something sad is not depression. It's human." Twice she sits down with the idea of composing, thinking *doloroso*, but both times her focus is vague and she abandons the effort without really beginning, the second time without playing or writing a single note.

She knows that it is a Tuesday when she opens the gray shoebox. The box is so ordinary that no one would bother to look inside. She keeps it casually on the closet floor, under a small pile of socks and scarves—the only jumble in the house that belongs to her, its neatest companion. Suzanne: made tidy by living her life in a series of small rooms in small flats and tiny houses whose only freedom was the space she made by keeping her belongings few and carefully placed. One thing under her control.

This box—unremarkable, on sight not worth opening—houses the tangible evidence. A small, private museum, it holds a history of particular love. A hiding place secret because visible and mundane, of four illicit and extraordinary years. It conceals no love letters. Those exist in ether, in whatever cyberspace contains deleted emails. *And maybe also on Alex's computer.* The thought thumps inside her chest like a missed heartbeat, but she tells herself, no, surely Alex—experienced in infidelity—was the more careful lover, covering his tracks, deleting their incriminating messages. Still, she wonders whether internet service providers and webmail accounts give passwords to bereaved spouses.

She rests her hand on the shoebox holding the material stubs of romance: concert tickets, boarding passes, train receipts, program notes, restaurant matchbooks palmed by a nonsmoker, flyers, hotel pens, and other small souvenirs of fraught geography, drives across hundreds of miles, aching airport good-byes.

Alex and Suzanne made love the day of the final of three performances of *Harold*, both before and after the Sunday matinee. His plane left that night, and he was scheduled to leave a week later for a two-month tour of Europe. So a few days later they each drove four hours just to have a long lunch in Bloomington, Illinois, talking music over the worst Indian food Suzanne had ever eaten but afterward would from time to time crave. He called every day from his tour, not missing one, and she holds now the scraps of paper with the phone numbers of hotels in London, Paris, Munich, Brussels, Amsterdam, Rome, Sienna, Madrid, Barcelona. She touches a small stack of transatlantic calling cards whose minutes were drained by long conversations. One of them ran out during a call to Berlin, from where Alex told her the story of Ovid, banished by the hypocritical Augustus for his scandalous writings on love. Ovid lived in exile on the Black Sea, without his beloved third wife, to whom he wrote for the remaining decade of his life but never saw again. There the poet lived without a library sufficient to do his work among a people whose language he could not understand. Over time his heartache did not heal, but he did learn the language well enough to compose a eulogy for the still living Augustus. "The eulogy and the language it was written in were lost centuries ago. Not a word survives," Alex told her.

"That's one of the saddest stories I've ever heard," she said, to which he replied, "Precisely."

She moved to Princeton while Alex was in Europe. The day after he landed they each drove five hours to meet midway.

Suzanne dresses for practice, veering from black so that Petra will not interrogate her more. The jeans she once had to wriggle into slip on easily. She pulls on a tee-shirt and sandals, pins up her hair, skips makeup when faced with her reflection's pointed watching. She does not want to see herself.

She almost doesn't answer the phone, but after years of waiting for audition calls—and then Alex's—it is hard for her to ignore a ringing phone. There's always the chance that the news is good, that the voice is beloved.

The voice on the other end says her name, repeats it and then asks, "Do you know who this is?"

"Who?" Suzanne echoes, but her chest tightens because she is almost certain that the voice she is hearing belongs to Alex's wife, that this is not good news at all.

"I need to see you."

Her chest squeezes itself, a vise, and her stomach contracts. "That's not a good idea. It's better that we don't."

"We have shared something important, no? There's a connection between us whether you want there to be or not." The woman pauses. "I need to see you. You need to come to Chicago."

"I have to go right now, somewhere to be."

"All right, but I'm going to call back if you don't call me soon. I assume you've dialed this number before? Talked to my husband in our home?"

"Yes," Suzanne whispers and hangs up.

Petra and Anthony are arguing when she enters the practice room, but their words lack heat. Suzanne unpacks her viola, tunes, rosins her bow, still trembling as she watches these two people capable of arguing ideas without emotion. Daniel, for whom all arguments are personal, has not arrived. When they were students at Curtis, Petra made the mistake of sleeping with Daniel. He struggled with her moral philosophy, with her assertion that she could be a loyal friend even as she was an unfaithful lover. "If you're going to ask me to sleep with just you, then we're breaking up immediately," Petra told him. A rough stretch followed: Daniel throwing rocks at the windows of the apartment, Daniel phoning drunk in the middle of the night, Daniel wetting Suzanne's shoulder with his real tears. It took about a month for his understanding that Petra was a friend worth having outweighed his desire to sing lead in a tragedy quickly turning trite.

Suzanne learned something about Daniel that Petra does not understand: for him everything is personal. If Petra and Daniel argue over politics or movies, and certainly if they argue over music, the differences in their opinion are, for him, indicators of moral difference. He either assumes she's inferior or fears he is. It's something Suzanne understands, feels herself when Ben mocks a piece of music she loves or makes a cutting comment about performance as a goal in itself.

But for Petra, arguments can be sport, and she and Anthony push back and forth the idea of performing the *Black Angels Quartet*.

"I think it's a perfect time to play an antiwar piece. Don't you agree, Suzanne?" Petra spins her gaze, glances at Suzanne.

Suzanne once played the piece, subtitled *Written in a Time of War*, in a course in which the professor was trying to teach his students about gesture, both physical and musical. She shrugs under her viola as she places her fingers on the strings, trying to steady herself as she warms up. Her right wrist feels weak, her biceps tired. There is a sharp pinch just inside her left shoulder blade.

"You don't have many opinions of late," Anthony says. "Funny thing is that I'm not sure it's such a bad idea. I'd like to feel some people out."

"Poll our electorate?" Petra asks. "See whether it would gain us more donors and audience members than it would cost us?"

Anthony takes no offense at Petra's words. "It's Princeton," he says, "so it's hard to say how it would play—I'm talking aesthetically more than politically."

Forcing herself to participate, Suzanne enters the conversation. "If we were to perform *Black Angels*, would we present it as a museum piece or translate it? I mean, the directions say amplify as much possible. Back then Crumb didn't have any idea what that would mean today. We'd blow out the back of the room."

"The huge score," Daniel says as he enters, "is reason enough for me to sign on. I like big pieces of paper."

"The physical size of the score *could* be a conversation piece for our," Anthony pauses as he searches for the word, "for our base."

"Well," Petra says, taking her seat, "you smell which way the money's blowing and let us know."

Today they practice Suzanne's favorite of their standards: *The Art of Fugue*. The clean counterpoint lifts her from her life, from space and time, from bad news large and small, from her anxiety, into an airy world of notes. They know the piece well, so despite its challenges, they play through and the hour feels more like performance than practice. They perform for themselves. They leave the piece as Bach left it: unfinished after the letters of his musical signature. Only Bach could take such a corny idea as weaving the letters of his name into his music and have it sound perfectly elegant.

The abrupt ending hangs above them, not menacing but haunting, not a guillotine but a ghost, and they know not to ruin the moment with speech. They pack their instruments quietly, nodding good-bye, silently sharing a rare secret performance. This love of playing is what holds them together across their differences of taste and personality. Even Anthony is in it for the music today.

Seven

When Suzanne and Petra arrive home, Ben is in the living room, playing the cello—something Suzanne has not seen him do in months.

The first time she saw him, he was hunched over a cello as though it were a child he was protecting from breaking waves. Though the instrument stayed silent, his fingers moved along the strings as though he were really playing, and his foot tapped time. When he looked up, Suzanne was unnerved by the dark eyes staring out under lashes so fair they were nearly white. He had reddish hair but no freckles, and he was more tan than pale. She had never seen anyone with his coloring.

"I could spend a night with that," whispered Petra as they stood outside the practice room he occupied but they had reserved.

"But you like ugly men," Suzanne said, though she assumed that what Petra suggested would happen, that Ben would fall for Petra for a week or forever. She assumed that she herself was too small and dark to attract his notice, but he fixed on her from the start, further unnerving her with his height as he stood and, as he spoke, with his rich Southern-melodied voice, itself cello-like. The first word he said to her in his molasses accent was *viola*, and she nodded that, yes, she played the viola.

"I'm writing some music for the viola," he said, the *o* open and then pulled long. "Maybe you'd run through it for me sometime."

Suzanne found her voice. "A sonata?"

"More like a group of caprices."

"A young Schumann," Petra said. "I hope you're not planning to live off your wife's performances and then throw yourself in the Rhine and get locked away for the rest of your short, stupid life."

Suzanne learned then an important fact about Ben: he doesn't swat banter back and forth. When a line is thrown his way, it sticks and he responds as though it were not a line. His words are always serious; he does not joke, and he does not flirt. To Petra's attempt, he said, "I'd take Schumann's compositions at any price. There have been few original composers. I'm not one for Romantic music, but I'd be happy if posterity could look back at my work and say that it was utterly new."

"Oh, my god, such an earnest young composer," Petra said sideways to Suzanne. Of Ben she asked, "Even at the price of poverty and extreme unhappiness?"

He lifted his cello, embracing it with his broad chest as well as his arms as he stood. "No one ever said we were meant to be happy. There are more important things."

"I'll do it," Suzanne interjected. "I'll play through the caprices for you."

"She's very good," Petra said, putting her arm around Suzanne like a loving father. "Though her name isn't Clara."

Ben ignores them as they enter now. He is playing something that sounds more like math than music—notes and tempo that do not amount to melody. They sit and listen, and it is a good ten or more minutes before he is done.

"Just working some stuff out," he says.

Suzanne rises when the house phone rings, then worries that she appears anxious to answer first. Her fear is dulled by Elizabeth's voice.

"We just decided to have a potluck tomorrow night. All of you come, and be sure to bring your friend Petra. She's fun; I like her."

"You're one of the few wives who does," Suzanne says, and it is true that most women despise Petra on sight.

"I can't believe that," Elizabeth objects. "She's terrific. Tell her she has to come."

"You just like her because she likes the same dreadful music you do."

"But she's a violinist."

"Classical musicians have famously appalling taste in popular music."

"You for one." Elizabeth snorts at her joke. "And there will be kids there for Adele to play with. My kids just love her, tell Petra that. Speaking of which, when are you and Ben going to give this town some more kids?"

Suzanne flinches, as she does every time the question comes up, not understanding how people can be so nosy, or so oblivious to the possibility that people who don't have children might not be able to. Or might have lost one. She could retort snidely—the impulse is there—but she likes Elizabeth, likes having a friend who is a grown-up party girl, careless about dates and times but thoughtful when she hears you're sick or celebrating. Elizabeth is free of malice, and Suzanne has never heard her say a mean word about anyone, not to them and not behind their back.

"We'll see you tomorrow," she says evenly, thanking Elizabeth before hanging up.

While Suzanne stares at the cabinet trying to imagine a dinner emerging from its contents, the phone rings again. She assumes it is Elizabeth, who always forgets something she meant to say and then phones back a minute later when she remembers.

Ben answers and passes the phone with a shrug. "Not Elizabeth."

Suzanne's pulse skips as she says hello, as if her body knows in advance who it will be.

"We need to talk," Olivia says. "Call me soon to let me know when you're coming to Chicago. You managed to get here plenty of times to see my husband. Make a way now. It's important."

"We don't talk to telemarketers." Suzanne is staring at Ben. "Please put us on your don't-call list."

"Call me soon or I'll call back."

Suzanne hangs up, steadying herself. Her heart feels like it has heavy, beating wings—a large bird trapped in her chest. Her eyes follow the lino-leum's lines of elongated stars, faded from their former silver to a dull gray, to the pantry, to the place where a wined-up Petra started to chip away to reveal the wood that they intended to reveal and refinish someday.

"It pisses me off," Ben says, "that we still get those calls. I thought you signed up for that registry, that it was illegal for them to keep calling."

"Shall we order Chinese?" Suzanne asks. Suddenly cooking seems impos-sibly hard.

Ben nods. "Hey, I wanted to tell you, I think I'm going to make a quick trip down to Charleston. My mother needs some things done around the house, and Charlie's not going to get them done alone."

Several ugly sentences form in Suzanne's mind: *Why doesn't she hire some-one? Why do you have to go? When are you ever going to do the things that our house needs done?* She closes her eyes, pushing away the person who would say those things aloud, the person she doesn't want to be.

"When are you going?" she asks.

"I was thinking next week, but I guess that depends on whether you want to go or not."

"But you've been working day and night on the new piece."

"Exactly. It will be good for me to step away from it, just for a day or two; you said that yourself."

"Too bad Suzanne can't go with you," Petra says as she enters the kitchen. "But I need her to go to the Children's Hospital in Philly with me."

Ben glares at her "You're not honestly considering going through with that, are you?"

Suzanne readies herself, fingers tense around the edge of her seat, for Ben's lecture on deaf culture and the dangers of rupturing Adele's social and cultural maturation. She waits for him to interrogate the meaning of a normal life, to emphasize the profundity of the deaf, to expound on the intricacies and beauty of American Sign Language, to argue that a full deaf life is better than a half-assed hearing one.

She asks herself whether she'll respond out loud: *You think of her as a theory and not as a person.* Or: *Petra is the parent.*

But Ben is tired. The parallel lines that run across his forehead groove more deeply than usual, and his face looks heavy.

Petra smiles. "So I need Suzanne next week."

Petra knows that she doesn't want to go to Charleston, not as long as she lives. They have talked about it a lot, maybe too much. But even when they discuss it, *Charleston* is a word Suzanne avoids saying, a name that makes her wince when it is spoken by someone else, particularly if the syllables are pronounced by a native, even by Ben—the first one drawled and the second clipped. For her it is a word that says, *You are poor; you are unfit; you do not belong.* And she can admit this: it is the city where she lost her baby.

She understands why people love Charleston's cobblestones and painted houses and marsh grass and salt air, people who view the bay from swinging chairs and admire the water rolling in to smother the vaguely rotten odors that leak from the earth when the tide is low. Charleston has things people want: galleries and festivals and good restaurants and money and ocean access and wraparound porches and flower boxes and the funky haunts made possible by the presence of art students, of white kids with dreadlocks.

People love the Charleston that cleans up its long history in the telling, makes it quaint, wears it as style. If the listener is not the Civil War aficionado the local speaker hopes for, the palmetto trees that saved the American Revolution can be mentioned, or the conversation can settle on the city's notoriously promiscuous and quite possibly bisexual female pirate. But across the time Suzanne lived there, she never could learn the city's secret speech codes—what things really meant, whether an invitation to drop by a home was intended or merely mouthed, whether a question about her musical preferences was meant to be answered in four words or forty. But she learned on her first visit one of the harshest codes: in Charleston the well-born make you say aloud things they already know.

"Your mother was Italian, right?" Ben's mother asked, the *I* long, the color on her cheeks artificial. And she said *Realtor* with a tone that made clear she already knew that Suzanne's mother wasn't the successful model that the affluent tolerate at their cocktail parties but the kind who scrape by between cash-flow problems, selling starter homes and condominiums that are cheaper to buy than to rent—the kind of places where Suzanne and her mother also lived. Still his mother asked, "So she must have done quite well?"

"And what does your father do?" asked Ben's sister, Emily, knowing already the most generous thing Suzanne could say was that he no longer worked. "Early retirement?" Emily pressed, cocking her head, her tone pleasant. Suzanne nodded, though everyone in the room knew the words closest to the truth were *unemployment* and *disability payments*.

Suzanne searched for sympathy in their eyes, some softening of facial lines or ease in their shoulders—something to suggest that they were, after all, nice people. She looked to Ben, who knew the language, but he was looking to the mantel, at the photo of his father standing in front of the small, fast yacht he had gone down on.

It was his brother who saved her, walking into the room with a surfboard. "Sort of like Ben," Charlie said. "And sort of like me. You've done a wonderful job, Mother, raising a composer and a beach rat, neither of whom has ever worked for money."

His mother passed Suzanne a plate of benne wafers. "You're very thin," she said, and Suzanne couldn't tell if the sentence was a compensatory compliment or recrimination.

Ben walked toward the picture of his father, rested his fingertips on the mantel in front of it. "Suzanne and her father are very different people," he said finally, after she had the cookie in hand, napkin underneath to catch the sesame seeds, no longer in need of rescue.

Charlie grinned at her, swiped his streaked hair from his eyes, young person to young person, bonded by similar tastes in popular music and a common enemy.

Ben cases his cello. "Suzanne?"

Suzanne hates that they have so many of their few conversations in front of Petra, but this time it feels like a mercy. "I guess I'll stay up here. I did tell Petra I'd go to Philly with her, and I should see my dad. Petra will give me an excuse not to stay very long. That is, if you don't mind going alone."

He shrugs. "No, that's fine. Probably easier since it'll just be a few days."

"Stay as long as you need to," she says, wondering if she can use his trip as a way to do what she probably has to do, which is to find out what Alex's wife wants from her.

When she thinks of her—*Alex's wife*—of how angry she could be, of what she might be capable of, Suzanne feels her whole world pulling away like a receding tide sucking sand back into the ocean. *Be prepared to lose everything*, she tells herself, and wonders how much she has to lose.

Eight

On Friday after rehearsal, Suzanne waits for Adele to get out of school, and together they bake a cake in the hot kitchen. Adele's choice is odd for a child: an Italian chiffon cake made with dark green olive oil and orange-blossom water.

"You have sophisticated tastes for your age," Suzanne signs.

"Maybe my taste is better because I don't hear. They say that, you know."

Suzanne presses her hand on her own breastbone, feeling something catch at the base of her throat. She composes herself and signs, "I think you're just a sophisticated kid."

Adele nods her pleasure at that, and Suzanne feels relieved. Adele loves to go to social events, but Suzanne has noticed that she grows anxious before them, slightly manic.

"You mix the dry ingredients, and I'll get everything else ready to go."

Suzanne sets the oven temperature, greases the Bundt pan, grates lemon and orange peel, gets out the mixer, separates eggs, measures milk, olive oil, vanilla. As long as she concentrates on the work of the moment, she feels almost normal. In those moments when she remembers everything—her lonely marriage, the baby she lost, Alex, Olivia, her whole crashed life—she wonders if she will ever feel happy again. She compresses herself back into the small, functional version of who she is and summons a smile. "Ready to mix?" She does not want to grow puny and bitter. She does not want her life to be already decided.

Adele folds the whipped egg whites into the batter, the spatula graceful with the turns of her thin wrist, which is limber like a conductor's. Her arm moves slowly and she looks transfixed as she smoothes clumps in the whites. Suzanne hears nothing against this silent symphony except birds and distant traffic.

After she centers the pan in the oven, she lets Adele lick the bowl and beaters. She knows she shouldn't—raw eggs—but she wants to share this rare fond memory from her own childhood.

"Don't worry," she says when Petra calls, "I washed the eggs before I cracked them."

"Can I meet you and Adele there?" Petra asks.

An hour later Suzanne drives across Princeton with Ben and Adele, as though they are a nuclear family. The entire car is fragrant with the still warm cake. "What's going on with Petra?" Ben asks, and Suzanne appreciates that he tips his face down so Adele cannot read his lips in the rearview mirror.

"The usual, I guess."

"She seems a little more out of control than usual."

Suzanne shrugs. She knows Petra is struggling with the decision about the cochlear implant and does not want to raise the subject again with Ben.

At Elizabeth's house, Ben presents the cake to the hostess.

"I wish Henry could cook!" Elizabeth says, and Adele and Suzanne exchange elbow pokes. Elizabeth hugs each of them in turn, pressing Suzanne into her pillow of a chest, kissing Adele on both cheeks, quickly embracing Ben.

The house and yard teem with chatting mothers, children hard at play, husbands arriving from work—most from jobs in New York and some from local employment—to meet their families for the start of the weekend. One of Elizabeth's children takes Adele by the hand, pulling her away to play. Suzanne makes her way through the house to the backyard, where adults talk in groups and children roam in small packs. Along the way she chats with people she recognizes. As always, making conversation with people she knows only a little feels like work, but she does that work. "A musician, yes. Viola," she says more than once. She wishes she could be more like Ben and Petra—wishes she didn't care—but she wants to fit in. If she cannot live an extraordinary life, a desire that crashed with Alex's plane, then she'll take the ordinary life she craved as a child. She needs to belong in this town, to be one of its families, to live a normal middle-class life. And so she tries. She answers the questions, compliments the women's dresses, inquires about the husbands' jobs, asks people about their tennis games and running times and where they take yoga. She finds a cooler on the porch and pours herself a glass of wine from a thick-walled, wet bottle.

In a far corner of the backyard is a quartet of chairs. One appears to wait for Suzanne; the others are occupied by Petra, Daniel, and Anthony in their usual arrangement.

"Can't you at least sit in different seats?" Suzanne asks as she approaches.

"We just can't get enough of each other," Petra says, patting the empty chair.

Suzanne sits and looks out to her right, where she can hear but not see a small brook on the other side of a boxwood hedge.

"A viola player and a cellist are standing on a sinking ship," Petra says. "The cellist calls for help, says he can't swim."

Suzanne finishes Petra's joke: "'That's okay,' says the viola player, 'just fake it like I do.'"

Petra lifts the outsized bottle of wine leaning against her foot and tops off Suzanne's glass, though it is still nearly full. "Keeping it close so we don't have to get up and down just to stay liquidated."

"Hydrated," says Daniel.

"And so I don't have to talk to those women. It's not like I even want anything to do with their stupid husbands, and if I did they should thank me. If one more of them says how ironic it is for a musician to have a deaf child, I'm going pistol."

"Postal," says Daniel.

"Right," says Petra, "homicidal."

The timbre of her laugh straddles the border between lighthearted and reckless. Suzanne knows, from experience, that this means Petra is a couple of hours into her drinking. She knows it's why Petra didn't come home, why she wanted to meet at Elizabeth's. Suzanne angles her chair so she can see the group of kids Adele is playing with. Adele seems to have given up trying to lip read—something difficult in groups and impossible with moving children—yet she appears happy in the company, handing toys back and forth with a boy her age, smiling.

"What do you think, Suzanne?" Daniel's off-center gaze suggests that he has drunk plenty of wine as well.

"We're recycling the argument over performing *Black Angels*," Anthony says.

Suzanne shrugs. "I'll play anything."

"Even Tchaikovsky?" Anthony exaggerates the lift of his eyebrows.

Suzanne smiles, though she feels as though she is watching them from far away. "Let's not get carried away."

"We know your theories," Petra says to her. "Romanticism yes, sentimentality no."

"My theories?" She wonders if Petra is angry with her or just wined-up and in the mood to quarrel with anyone. She reminds herself that Petra's arguments are rarely personal, but her friend's sentences have sharp points tonight, and her voice is pitched higher than usual. *Theories* is a word they usually reserve for Ben—a shared defense disguised as mild disdain.

"I think we should play the *Black Angels*." Daniel speaks without looking at any of the others. "If we can't do something, say something, about what's going on in the world, then what use are we?"

Petra shrugs. "Either way. There's always a war somewhere, no? Besides, this isn't my country. I have the luxury of being an observer."

Suzanne listens to their arguments but continues watching Adele at play. Adele interacts through objects—handing the other children found leaves and flowers, accepting a bubble-blowing wand. Suzanne wonders if she will always have to give to fit in, and how that giving will change as she grows up. She imagines Adele with the implant, almost hearing, learning to speak but still noticeably different. She wonders whether Adele will be more fully accepted or instead rejected. With the implant, she'll be neither hearing nor deaf but instead an inhabitant of the one category children will not tolerate: indefinably different. Suzanne is not sure adults accept that kind of difference much better than do children, even as she hopes that children are nicer these days than they used to be, that better parents have made better kids.

Anthony waves for her attention. "Suzanne, what do you think?"

She sips her wine, which tastes too much of its cask. "Here's my opinion, then. The contribution of art to society is its existence more than its content. It's not the job of art to comment on current events. It should matter, but it should inspire by existing, by exploring what's beautiful, what's timeless."

"Oh, my god, you sound exactly like Ben." Petra's words slur and she blinks frequently, her expression prickly. "I think I'm going to puke."

Years of experience with her drinking father tell Suzanne that it's useless to reason with Petra now, but she is tired of one-way niceness, of covering for Petra with Adele, of defending Petra and Ben to each other, of always being the grown-up. "You wanted to know what I think, and that's what I think. Take the Holocaust, the role of music. What was miraculous wasn't people writing music about how awful the camps were. What was miraculous was the people in the camps playing Bach, saying, *You can't take this away from us*, saying, *This is beautiful no matter what*."

"So no music can ever comment on the world? Just itself? That's masturbation." Petra says the word too loudly, and a nearby couple look over their shoulders, the woman shifting them away.

"Let the rock stars protest war," Suzanne says. "People actually listen to them anyway."

Petra looks straight at her and pauses before she says, "You're such an elitist."

"If you're mad at Ben, Petra, then argue with him. But, sure, I agree with him on this. We live in a culture that doesn't value what we do. To meet it halfway is to give up. If holding up the best music ever written as a great human accomplishment makes me an elitist, then I am a snob, a monk in the tower protecting the books from barbarians."

"You're self-absorbed, that's what you are," Petra says. "When's the last time you thought about the war or even anybody else?"

Suzanne's anger expands and then fast shrinks back into the small, dull pain of feeling alone in the world. It's what you are left with when the person in the world who best knows you dies, something that has now happened to Suzanne twice. Next, she thinks, she'll lose Petra and then Ben. Being without them would make her even more alone than she is when she is with them.

Anthony's wife strolls toward their group carrying two small plates and forks. Jennifer wears thin gold jewelry that seems too delicate for her sturdy frame. She holds a law degree that she's never used, and her family's money is no longer looked down on as new money—it's been three generations, and even in Princeton people no longer care very much where money is from so long as it is plentiful and tastefully spent. That the money is spread thinner now is a more serious problem and the reason the quartet is always under pressure to become more reliably profitable.

Though Jennifer dictates to Anthony most of his life, from where he dines to what brand of shirt he wears, in front of the others she waits on him as though she is a well-dressed servant. She hands him a plate holding cake with sliced strawberries and asks if she can bring him coffee. He stands to give her his chair.

Watching the children play, Jennifer explains her child-rearing notions as though they are all gravely interested—as though Daniel and Suzanne are parents and Petra is a by-the-book mother instead of who she is.

Jennifer tells them she has plans to market her ideas in the form of a chart she's designed to track her own children's behavioral progress and quantify their rewards and punishments.

"It's like a game for them," she says. "Each child is a different color of cat, and the chart looks like a board game except it's vertical and magnetic so you can put it on the refrigerator. Very colorful. Their pieces get sent back spaces for particular offenses—like three spaces for whining—and they also receive surprises along the way, such as a trip to Thomas Sweet for a day without sibling rivalry."

Suzanne pictures her life on the board, her childhood ambitions punished with poverty, her adultery with pain, her need to fit in with shunning. Her cat would fall backward right off the chart.

Anthony, who may or may not approve of his wife's meting out of childhood's pleasures, smiles. "Jennifer's research suggests there's a national market for this kind of thing."

Petra leans over, tipping her low-slung lawn chair to a dangerous angle. "Great," she breathes into Suzanne's ear. "Now children in all fifty states can hate her." She rights herself, pushing off the grass with her hand.

Suzanne smiles, relieved to have her best friend back on her side, if only because they now face a common enemy.

"I don't understand." Jennifer points to the rather flat piece of layer cake she's just taken a bite from. "The recipe was three pages long, describing every test the kitchen made. I followed it exactly. I even beat the eggs and sugar over simmering water until the mixture reached exactly 110 degrees. I have a new thermometer—the good kind."

"You took your cake's temperature?" Petra smiles at her.

"It looks delicious," Suzanne says quickly. "Ben always prefers a moist fallen cake to one that's cooked too long."

Daniel nods. "It looks great, Jennifer. I'm going to get a piece later after I finish my wine."

"The glass or the bottle?" asks Petra.

"That's not the point." Jennifer looks at Anthony, then Daniel, searching for support. "That's not the point. If you follow the rules, you're supposed to get what you set out for. A recipe is a pact."

"Like music." Anthony rubs his wife's rounded shoulder with his free hand. "You can't give an audience a pleasant beginning and then hit them with something they don't understand. Same thing with marriage."

"I suppose you think life works that way," Petra says, her words loose but her face clamped. "Follow the rules, advance three spaces, collect your reward. Americans who were popular in high school always think like that."

Dusk lurks above them and then settles, as though the darkness is not a declining of light but a tangible thing losing altitude. Once lowered, it leaves Suzanne slightly chilled. Adele sits with another child, a girl whose mother, Linda, is a widow.

"She's beautiful," Daniel says of the woman, who stands beyond the girls.

"She doesn't look it, but she's ten years older than you are," Suzanne tells him, her voice sympathetic.

"That doesn't matter to me."

While Petra's drinking words slur unpleasantly, Daniel's overlap melodically, as though he is speaking a Romance language Suzanne half understands.

"She has two children, all the time."

"I love children," he says.

"Daniel," Suzanne says, her voice now like snapped fingers, "she doesn't drink. She quit when her husband died, because she always has to be the responsible one."

"Ah, well, now that might pose a problem." Daniel grins, boyish, but still he watches Linda play with her daughter and Adele. The three hold hands and turn in a circle. From behind, Linda, slim-hipped, looks like a tall child.

"Ashes, ashes, we all fall down," Linda's daughter sings as the three collapse to the ground laughing.

Ben walks up behind Suzanne, holds the back of her neck in a loose grip.

"That's a bit morbid," says Jennifer. "The father died on 9/11."

Petra's words collide with each other: "Did you hear the one about the terrorists who hijacked a plane full of viola players?"

Anthony helps Jennifer from the low chair and murmurs good-bye as they walk away to collect their children.

"Have some more wine, Petra." Ben's voice is like metal.

"Let's go," Suzanne says.

"But Adele is having fun. She never gets to play with children."

"Then let Ben drive you home, and I'll stay with her."

"And then come back for you?" He sounds annoyed and his grip tightens perceptibly.

"And then come back for Adele and me," Suzanne says resolutely. She's about to ask Daniel if he wants Ben to drop him off also, but he's already up and walking a straight line toward Linda.

As soon as Ben and Petra have left, Suzanne wishes she and Adele had gone with them. The party empties while they wait for Ben to return, and Adele quickly runs out of children to play with and settles in Elizabeth's living room with a book. Suzanne helps Elizabeth process some of the dishes, including her own empty cake plate. At one point she turns to Elizabeth, suddenly compelled to tell her—tell someone—about Alex. Instead she pours the wine left in her glass into the sink. She reminds herself, sternly, that she can never tell anyone, that not telling is part of the cost of what she has done.

When Ben returns, finally, the kitchen is clean and Elizabeth's family has gone to bed. Elizabeth dances with Adele in the living room to music with the bass turned up.

Ben wipes his feet on the mat just inside the kitchen. "It was hard to get Petra to stop talking and get inside."

Suzanne shrugs. "Too much to drink, I guess. Shall we go?"

Adele begs to sit in the front, but Suzanne insists she sit in the statistically safer backseat. "I'll sit with you, so we can chat."

As they drive across to their side of town, Adele leans her head into Suzanne's arm, sleepy and sweet.

Figuring Petra has passed out, Suzanne puts Adele to bed, brushing her teeth for her because she is too tired to lift the brush herself, tucking her in, kissing both soft cheeks.

When she gets to her bedroom, Ben is packing.

"I forgot you're leaving tomorrow."

"You seem to have a lot on your mind lately," he answers, his tone neutral.

She stalled him after Alex's death—several days, a week, strange that she cannot remember exactly. She stalled him not because it would have made Alex the last—she hadn't seen him for a month when he died—but because she feared some emotional ignition. She was afraid she would burn white heat and confess every wrong thing she has ever done. But she could not, or did not, stall longer, and she and Ben have made love several times since. She was surprised by how easy it was to give away nothing. Now she reaches for his hand: they always have sex the night before one of them goes away. It is almost a superstition, a required act. Even when it was her leaving to see Alex, she and Ben would sleep together. The next morning, shaving her legs in a bubble bath, she would separate the two realities into Ben-time and Alex-time, two things that were both true but were divided by water and had nothing to do with each other.

Tonight Ben has left the light on in the bedroom closet so that he can see her. And she can see him, the ropes of his stomach muscles leading up to the broader muscles of his chest, shoulders, arms reaching to hold her hips, guide their motion. A still-young man who has stayed in shape to play the piano and the cello even though he abandoned performance years ago. She presses her hands on his chest, for balance and for leverage, and she and Ben let themselves go completely, eyes still open. It's the closest they ever come to seeing each other, to really speaking.

In the morning she sleeps through his leaving, his good-bye only a short note on the kitchen counter.

Nine

It sits on the center of Petra's palm, looking more like a computer chip than the swirled snail of the hearing inner ear.

"The implant imitates the cochlea not in appearance but in function," the doctor tells them.

He has the good looks of Spanish youth, reminding Suzanne of the tall, healthy musicians she played *Carmen* with one summer in Seville. They attacked the music, grinning with the schmaltz of it, taking her later for wine near the university that was once Carmen's tobacco factory. "Tourist season," they shrugged, and she felt happy. She was not a tourist but a musician leading an extraordinary life, a woman meeting her lover in Lisbon two days later.

The doctor's smile does not seem disingenuous, but it is easy, offered without real thought. "It both will and won't make her hear, depending on how you conceptualize hearing."

Petra repeats her question: "Will she be able to hear?"

"The implanted electrodes introduce signals that are carried by the auditory nerve fibers to the brain, allowing sound to bypass the damaged portion of the ear. Is this hearing? Yes and no. The sound processor translates microphone signals into electrical stimuli. These elicit patterns of nerve activity that Adele's brain will interpret as sound."

"So the answer is no; she won't hear." Petra leans back in the armchair, folding her arms.

"More than ten percent of patients receiving the implant can communicate without any lip reading at all. They can converse with their eyes closed, you understand, talk on the phone. Most recipients can communicate fluently in spoken language when it's combined with lip reading. Many can distinguish pitch. The numbers are only getting better."

Petra shifts forward again. "But aren't the outcomes much better in people who have lost their hearing? You know, who remember what speech sounds like and already know how to talk."

"Of course." The doctor still smiles. He is not talking about his child, and he speaks with energy and good cheer. "But we are having tremendous success with those who have been profoundly deaf from birth, provided—"

Petra laughs. "'Profoundly deaf.' That's funny."

"Provided that we implant close to the optimal age range and follow up with education and therapy. If we can implant Adele in the next six months—sooner is better, understand—I have every reason to believe that she will live a normal life in the hearing world."

"'A normal life.'" Petra laughs again. "Can you get one of those for me, too?"

The doctor smiles, aware that she is joking but not quite getting it.

"When do you need to know?" Petra asks.

"We can complete the presurgery therapy and schedule the procedure with about two months' notice."

Petra stands, her posture erect but awkward, one hip stuck out too far, like the marionette of an unskilled puppeteer. "I'll call you in four months if I decide to do it."

The doctor's smile is gone. "Your daughter really is an excellent candidate. Think about what her life will be like without speech. It will limit who her friends are, who she can marry, what kinds of work she can have. She's such a smart little girl, so lovely and sweet."

"I think about that all the time. Can you really think that I don't think about that all the time?" Petra pulls on Suzanne's hand, her voice calming some but still loud when she says, "You need to get me out of here."

"Wait," says the doctor. He writes a room number on a piece of paper. "Go back out front, cross the courtyard, and enter the other wing. Some of the therapists are in with a group of children. Go see what they're doing before you close your mind."

The doctor has misread Petra. Petra is impulsive, but her impulses are complex, and she often clings to an idea most tightly right before she throws it down. Every time she decides to quit drinking for a stretch, she begins with a bender. If she's arguing with the doctor against the implant, it's because she's leaning toward the surgery.

"Poor little irony," Petra says when they reach the hedge-lined courtyard.

A couple passes them, and Suzanne's legs shake under her weight. She avoids eye contact; she does not want to see people who are visiting terminally ill children. Perhaps, she hopes, Adele's deafness works like a charm, protecting her from early sickness and death, her ante already in the pot, her dues already paid.

Suzanne nods to a bench. It is important that Petra calm down before they see the therapist and children. Suzanne is sympathetic, knowing that

Petra may hear what she hears all the time: "How ironic: you're a musician and your daughter is deaf."

Because everyone knows a bit of Beethoven's story and because so many rock musicians have lost their hearing to earphones and amplifiers, people associate deafness and music, even if they label it as irony. Some suspect, even, that the mind's ear hears more perfectly than the actual ear. There's the story about Schubert: he claimed the piano was more distraction than help in composing. Someone with perfect pitch needs only pencil and paper to write music.

"The Beethoven effect," Suzanne says.

"What people forget," Petra launches a speech she has given before, "is that hearing loss was more common in Beethoven's day—as likely to strike a musical genius as anyone else but not *more* likely. They forget that or else they want to overlook it because they think it's romantic. Even you, even you think it's romantic that she's deaf."

Suzanne exhales. "That's not fair, Petra."

Suzanne often argues that Beethoven composed his best stuff late in life not because of his hearing loss but despite it, building on decades of work and study and thought. It is that way with most composers, at least those who aren't stunted prodigies. Beethoven hated being deaf, railed against it. He wanted to hear his Ninth Symphony not just in his mind but with his ears.

Petra wraps herself with her arms and rocks back and forth intensely. "I know what," she says. "You decide. You're so good at deciding everything— you decide. I'm leaving it up to you."

Suzanne feels her anger rise as heat into her face, the tops of her ears growing warm. She tries hard, all the time, to help Petra as much as possible without ever tricking herself that she is a parent, that Adele is hers, that she has the right to decide anything important. Especially in this she has kept a studious distance, even when it wasn't easy, trying not to even have an opinion. Yes, she's gathered information and listened, but she never allows herself, even for a moment, to forget that Petra is Adele's mother and she is not.

Before Petra's frantic phone call when she realized that Adele could not hear, Suzanne had not given much thought to the ear. When musicians speak of the ear, they mean little more than the ability to identify or produce pitch, tempo, and dynamic. Like everyone else, they complain that their ears are too large or too small, that they stick out or lie strangely flat; as teenagers, they pierce them thoughtlessly. Rarely do they contemplate the ear as their most fundamental organ, their talent, tool of their trade.

Petra's call was followed by others as the doctors, including specialists Petra could not afford, debated the type and cause of Adele's deafness. From a helpless distance, Suzanne looked at drawings of the ear. She learned the beautiful names of its parts. Visible to the eye are the helix, the antihelical fold, the tragus dipping over the external auditory canal. Deeper, past the secret passage of the tympanic membrane, through the drum, sit like atolls the malleus, the incus, and the stapes. So gorgeous and intricate is the ear that it is miraculous that anyone hears at all. For most of those who do not, she learned, it is not that the ear shuts to sound but that, for various reasons and reasons that often remain unknown, the deaf person does not translate the acoustic energy of sound into the electrical signals carried to the brain by the thirty thousand fibers of the auditory nerve. That is the nature of Adele's deafness, and no doctor could explain why except to say that the four parallel rows of hair cells in each of her ears were incomplete or had deteriorated. A tiny imperfection with profound consequences.

"Could it be something she took?" Ben once asked.

Suzanne yelled back at him that no, Petra had not cost her daughter her hearing. "She took nothing, drank nothing, breathed nothing noxious. She avoided cats and people who coughed. She washed her hands." By the time she said *hands* she was crying. Suzanne knew, even as she was doing it, that she was defending not Petra but herself. Surely Ben had noticed his mother and sister commenting about her exercising while she was pregnant, about what she ate, about the half cup of morning coffee. "Everyone wants to blame the mother," she finished, but Ben was already walking away, his response to almost every fight, his response to most of her strong emotions.

Sometimes after talking to Petra Suzanne dreamed of riding a raft through the turns of the ear. She asked every musician she knew whether they knew that the basilar membrane running the height of the cochlea distributes vibrational energy longitudinally and by frequency. Only one person she asked had known this before she told him, and that was Ben. Ben was the only musician she talked to who had thought seriously about hearing, considered the ear in composing. At Curtis he composed a piece that alternated the lowest frequencies that cause the most vibration at the apex of the cochlea and those very high frequencies that cause the most vibration at the cochlea's base. He called the series of movements "Ear Dances." Just before they moved to Princeton, Suzanne dug through every box in their garage, but she could not find the composition.

"We're talking about Petra, not you," Ben said when she asked him if he knew where it was. "Don't turn into one of those women who go daffy on their dogs when they don't have a baby."

"Adele is not a dog," she said, but as is common with the most cutting of remarks, she not only hated him for its cruelty but believed in its accuracy.

Suzanne sometimes thinks that if Ben had not said that single sentence she would have forgiven everything else, endured the emotional distance that was there from the beginning, stayed more or less happily married, resisted Alex's gaze. Other times she thinks the two events are unrelated, that she couldn't have refused Alex even if she had been happy, that she would have fallen in love with him in any circumstance. Nothing breaks cleanly. Sometimes she thinks her marriage ended the day she met Alex, but it's also true that her marriage never ended but goes on and on, that she is married still.

And now she hopes that her loss—her mother, her child, her lover—protects her from more loss, the way she hopes Adele's deafness protects her from premature illness. *Dues already paid.* But she knows this is a false superstition. Everyone who reads the news knows that life can take everything from you. Some people lose one child in a flood or famine; others loose all six plus everyone else they've ever known. Luck doesn't spread evenly, not good luck and not bad.

"Petra?" she says. "What's the name of that composer for recorder? Seventeenth century?"

Petra smiles. "Oh, yeah, from that awful tutorial."

"Remember, he grew rich as a bell tuner? He traveled everywhere because he had a special feel for them, for that shape."

"The bell whisperer," Petra laughs. "So, okay, let's go see the kids and the bells. And yes, I know I'm a bitch."

Suzanne puts her arm around her friend's square shoulders. "You're scared."

"I am scared." Petra still smiles but also swipes her eyes. "But let's do this. I want to see."

Inside the other wing of the children's hospital they follow the information boards and signs to the fourth floor, then down a gleaming hallway that does not smell like hospitals usually smell but instead has the neutral odor of an office building.

The door they seek is open, and they stand wedged together in its threshold, watching a small circle of children made blind with plush black eye covers. They respond with push buttons to chimes played by a woman in a lab coat. The children range in age from maybe three to nearly adolescent. When they remove their blindfolds, the woman turns. She's in her forties, blond and elegant with stern features calmed by an ample smile. She smoothes her already sleek hair with her hand and then extends that hand to Petra, saying her name as a question.

The children zip backpacks, collect belongings, make their way to the door in pairs and small groups as Suzanne and Petra stand aside for them. Some say good-bye to Dr. Ormand; of these, some sound almost like hearing children while others speak with the exaggerated roundness of the deaf, of those who have learned to speak by shape and not by sound, who have learned to speak with other people's fingers on their mouths. One boy, about Adele's size, walks alone. He is humming, carrying the simple tune well, and grinning.

Suzanne nods. "Can they hear the chimes?"

The doctor motions them into the room, and they sit at the table where the children were being tested. "I'll have to tabulate their answers to tell you about this group today, but the answer is yes. Pretty much. They can perceive the sounds. It takes work and therapy—a lot of it—but within a few months of implantation all of these children could correctly identify whether a chime is sounded or not. Most of them can accurately identify differences in volume, if those differences are substantial. They can't distinguish differences as subtle as those described by the Weber-Fechner or Powers Law, but they can distinguish loud from soft."

"Blindfolded?" Suzanne asks, for Petra.

The doctor nods. "And most have some control over pitch. Again, they may not be able to discern an A from an A sharp in the same octave, but if you play two notes an octave apart, or even considerably closer, almost all of them can tell which is higher."

"But what's it like?" Petra asks. "What's it like for them? Is it like hearing?"

Dr. Ormand shrugs. "I don't know. I was born hearing. There are some good books, memoirs that I can recommend, but I'm not sure we can ever understand. What I do understand is that these children will have a more normal life than they would have if they hadn't been implanted."

"What's normal?" Petra asks, sounding again like Ben.

The doctor smiles—a professional gesture more than a genuine response. "There's a philosophy department over at Temple."

"That one boy," Suzanne says, "he was humming 'Frère Jacques.'"

"Again, it takes a lot of therapy and follow-through, not just here but in the home and school, to train the children how to interpret the signals their brains are receiving. But yes, some of them can perceive music and even sing well. That's likely determined by innate talent underlying the deafness."

Suzanne asks, "Is it really music to them?"

The doctor shrugs. "There's probably a music theory department at Temple, too."

Suzanne does not know how to phrase her question more usefully, to explain that it's a real question and not, like Petra's, just an expression of stubbornness.

"There's work being done in Canada that suggests that maybe ten percent of music can be experienced through the skin, even in people who can't hear at all. The researchers there designed a special chair that allows the deaf to have an experience of music. Not your experience but *an* experience. Add an implant, and yes, I would call it hearing music."

When they stand to leave, the doctor hands Petra what they have come for: a thick stack of pages containing findings that suggest that Adele, if implanted, could talk on the telephone. That she could—more or less and depending on definition—hear.

"On the other hand, I should warn you. In your home country, in Sweden, where good candidates are implanted early and are not allowed to sign in schools, plenty of kids yank out their earpieces as soon as they get home and use sign language. I've read your daughter's evaluation carefully. She's just a little older than I'd like, but otherwise she's as good a candidate as they come. But the cochlear is not a panacea. It's a big decision."

"I want her to hear me play violin," Petra whispers. "Is that selfish? When I found out she was deaf, that's what I hated the most. All the music I played for her while she was inside me—she didn't hear any of it." She is crying now. "I want her to be able to do anything, whatever she wants, to be happy."

The doctor's face is still—not unsympathetic but dispassionate. Suzanne recognizes the expression from the doctor who told her that her baby would die inside her, handing her a box of tissue but not laying a hand on her shoulder. Dr. Ormand has heard these things before, and it isn't her job to make parents feel better.

As they walk back down the hall, Suzanne finds that it now smells exactly like a hospital and quickens her pace.

Ten

Suzanne drops off Petra downtown and steers south, where her Irish father lives stubbornly among Italians despite the fact that the last Italian willing to give him the time of day divorced him with cause two decades ago. She lets herself into his building and then into his third-floor flat.

He sits in the crooked frame of his window, exposing only a fraction of his profile. At this angle, though, his hand is larger than life. And Suzanne cannot forget that it is this hand that her mother saved her from, rousting her from sleep only days before her ninth Christmas, whispering close to her ear, "Quietly, quickly; come, Suzanne." Her mother's lips brushed her ear, and her face smelled clean, like mint. After that night, any time Suzanne spent with her father was counted in hours and not in days, and she understood that this was for the best.

Now his hand has stilled and the many serrated edges of his tricky personality have dulled. Years of heavy drinking have bored holes through his intelligence. As his brain's nerves and synapses seek passage around these empty plugs to form a coherent story of the world, he revises the past and sees in the present mostly conspiracy and threat, whether from a new wrinkle in the tax code or the transport truck that bears toward his fender as he drives thirty miles per hour on the freeway.

She cannot bear to visit more than a few times a year. Ben never offers to come with her—and she never asks him to—so she always comes alone, with food prepared in a foil casserole pan.

Her mother, after they left that night, became a producer of frozen casseroles. She worked long days all week, in an office during the day and in the evening trying to sell houses in a sliding city, in a city whose residents had yet to discover that they wanted, after all, to live in town. So on the weekends her mother cooked for the week, freezing meals in foil pans for Suzanne to thaw and heat on Monday, Tuesday, Wednesday. As she grew older, Suzanne offered to help, to cook on weeknights. "No," her mother would say, "your time is for practice." When her mother died, she left a freezer full of neatly stacked dinners.

Eventually Suzanne ate this posthumous food, not out of nostalgia or tribute but because she was broke and needed to eat. The final meal was an improvised ratatouille stirred with noodles, made from an eggplant gone bitter, so the last taste of her mother was disappointment. Suzanne fell apart crying, wishing she had saved the delicious spinach lasagna or cacciatore for last.

"What are you looking at?" She starts to add the word *Dad* to the end of her question, but the consonant sticks on her tongue, and the question ends with a small thud.

"The garbage men. All they do is stand there and smoke. Company's owned by the brother of the guy who owns the building. It's a racket. My rent money goes to them so they can stand around and puff their Marlboros when all I can afford is generic. One of these days I'm going to do something about it."

Suzanne nods, but her father's attention stays trained through the window.

"One of these days I'm going to write a letter to someone. Maybe the newspaper, or that television station. Someone ought to investigate this racket. Maybe I'll get a petition going around the building."

"I just came to look in on you." Suzanne crosses the small efficiency unit and puts the lasagna in the half-sized refrigerator. "I have a friend waiting for me, so I can't stay."

"I suppose you'll want me to wash that pan after I eat."

"No," she says, and when he looks at her, she musters a smile. She says what she says every time: "It's the kind of thing you can throw away if you don't want to keep it."

"I know you mean well, but that's the problem with this country. Everyone thinks you can just throw things away. Pans, paper, marriages, babies."

She feels a twitch in her ribs. "Well, you can wash and keep the pan if you want, and maybe you'll like what's in it. I grew the basil—no cellophane bags involved."

She waits, but her father sees only the workers who have caught his ire.

"I'll see you next time," she says. "Take care of yourself."

Alex often asked her why she would drive to Philadelphia and back when she could have Chinese food or pizza delivered to her father with a phone call. Yet he understood, as much as anyone could, that her relationship to her childhood is more complicated than that.

Her car is parked to the left, past the garbage collectors, but she turns right to circle the block rather than cross her father's field of vision and earn a role in one of the myriad small conspiracies against him. Though she strides, neck tall and straight, she feels like a teenager disappearing around the corner to sneak a cigarette. Or an adulterous wife walking an extra block, hoping her lover will call her cell phone like he said he would.

Over her the sky is mostly the same concrete gray as the buckling side-walk, though sun glows through the connective tissue between cirrus clouds, making their edges glint like metal. She can hear from above the sound of knives scraped against a honing stone and is terrified that she doesn't know whether the sharp sweeping noises come from an upstairs apartment or from the hot-steely sky itself, an auditory announcement of impending cosmic retribution.

An Asian woman trundles three children wearing summer shirts through the narrow door to a vegetable market. She makes brief eye contact with Suzanne but does not smile. Suzanne quickens her steps, anxious to be sealed into her car, its roof between her and the sky, the vent blowing cool air through the dashboard and the radio pushing out any music at all.

Eleven

Pop songs from the 1960s crackle from the car speakers as Suzanne zigzags northeast on mostly one-way streets, toward the restaurant where she'll meet Petra. She touches the hospital literature that Petra left on the passenger seat. The cover page is a medical illustration of aural anatomy. As always, it looks so much like a seashell that Suzanne is tempted to ascribe pattern not just to the universe but to her own life.

On that first day in Charleston, after Ben's mother and sister finished their stylized interrogation over cucumber-and-cream-cheese sandwiches and too-sweet iced tea, his brother, Charlie, took her to Folly Beach. Ben declined the invitation, choosing to stay behind to read theory for an upcoming exam.

At the beach Charlie taught Suzanne to ride a wave with her body. Over and over she swam out, the saltwater and sunscreen stinging, her eyes nearly closed. Over and over she stretched herself long, catching wave after wave, at once thrilled by and afraid of the water's lift and slam. Joyously tired, the way the beach would always leave her, she soaked in sunshine, waiting for Charlie to come in from surfing the farthest break line. She felt his shadow over her before she saw or heard him. When she sat up, he placed two shells in her palm.

"It's funny, isn't it? The one that looks like an ear makes no sound."

He held the other one, a large conch, to the side of her head, and she heard the false sea in one ear and the real ocean with the other. They sat together after that, listening to the waves, the squawking gulls.

After a while, he said, "You sure you want to marry into this family?"

"I want to marry Ben." Suzanne had never said it aloud before, perhaps had not even thought it. But as she said the words, she heard them as truth.

"Hell, he's so hot, so do I!" Charlie laughed, but then his face settled into something serious, an expression Suzanne couldn't read. "Does Ben ever talk about our father?"

Suzanne touched Charlie's forearm, briefly, and shook her head. "Just a very little. A childhood memory or two. And that he drowned during a storm."

"Out there somewhere." Charlie stretched his arm toward the blurred horizon, where the pale sky met the darker ocean. "It's kind of weird, don't you think, that my mother keeps a picture of the boat on the mantel? There are other pictures of him, where he's not standing in front of the boat he died on, but that's the one we all have to look at."

"I'm sorry" was all Suzanne could think to say, and she held the conch back to her ear as she studied the translucently thin shell in her palm, noting its imperfections, that it was chipped in two places.

She wedges the car into a tight parallel space on South Street and walks the few blocks to the Afghan restaurant where she will meet Petra, the restaurant where Alex asked her about her two most crucial choices in life: instrument and husband.

The establishment is small and made smaller by dark red decor: walls, carpet, chair cushions, tablecloths all versions of the same hue. Lining the foyer are teapots, samovars, rice pots, long-handled spoons, daggers, an antique machete—objects of cooking and objects of war—together with framed reviews as well as articles about how violence in Afghanistan goes on and on. Last time she was here, Suzanne asked Alex if it was wise of the place to associate death with its cuisine. "It's fine," he said, "because people want to be told what they already think. If the restaurant displayed pages of Afghan poetry or pictures of Afghan children watching television, people wouldn't come back. Food and blood aren't a problem. They're what people expect."

It is late for lunch but early for dinner, and Suzanne has the place to herself while she waits. She points to a table near the window, and the old man who seats her and will probably also cook her food leaves her with a menu that she does not study. She plans to order the precise meal she ordered the last time she was here. She cannot remember what Alex ordered, which feels like a crushing loss. If she can't remember every detail, perhaps it is less painful to remember nothing.

What she does remember is their conversation, nearly perfectly. The place was more than half full that day, mostly with a workday lunch crowd, including someone celebrating a birthday at a table of six. Someone hummed the birthday song and, in a spontaneous coming together, everyone in the restaurant sang. This struck her as funny, and she laughed until she contracted the giggles.

While she stifled her laughter, Alex asked her, cold, "Why did you marry your husband?"

She felt her mirth drain and somberness cross her, shadowlike. She thought about his question—how she might answer it—for what felt like too long.

"There were several reasons," she told him finally, "including how serious he was about music. Really committed and really talented. I thought we would have this life of music, even that we would be at the center of something, though I guess there hasn't been anything to be the center of for a long time. Not like eighteenth-century Vienna, nineteenth-century Paris." She paused before striking a more embarrassing truth. "I also thought he would take care of me. He was confident and from a stable family with some money. Old Charleston. And he seemed like he was going somewhere, that he could make me safe and take care of our children. You know how I grew up."

Alex nodded, simple understanding.

The other reasons, which were even less tangible, she kept to herself, not so much to protect Alex's feelings but because she had no words that wouldn't get them wrong.

Alex sipped tea, then looked into the bottom of his cup. "I married my wife for a similar reason. She was competent and elegant. She knows how to organize the bills and cancel a magazine subscription and make sure the car gets properly serviced and the gutter cleaners are called the month they're supposed to be called. She knows how to dress for a morning meeting versus a cocktail party. She knows how the world works and how you're supposed to live in it—the things I didn't know. When you have a childhood like ours, normalcy is irresistible, no?"

Suzanne nodded. "You want things to work like they're supposed to."

"You want the house to be warm in winter and things to start when you turn them on and turkey to be roasting in the oven on holidays." He turned his eyes but not his head sideways before continuing in a voice carrying traces of the accent that he had all but eradicated but that returned when he talked about his childhood. "When I was a kid, what I wanted maybe as much as anything else was automatic sprinklers like I saw in the middle-class neighborhoods. I thought those people were rich and that they knew how to do things. Our yard was a patch of dirt with a little strip of dead grass. My wife knows how to open up the yellow pages and find a landscaper. She knows how to *program* the automatic sprinklers. She buys flowers from the nursery and makes the front of the house look nice all the time. She has made my work possible, by and large, and she knows how to put herself together for a fund-raiser and how to talk to those people I can't stand, how to ask them for money."

Suzanne swallowed her jealousy not just of his wife but of him. "Then why are we here now?"

"Great sex or a nice lawn? Grass isn't all it's cracked up to be." He squeezed her hand over the table. "Seriously, automatic sprinklers is a pathetic goal, the bent dream of a poor kid. Anyway, I'd argue that our spouses didn't fully deliver on their end of the bargain, though probably yours more than mine. But that's not my reason, and I don't think it's why you're here, either."

His directness made Suzanne nervous. It was the sort of conversation that could be irrevocable, that could change her life if she wasn't careful. And still she felt gnawing envy of Alex's wife, of his success, of his entire life. Around them the good cheer from the shared birthday song lingered, and people's words bounced, jovial. She set down her fork and waited for Alex to finish his answer, worried that he would describe their relationship as a symptom of mental illness or an act of self-destruction. "Why are we here?" she asked, her question almost a whisper.

"Because we fell in love," he said, holding her forearm now, rubbing the inner crook of her elbow hard with his thumb. "We're here because we fell in love."

He asked her about her life's other defining choice—why she had chosen the viola—and she told him the story of Charlene Ling.

"My mother put a violin under my chin when I was eight."

107

"Two years too late," Alex interrupted.

"An unrecoverable edge," she continued. "But I had talent and a good teacher and I might have kept going with it, except I had the misfortune to attend middle school with Charlene Ling."

"Arguably the best violinist in the country after Felder. But that's good fortune that you switched. You were made for the viola."

"Aside from all the jokes." Suzanne smiled. "If you happen to play in the school orchestra with someone on her way to being the world's best, you don't think, 'I'll be second best in the world.' You think there's a Charlene Ling in every school in every city in every country and that the world doesn't have enough orchestras for you to have a chair anywhere."

She did not add that the greatest anxiety of many female musicians is not stage fright but the creeping fear that they will wind up spinster music teachers surrounded by instrument-wielding children who aren't theirs and a pack of mewing cats who are.

"But you didn't give up music."

She shook her head. That had never been an option for her, not ever. "Switched to a less competitive instrument, at least at my school, and got to be first viola instead of second fiddle."

Alex lifted his chin to acknowledge her small pun, but he let her continue talking.

"I figured I'd be visible, marry a visiting conductor, and travel the world happily ever after with my famous husband."

"The cult of the conductor. Everyone wants us." He paused from his food, spread his hands, grinned. "And now you have me."

Suzanne shrugged, thinking still of his wife, the woman who knew how to dress, how to get things done, how to raise money. "I do and I don't. Anyway, I was twelve then, prone to romantic fantasy."

"And so then what happened?"

"I fell in love with the viola."

Suzanne hears the door push open, a jangle of bells.

"Sorry I'm late," Petra says, sitting down, grabbing the menu. "I'm starving."

With sudden clarity that constricts her lungs, Suzanne remembers what Alex ordered that day: tomato-lentil soup and a rice dish with dried fruit and nuts. This is what she asks for when the old man comes to take their order.

Petra orders her meal and bread for the table. "Do you have a wine list?"

"Sorry, no liquor license," he says, retreating with their menus. "I'll bring you tea."

"Is that why you picked this place?" Petra asks, joking but her voice stretched just a little tight.

"I'll buy you a bottle on the way home if you'll indulge a side trip."

Suzanne tries to feel Alex in the smell of the steam rising from the raisin-studded rice, in the tanginess of the soup, in the texture of the soft, warm bread she tears with her fingers. She wishes she had asked that day, when she could have asked him, what he meant about his wife not holding up her end of the bargain. She wishes she had asked to see a picture so that now she could match a face to the voice she has heard through her phone. She wonders if Olivia simply wants to torment her or if there's more, and she wonders how far she'll go. *A woman who knows how to get things done.*

"It's time to swallow, honey."

Suzanne looks up. "What?"

"You've chewed that bite like sixty times," Petra says. "Tell me it's not a diet. You're getting way too skinny."

Suzanne shakes her head. "I'm not trying to lose weight."

Twelve

After Suzanne wrestles the car from its tight space, she heads not to the freeway but up Broad, toward Temple and then beyond into the monolithic slum that is north Philadelphia. This is the place that inspired Alex to get the hell out, that forged his strength as it scarred him, giving him a place to be from and to overcome. She shudders at how easily he might have been stuck, the terrain of his childhood as much quicksand as mud. How different his life would have been if his talent had been less enormous, if he'd been a sliver less obstinate, if his music teacher hadn't tossed him a life rope, if his aunt hadn't owned a piano and three classical records.

He'd listened to those scratchy records—the Chicago Symphony playing Beethoven's Ninth, Horowitz playing the Beethoven sonatas, and the Berlin Philharmonic playing Brahms' Third Symphony—again and again on an old Magnavox record player that looked like a suitcase, risking his father's formidable wrath, insatiable for the music whatever the consequences.

Every chance he got or could make, he was at his aunt's piano. At nine he was picked up by the police for breaking in to play while she was at work, after which she gave him a key and told him to hide it from his father. At fifteen he spent nearly every dollar he earned washing dishes at a Bavarian restaurant to take the train downtown to volunteer as an usher at the Academy of Music. At thirty—already prominent, in some circles famous—he attended the funeral lunch of his father at the same haus of strudel and beer, a smirk on his face, the weight of childhood terror beginning to lift.

Suzanne navigates her way to Olney, the once working-class German neighborhood now solidly destitute and black and not a place visited by people who look like she and Petra. Alex told her she was the only person he knew he could take on a date to a ghetto. She started to joke, to say she wasn't that low-maintenance, but instead she held his hand and said there was no place she would rather be. He had that effect on her, made her want not to sound like everyone else. Sometimes she was careful with her words because she was afraid of disappointing him—boring him, losing him—but more often it was because she felt different with him. Like him, she had come from common, seeking something more, something harder. They were not like most other people. She and Alex came together because they fell in love, but their shared class was part of that. Not many people from any class but the top really make it, not in music, not in anything.

Suzanne parks in front of the row house where Alex endured the slow years of his youth.

"Did you ever live here?" Petra asks.

Suzanne says yes, she did, and it's true in its own way. It is that much like places she did live, although her run-down neighborhoods were south of the city instead of north, and not often did she and her mother rent an entire house.

This street was and is a poor one, yet it is lined with alders and a few spindly oaks and is better than some. Many of the houses have porches or at least stoops, marking this a better block than those where the row-house faces drop straight into the sidewalk, a juncture marked by a decaying line of caulk. The dirty house looks as though it was once yellow, but Alex said it had always been that way—never yellow but looking like it used to be.

Its windows draw an inscrutable face: two small eyes and a large off-center mouth, the door a long scar.

Alex could have directed the Philadelphia Orchestra had he wanted to, but he'd sworn to himself that he would never again live in this city, the place that had produced both him and Suzanne. He'd had a real chance—one in three—of leading the New York Philharmonic, but his stubbornness had gotten the better of him. He'd been done in, as he had known he would be, by conducting an all-German program, Wagner to boot. He'd chosen the program out of spite, after some newspaper made a comment about his last name and parentage. He said he'd never regretted his defiance until he met Suzanne, and then it bothered him that they could have lived an hour's train ride apart instead of enacting the geographic comedy they did.

Suzanne thinks now that if he'd put together another program—Ravel would have been safe in Avery Fisher Hall that year, or Delius, or even Copeland for that matter—he would not have gone down on a plane headed for Chicago. Wagner wasn't even in his top ten, but he wanted to make a point. To Suzanne he always gave French music, including every recording of Debussy in print, all the Ravel recorded in the last twenty years.

She reaches for the CD case on the floor under Petra's legs.

Petra grabs the case and flips through it. "What do you want?"

Suzanne considers the question, then says, "Anything by Verdi."

Though she does not love the melodramatic libretti he grew to rely on, she loves Verdi for saying that he would accept the public's criticisms and jeers only if he never had to be grateful for their applause. This he said after the flop of the comic opera he wrote the year both of his children and then his wife died.

Suzanne bites the corner tip of her tongue, wincing but not releasing it. She tries not to ask herself if Alex would be alive if he'd given the people what they wanted.

"Dear heart," Petra whispers, crooking her neck to see in the sideview mirror. "Memory lane is great and all, but I don't think we should be hanging out in this neighborhood."

"Forget the Verdi. Play the *Kinderszenen*. Did I tell you I heard Matsuev play it in Paris? One of the most beautiful things I have ever heard. He played it first, and I almost wanted to leave before the Chopin."

"You and your Schumann." Petra laughs.

"He played *four* encores that night. I doubt I'll ever see that again."

They make good time to Princeton, where they pick up Adele, groceries, and wine, in that order.

The phone is ringing as they enter the house. Suzanne feels a chill of brief panic but forces herself to answer.

"I thought I'd get the machine," says Ben.

Suzanne starts to ask him why he didn't call her cell, but she stops because she does not want to hear the answer: he doesn't actually want to talk to her. It's how he always is in Charleston. She wants to tell him not to bother calling, but that's not the kind of thing married people can say to each other.

Perhaps it is only because Petra mentioned Schumann when Suzanne and Ben met, but the association has stayed firm in Suzanne's mind. She wonders now, even, if she married him because of it, at least a little. In those Curtis days, when she thought of Robert and Clara Schumann, it was not the later marriage, when he was institutionalized and being driven mad by a constant A in his ear—an inescapable thrumming note he swore was real—and his virtuoso wife left her children with relatives to support the destitute family by touring. And she did not think much about the mature Clara Schumann, outliving first her husband's sanity and then, by another forty years, his death. Rather she imagined the young, happily married Schumanns triumphing over the obstructions of Clara's father, writing scores, using their newspaper to decry the cheap and commercial while championing the innovations of Chopin and shoring up the reputation of Bach, opening their home and their piano to the likes of Johannes Brahms. Suzanne pictured a busy home, filled with children and visitors and new music. She pictured people at the center of the musical world of their day—contributing, shaping, weighing in. They mattered to music, and music mattered to them.

Of course Ben is not like Robert Schumann at any age, though they hold in common three traits: a disrespect for received notions of form, the choice of the cello's voice to soothe anxiety, and the decision to eschew performance for composition. The story goes that Schumann ruined a hand with a home-rigged metal device he crafted to shorten the time it would take to develop finger independence. It's a tale often repeated by piano teachers to illustrate the truth that shortcuts don't work, that music accommodates no cheating.

Yet Suzanne has always suspected the story is a half truth, an excuse authored by Schumann himself, or perhaps by history, to explain his choices. It was well and fine for Clara to play for the public, but Schumann would rather spend those hours composing new music or writing about it.

Suzanne wonders how they did it all. They were, after all, parents of eight children, five of whom survived childhood. It's always mentioned that way in the history books: five surviving children. Maybe the thinking is that parents in the eighteenth century expected several of their children to die, but can it really be that they didn't suffer as much? Suzanne has imagined the Schumann household in the days following the death of a child and wondered if music was played and, if so, which pieces and by whom. After she lost the baby, she couldn't play for six weeks, and she and Ben barely spoke to each other for much longer.

"How's your mother?" she asks him now.

"The same, okay, and my sister. They said hello."

Petra takes the bag of groceries from Suzanne and drops a stack of mail on the cypress buffet in front of her.

"How's Charlie?"

There's a static-filled pause, as though Ben is calling from across the world.

"I don't know. I guess he's okay. He hurt his knee and couldn't surf for a while, which my mother of course sees as providence."

Suzanne musters a laugh, which is followed by another long pause. It grows longer, and Suzanne flips through the mail, determined not to speak first, not to carry the conversation that Ben initiated by calling. She sorts junk mail from the bills, which she stacks neatly, then pauses at a manila envelope with no return address and an Illinois postmark.

"I just called to say hello," Ben says.

"Okay, thanks for that. I'll see you soon, yeah? Or are you staying?"

"I think I'll head back early next week, probably drive straight through."

"Stay longer if you want." She pulls at the envelope with her teeth, tearing it unevenly open in her hurry.

"I promised Kazuo I'd be back by weekend after this, so maybe I'll stay on into next week, if you're sure."

"All under control here," Suzanne says flatly.

They say good-bye, and Suzanne extracts the contents of the envelope with a shake and a pull: a music score. It looks like any other computer-generated score except that it is smaller in size than most, with more lines to the page, and so rather elegant, its glossy black notes close together. There are a few penciled notes and instructions, written in two hands—one unknown to Suzanne and the other unmistakably Alex's.

The page is trembling when Petra startles her from behind, her breath in her ear. "What do you have there?"

"I think I'm holding the score to a viola concerto," she says because there is no other answer. "I've never seen it before."

Petra plucks the sheet from her hand and takes it to the piano. Standing in the kitchen with her eyes closed, Suzanne hears Petra play the agitated opening theme.

In the four weeks since Alex's death, Suzanne has survived minute to minute, breath by breath, muting herself, fleeing to the past as often and as fully as she can, hiding in the shallowest present she can make, as numb as she can will herself to be.

Now, on the one-month anniversary of the plane crash that killed her lover, as she listens to Petra play the horribly beautiful music, feeling returns to Suzanne like the excruciating tingle of blood circulating in a limb that has fallen asleep. *Pain*.

II. Agitato

Thirteen

She must have watched Suzanne come up the walk, because Olivia opens the door even as she knocks. Usually Alex called her *my wife*, or simply, with the power of an incantation, *she*. As in: *She just pulled up; I have to go.* Or: *I can't get out tonight to call; I think she is suspicious.* Or, some days: *She is making me angry enough to leave her; do you think the quartet would consider relocating?*

Still, Olivia's is a name Suzanne has heard often enough, and yet she is unprepared for the woman. She is unprepared for the elegant lines of her face or the way her straight posture, combined with her height, makes her regal. A Greek rendering of a goddess, an Athena, stepping past middle age with grace. Her hair is not graying or salt-and-pepper—the words Alex casually tossed—but gloriously silver and black, sleek, coiled into a smooth chignon at the nape of her long neck. Alex did not warn Suzanne that Olivia's dark eyes are so large they relegate her other features and drain her face of specific age. Before her now, Olivia dwarfs Suzanne in inches, in poise, and, Suzanne fears, every measure that matters.

Suzanne feels like something flimsy and easily crumpled. Toss her in a can, or just light a match nearby.

She finds her voice. "Olivia," she says, because "Mrs. Elling" seems even more preposterous.

Olivia wears her smile evenly, and someone else might take it for warm. Her handshake is cool yet full with touch and generous with energy as she says, "Ours is a peculiar meeting, no?"

Suzanne only nods. Under Olivia's aggressive composure she feels frizzy and unkempt, lacking in grace, sour smelling from the too-warm airplane. Her once smart travel dress has lost its form through many washings and now hangs loose, a frumpy sheath that makes Suzanne look thick-waisted though she is not. Olivia wears gray trousers and a pale green blouse, both crisp and wrinkle free. As if to prove her unworthiness, Suzanne says, "You are not what I expected."

"It's funny that you should say so, because you are precisely what I expected." Olivia pulls the door open wider, stepping back for Suzanne to pass.

As Suzanne penetrates the Elling residence, she recognizes objects often described to her, but the house is much larger than she anticipated, larger than the house she pictured when Alex told her that he loved his little place with its peek at the lake, that his little house was all he needed until she was all he needed.

I am sitting in the red chair, he would say. *The plate glass is old, and so the gazebo in the yard looks like it is melting in the sun. Trace the lines of your right hand and describe them to me.*

Or: *I am sitting in the red chair, leaning back. Lie on your bed and tell me what you are wearing. Is your pillow soft or hard? Are you on your stomach or your back? Turn onto your stomach.*

Or: *I am sitting in the red chair. Take out your viola and play for me. Be sure to put the phone close so I can hear. Brahms today. I want to hear you play Brahms.*

Olivia offers her the red chair, and Suzanne perches on it. The old plate-glass window looks wavy, and when the sun emerges from a passing cloud the gazebo in the yard looks as though it is melting. But Alex misled her about the house: it is not small. It is bigger than anywhere Suzanne has ever lived.

As Suzanne scans the living room, she notes that if Olivia failed to keep some part of the marital bargain, it is in an unseen way. The house is kept. The room mixes deep red, pale blue, and dark wood, a combination more attractive than Suzanne would have thought. The furnishings match in style and in proportion, as though planned and purchased at the same time—something Suzanne has never known outside Ben's mother's home, whose furnishings Suzanne finds overly ornate and oppressive, dusty feeling even when clean. The room she sits in now is airy and uncluttered, but the chairs and sofa are substantial within their clean lines. The colors are balanced, and the total effect is of composure. It is a very nice room, a place where someone would want to live, even more so if that someone grew up unhappy in a dingy row house in north Philadelphia.

Suzanne lets her weight shift from her legs and leans back, sinking slightly into the red leather curved by a body larger than her own. She sits on Alex's chair, small within the depression made by his absent form, looking through his window, listening to his wife offer her coffee.

"No, thank you." She settles further into Alex's depression, trying to feel the shape as his embrace, wondering if she will smell him if she presses her face into the leather. *A dirty shirt*, she thinks, *or his pillowcase*. She wonders if she might be able to take something with his scent.

"Not taking a cup of my coffee doesn't absolve you for sleeping with my husband," Olivia says, her voice as cool as if she were talking about something that didn't matter. "You did that. Maybe he was even going to leave me for you and you were going to let him. You know that, and I know that. You might as well have some coffee if you want some. You look tired."

Suzanne feels the fatigue as gravity pulling at the corners of her eyes, as a weight in her cheekbones. On the plane—her first flight since Alex's death—she wanted to sleep but was afraid that if she relaxed her mind, she would imagine the crash, feel Alex's last terrible moments of life. And so she read with focus chapters of the autobiography of a man who lost his hearing and was fitted with a cochlear implant. A technophile, the author seemed most interested in how the implant made him a machine, in his need for software updates, in the pat irony that something artificial in the end made him more human. He was someone who grew up able to hear, who was restored rather than reinvented.

Suzanne read the description of the operation twice—how the surgeon bores through the base of the skull with a diamond-studded drill bit, how the nurse pours distilled water over the implant to protect it from static electricity, how the cut bone is reconnected with metal sutures. When she pictured not the man writing his story but instead the delicate place behind Adele's small ear, she decided not to give the book to Petra. She slapped it softy shut and felt the coming of sleep like a slip of satin across her face. But the wisp of irrational thinking that precedes a nap floated down too late, coming as the pilot announced the plane's final descent into Chicago, city of her lost lover, city of what she assumed was now her mortal enemy.

"I take it black," she says. "No sugar."

Returned with the service tray, Olivia asks, "What did you tell your husband this time?"

There is nowhere to set her cup without first standing, so Suzanne holds it on its saucer, a feat that requires both hands, and tries to sip the coffee down quickly, although it is very hot and the cup is very thin. "Nothing yet. I left while he was out of town, but I'm going to tell him the truth."

Olivia's composure breaks just slightly, a subtle collapse of her chin and slight alarm in her cool gaze. "The truth?" she repeats.

"A version of it." Suzanne wants to stop there but knows that Olivia has brought her here to get something from her. She hopes that the more she gives Olivia up front, the less she will take in the end. "I'm going to tell him that I've been asked to arrange a posthumous viola concerto by Alex Elling. He'll ask why me, and that I will lie about."

When Olivia leaves the room to get the score, Suzanne rises and sets her cup and saucer on a side table across the room. She lifts a throw pillow from the sofa, presses it to her face, breathes in fabric. *No Alex.* She turns to the small fireplace, its narrow mantel, and there, in a dark wood frame, is Alex's son. She has feared this son, terrified that he will look like his father and crack her heart. This is only his picture, and already it is worse than she feared: he does not look like his father but rather an even blend of his father and mother. Half Alex and half Olivia—proof of their union, proof of Alex's permanent connection with Olivia, who has his pillow case, his dirty shirts, his chair, his large house, his child.

Olivia, who has returned holding a large folder. "You didn't know he was composing."

Suzanne shakes her head as she turns. Olivia reestablishes herself on the sofa, trousers holding their perfect center crease, blouse fresh. She is not a woman who rumples, and again Suzanne feels unkempt. Slovenly, her father once called her mother, who was working too hard and succumbing to

123

the flu. Once Petra called herself a *salope*. "You know," Petra said, "French for sloppy. Even sounds like it." But later Suzanne read the definition in a French dictionary: *bitch, slut, whore*. She tries to smooth her hair with her hands, hoping their oil will calm the frizz, wishing she had taken the time to put it up.

"Do you suppose he told you everything?" Olivia does not quite face Suzanne as she speaks, offering instead a three-quarter view.

"Most things, yes, I did think that."

"*Did*." Olivia's mouth pulls to one side, but the expression seems too sympathetic to be a smirk.

Suzanne presses a little harder; she wants to understand more than she wants to protect herself from this woman who certainly means her harm. "I don't know why he would keep such a thing hidden from me."

Olivia runs her hand up and down the envelope in her lap, just once in each direction, a tic almost under control. "Maybe he was embarrassed, insecure of the quality of his composition."

"Alex wasn't subject to self-doubt. He was one of the most assured men I have ever met."

"Part of the attraction, I'm sure, but maybe he valued your opinion even more."

There is some truth in this. It took a long while for Suzanne to overcome her belief that she wasn't good enough for Alex, that he would leave her for someone more sophisticated, prettier, more talented, better bred. But finally she noticed that Alex depended as much on her as she depended on him. If she was critical or even neutral about a program he was considering he would grow agitated, or sometimes sullen, and later she would discover he had swapped pieces to win her approval. Once when he mused that he was going to start a program with Franck's "The Accursed Huntsman," Suzanne laughed and said, "Didn't Franck's students call him Pater Seraphicus?" The final program did not include the piece. And, more and more, particularly in the last year—the final year—Alex asked her opinion about questions of orchestration. *How necessary is the brass strength? Heavier on the percussion? Can you hear the timpani? Would it work with strings only?* She wondered sometimes if he was trying to push her to start composing, if despite his stated objections to composition he wanted her to do what she aspired to do. Now she wonders if he asked because he was the one beginning to write his own music.

Olivia watches her, raptor-like. "Or maybe you didn't know him quite as well as you thought you did. Maybe you misread him."

Yes, Suzanne thinks; she has spent her life getting everything wrong, not understanding what was right in front of her. She's always felt like that: everyone else receives a graduation-from-childhood key to decipher human nature, but no one ever told her to get in line.

"Why didn't you just send me the whole score?" Suzanne asks, returning to her chair, Alex's chair. "Why make me come here?"

Olivia's expression lowers. "I knew about you all along, you know, even your name, almost from the very beginning. I've heard your CD, seen your picture. Now you have to know who I am, what I look like."

Suzanne remembers one of her early assignations with Alex, an orchestrated meeting in the improbable city of Cleveland. She thinks of Olivia home alone, or with the son, knowing where her husband was, why and with whom.

Olivia's sideways smile returns, and now it looks as though it could be a smirk. "And we are just getting started."

Since retreat does not seem open, Suzanne pushes forward. "Can I see more of the house?"

"Tomorrow, after my son leaves town and you come back. I do apologize about the hotel, but you should have waited until tomorrow, as I said. I would have paid the difference in flights. Money is nothing for me in this."

Suzanne nods, though the idea of money being meaningless is not something she has ever understood. Maybe the closest she has come were those times with Alex, those times she said, *Let's get the real champagne* or *This meal is on me* as though she were a person who could say such things all the time.

"And tomorrow, when you come back," Olivia says, "I'll show you his study. I'll show you where he ate the breakfast I cooked for him every morning he was at home. I'll show you our bedroom." She says *bedroom* slightly more slowly than her other words and then pauses. "I imagine he told you we rarely slept together."

The word *rarely* bites Suzanne. *Never* is what Alex told her. *I haven't slept with my wife in seven years, and I will never sleep with her again.* She believed him, nearly completely, even as she knew it was the kind of lie people tell in situations like theirs, even though she could not say the same thing. Still she believes him, and she suspects that Olivia is trying to trip her up, to erode her faith in Alex. *She is trying to inflict pain.*

"It's not a subject that came up. It was never about you." Suzanne can feel the small square of her own chin, pointed straight to the ground instead of lifted as it is when she curves over her viola. It is pointing down so she will give away nothing. In her posture she holds her version of Alex away from his wife, holds it for herself.

"Really?" Olivia asks, gazing through the glass waves of the window as if, though surely not, she is disinterested. "Because for me it was always very much about me. A difference in perspectives, no?"

"We just didn't talk much about other people, except for musicians." Suzanne steps forward to take the envelope with Alex's score, anxious to be alone with it, the one thing Alex may have left that is hers alone: music written by him for the instrument she plays.

People often call a musical score a piece of music, but of course it is only the two-dimensional representation of a complex experience. Yet unlike a photograph or a birth certificate, it is a representation that preserves not just a moment but the full music itself, protecting it intact through years of neglect or disinterest, making it possible at any moment, allowing it to be played centuries later. *Cryogenics for songs and symphonies*, Alex said once. Are not lost Verdi operas found and played? Do not university choirs perform chorales not heard by any ear since sung by medieval priests?

If she can play this score, breathe life into the composition, she can resuscitate Alex, at least *an* Alex. The music in Olivia's hand promises a communion between the living and dead, a way to share time with the man she loved. She takes the envelope.

"It will be difficult," Olivia says, "to fill in another person's gaps, figure out what someone else meant, was thinking and feeling. He'd only just begun the orchestration. But it shouldn't be too hard for you." Olivia produces again the full but flat smile. "Since you knew him so very well."

Suzanne gestures to the coffee cup, to be polite, to deflect Olivia's clinical gaze.

Olivia waves away the suggestion. "I'll take care of it. It's nothing, in the scheme of things," she says. "And you, you will start work tomorrow and stay until you can play the solo for me. Then you'll go home and work on the arrangement, and then we'll see about getting an orchestra."

"You're asking me to do something I can't do. I can play the solo for you, but I'm not a composer."

"You started to be; you wanted to be. You've had the theoretical training. You help arrange music for your quartet."

"A full orchestra has eighty instruments. I don't know what to do with the brass, the winds, the percussion."

"You took advanced instrumentation and orchestral writing. I've seen your transcript; did you know that? I know every retreat and fellowship and residency you've ever been offered."

Suzanne does not want to respond to this, but instinctively she mouths, "How?"

"Did you think I wouldn't want to know whom my husband was sleeping with?" Olivia shrugs. "You do the best you can, and we'll see if we can get it premiered. Maybe here—his orchestra—or else Philadelphia. Which do you think for Alexander Elling's unveiling?"

"You are deluded if you think a major orchestra is going to perform anything I arrange."

"Maybe your husband can help you." Her whisper is loud. "So Chicago or Philadelphia?"

"Chicago—that's an easy choice." But even as Suzanne says this, she hesitates. Maybe Alex would have wanted it performed in Philadelphia, after everything, despite his venom for the city of his scarred childhood. Maybe he would have viewed it as the ultimate triumph over that childhood.

She is already considering Olivia's question—where the concerto will be performed and not whether it should be. That, she understands, is how powerful Olivia is.

Fourteen

Because she does not want to ask Olivia to use her phone, or even to have Olivia see her phone for help, Suzanne walks several blocks with viola and roller bag so that she is out of view when she uses rationed cell phone minutes to call information and then for a taxi. This is not a neighborhood of taxis, except perhaps those arranged by homeowners for early-morning trips to the airport, and the wait is nearly thirty minutes. The minutes sag as Suzanne sits on her suitcase at the corner she named for the dispatcher by reading the street signs, imagining in each upstairs window of each house a pair of eyes, watching her. She looks as though she has been evicted, or perhaps as though she is fleeing an unstable marriage.

The driver, a large, dark man, smiles broadly at her, taking the trouble to get out, put her bag in his trunk, open the back door for her. She keeps her Klimke and Alex's score, resting them on her lap. She names a hotel where she has been with Alex—emotionally dangerous, and probably expensive, but there's comfort in the familiar and relief in having a place to name, as though she belongs somewhere and is doing what she is supposed to be doing. She sinks back, her hands lightly weighting the score on her viola, and gazes out the side window. Her view crowds as they move from the large, widely spread estates near the lake to the smaller and more varied houses of the inner suburbs, which give way to the less orderly shapes of the city itself, a city that still feels small to Suzanne, who grew up knowing wide Philadelphia and tall New York. Occasionally she meets the driver's eyes in the rearview mirror. Finally she asks him where he's from.

He grins and says, "Haiti" in a series of short syllables, three or four of them rather than two.

"Port-au-Prince?"

He shakes his head, the gesture large and amused. "No, no, I am a village boy."

"But now Chicago," Suzanne says.

On the night of one of her ugliest fights with Alex, their taxi driver had been Haitian, though they had not talked to him enough to find out if he was from capital or village.

The evening had started well, the weather beautiful enough to walk to the Upper West Side venue from Alex's Murray Hill hotel, where they'd spent the entire day. They were on their way to a performance that Alex had to attend. It would be awful, he warned her, but it was one of the reasons he was in town and a favor to a friend as well.

In a dark purple sleeveless dress, Suzanne felt as she often did walking next to Alex: beautiful and important. Whenever she turned a man's head, Alex put his arm around her or reached to hold her hand, and she felt specially claimed. Mostly, though, they walked with a slight gap between them, a space that felt not empty but magnetized. "Anyone who looks at us can see that we are lovers," Alex said, and she believed it was true.

As they crossed Central Park, Alex asked her about Ben's work.

"He's working on something new," she told him. "He wants to extend some of what Janáček was after in his last pieces. He's connecting largely through the math, using certain identity permutations."

"You husband sounds like an interesting guy."

Suzanne faltered in her response, unsure what Alex was after. Finally she settled on a quiet "Yes."

"Is he good? Is he a real composer?"

Suzanne nodded because yes, Ben was a talent.

"At least he's not into minimalism."

"No one really is anymore," Suzanne offered.

"It's still played enough. Just yesterday I saw that guy advertised in the *Voice* as 'being on a first-name basis with Philip Glass.' Made me ill just reading that."

"The public's always a bit behind the game, no?" Suzanne drifted closer so that her arm brushed Alex's, hoping to bring him back from his line of thought with her physical presence.

"It's as big a problem in music as in art. Once you're about an idea and not about the medium, you're in trouble. Composers should leave the concepts to the philosophers and writers, who might have the talent for it. Take a look at what's being performed. Operas based on David Lynch movies—is that all they can come up with?"

She wanted to tell him about the beautiful composition she'd played at a conductors institute the previous summer—penned by a young music professor in South Carolina—but she didn't know how to make a space for her own ideas in Alex's black-and-white pronouncement. She imagined him disparaging academics and thinking her naive. It wasn't until later in their relationship that she realized he valued her opinions, that he wasn't testing her to see if she was smart, that she didn't always have to be on her intellectual toes the way she had to be with Ben. So on that day she laughed and held his arm, wanting only to maintain their closeness. "Is that why you don't compose?"

"That's part of it," he said, and they walked on, exiting the park and heading farther west to the small auditorium, which was located in a 1970s office building whose exterior in no way suggested that it held a performance space.

Even when they were not in Chicago, people at concerts recognized Alex, and Suzanne was already practiced in being with-but-not-with him. When two men came to shake his hand, she excused herself to the bathroom. Between conversations he slipped her a ticket, and she went first into the auditorium, Alex joining her just moments before the lights dimmed. He did not take her hand but pressed his leg against hers in the dark.

The first piece was an appalling exaggeration of serial music. The composer played electric violin and was accompanied by a dancer of sorts—the program called him a movement artist—encased in black leggings and turtleneck. Summoning her natural compassion for any performer, the empathy borne of kinship, she kept her eyes forward, afraid that her smile might turn to laughter if she glanced at Alex. To make time pass, she counted the ratio of heads to empty chairs in the rows in front of them: the theater was not quite half full.

The beginning of the main fare suggested something better. The composer-pianist had broken apart Bartók's piano sonatas, filling in the spaces with his own measures. The music was beautiful and made new, as though the composer had cracked open a geode, separating the sparkly, faceted pieces, revealing something previously hidden. But then the silent woman standing near him onstage made a circle of her mouth and let out a chilling note before chanting in a strangely high monotone: a poem by Wallace Stevens, word by slow word. She could imagine Ben, an opera hater who believed that words and music were incompatible, noncomplementary languages, standing indignantly and huffing from the room before the chanter made it through the poem's first stanza. She felt Alex, who usually sat preternaturally still at concerts, flinch in the seat beside her, a spontaneous aversion he covered by switching the cross of his legs, folding his arms, sinking back further in his chair as though anxious for an extra inch between him and the horror on stage.

The reception was held on the second floor of the same building, in a large conference room whose burgundy, blue, and rose paisley carpet belonged in a movie-theater lobby. The swirling patterns and the quick glass of inexpensive champagne tilted Suzanne's perception, and she felt ill at ease as the room filled. She skirted its circumference, sampling warm grapes and cheese and miniature quiches, hoping the food would serve as ballast. She determined to be happy and charming, to be what Alex wanted her to be, to be the woman he had flown from Chicago to be with.

When she felt a little better, and when enough time had passed that she and Alex could slip away, she found his head among the crowd and wove her way to the center of the room, where he was talking to a tall brunette in a red dress. The young woman was pretty in the way that Suzanne had been at twenty-two. Her hair was the same unusual shade of brown, and she had narrow hips and breasts of a certain shape and lift, though she was half a foot taller than Suzanne had ever hoped to be.

Suzanne felt her pulse in her carotid artery, felt fingers of heat climbing her neck, touching her face, which she knew must look red. *Jealousy*, she named for herself, hoping to douse it by identifying it. She felt low to the ground. She'd worn ballet flats instead of heels because of the long walk, but now she had blisters on the backs of her heels anyway. She tried to smile.

"I don't think I ever understood that poem until today," the young woman was telling Alex.

The comment would ordinarily have infuriated Alex, but instead of walking away, instead of soliciting Suzanne as a mocking conspirator, he discussed the poem and delivered trivia about Stevens. He was smiling more than usual—it was something he usually forgot to do—and smoothing his hair with his free hand the way he had those first few times he'd spoken to Suzanne. She'd been warned right away, by one of the bassists in St. Louis, about Alex's reputation as a womanizer.

Alex turned to her now. "And what did you think of the Bartók?"

Suzanne wanted desperately to say something smart, but her mind felt wavy. She tried to assemble a sentence to explain how she felt the composer had cracked open the sonatas to find something new and beautiful inside.

"But the poem," the tall young woman said. "Don't you think that's where the real innovation lies? Anyone can do deconstruction."

Her pulse still throbbing in her neck, Suzanne reached for something to say. "I think words and music are incompatible, noncomplementary languages."

The woman laughed, tossing her hair behind her shoulder in a move that elongated the triangle between them, bringing her closer to Alex and making Suzanne the outlier. "It seems we're not in the presence of an opera fan."

Suzanne took two steps back, then turned away, murmuring to be excused.

"But perhaps a fan of yours," she heard the young woman say.

Fifteen minutes later Alex found her sitting on a bench at the side of the empty lobby downstairs. He was buoyant as he said, "I've been looking for you."

"Not very hard," she whispered.

"What are you talking about?"

She shrugged. "Let's go, okay?"

He held open the door for her as they walked out to find dusk settling. She didn't intend to, but when he put his arm around her bare shoulders, she condensed into herself. He dropped his arm and stepped in front of her, blocking her. "What's wrong?"

"I feel like I can't say anything about music to you, and then there you are pretending to like the concert."

"What are you talking about?" His voice lifted, his father's accent angling into his words. "I always ask your opinion about music, and I'm pretty sure we both thought that concert was about as bad as it gets."

"But you were telling that woman otherwise."

"Don't be jealous. Don't do that."

"It's hard to imagine you'd let her comment pass without a sneer if she wasn't young and pretty." Suzanne tried to step around him, but he held her shoulders tight with both hands. Her throat constricted as she softly croaked, "You let her make fun of me as though I wasn't even there."

"She's a stupid girl. Stupid and pretentious. And I was 'letting her comment pass' because her father happens to be a philanthropist with a love of classical music. If you haven't noticed, it takes money to run an orchestra. A whole fucking lot of money. Would you even have been interested in me if I wasn't successful?" He dropped his grip on her shoulders and spun to the street, hailing a cab. "I can't believe this."

Two taxis passed before one stopped. In the back of the cab, Alex glared down his nose at her, then out the window, then back at her while the cab driver tried to make a left turn through heavy pedestrian traffic.

"Can't you just drive around the block?" Alex yelled at the man.

"Almost got it, sir."

"I'm sorry," Suzanne said, her mouth heavy with silent crying. "But it was a fair response."

"What the hell do you think I'm doing here? You think I flew to New York to see that crap? Or was it for the disgusting finger sandwiches?"

"I just want to be sure you'll tell me if it's ever over. I don't want to be pathetic." She was crying aloud then.

The cabbie made eye contact in the mirror as the car gained speed heading downtown. Out the window the street looked shiny with reflected orange light.

"It wasn't ever going to be over," Alex said.

"Wasn't." Her throat ached as she spoke. "I just don't want to be a notch, one of many."

"The last of many, Suzanne. You were going to be the last of many." He turned from her, leaning forward, his arm a barrier. "Where are you from?" he asked the driver, cold and steady, as though Suzanne was not in tears, as though she was not in the car at all.

"Haiti," said the man, "but now New York. I've been here a long time."

Back at Alex's hotel, Suzanne sat on the bed, contemplating catching the train back to Princeton even though she had made an excuse to be away for the night.

Alex sat at the desk, a map open under a lamp's tight circle of yellow light, furiously writing on a notepad. He circled something with a flourish and threw the pad at her, its corner catching her leg. A tiny pain. "There," he said.

On the lined paper he had written the location and date of every one of their assignations. There had been fourteen then, some lasting only a few hours and some spanning several days. The ink tallied the total miles driven, distances flown, circled the already staggering total. The precision of his memory stunned Suzanne. He remembered even a meeting she had forgotten: three hours in Wilmington, Delaware, on a bitterly cold January afternoon.

"The next time you have any doubts about how I feel about you, take a look at a fucking map."

He'd grabbed her shoulders again then, removing her clothes with no hesitation, making love to her until neither of them was angry anymore. The next morning she woke to his renewed touch. His fingers combed her hair. His lips grazed her eyelids. "I'm sorry I get so angry," he said.

She turned into him. "I'm sorry I get jealous."

"I know my reputation, my track record, but you have to believe that I love you."

"It's not just jealousy, either, I think. It's those people. When we were alone I felt beautiful."

"You are beautiful."

"But then we're there and suddenly all I can think is that my pretty purple dress cost thirty dollars and everyone can tell."

"There was no other woman in that room for me."

She didn't tell him that for almost a week before he arrived her concentration turned to powder, from the fear that he wouldn't come and then from the excitement that he would. She didn't tell him that she barely slept for several nights and had to force herself to eat, that she spent an entire afternoon trying on dresses before buying the purple one. She just nodded and said, "I also hate even the idea that this is some ordinary affair, that this is anything other than the love of my life."

That night they had dinner with Piotr Anderszewski after hearing his airy Bach partitas from the center of Carnegie Hall's tenth row.

"I am the love of your life," Alex said when he put her on the train home, and she decided that she would refuse her jealousy from then on, that she would believe what he told her. She thought of it as a leap of trust, and the trust was no less firm for the size of the gap that had been crossed to land there.

Now the Haitian driver drops her in front of the Intercontinental, so she is alone when she realizes that the lie Alex told her that day in New York had nothing to do with the woman in the red dress. He lied to her about something more important than a flirtation: he lied to her about music. If he wasn't already composing that day, certainly he was planning to, and he hid that from her even after she asked, "Is that why you don't compose?"

She passes quickly through the heavy revolving door, around the central staircase leading to the mezzanine, across the lobby floor of mosaic tiles, embedded as tightly as memories. *You are the last of many.* When she checks in with a friendly woman in a blue blazer she smiles and says what she must: "I only need one key."

Mercifully her assigned room has a different layout from the one she shared here with Alex, but the decor is similar enough to hurt her. Locked in, she realizes that she is fully alone for the first time in a long time, that there is no need to perform. She has held together in front of everyone: Ben, Petra, Adele, the quartet, the town, the people on the plane, Alex's wife, even the cab driver. Now she dissolves. Her crying is as long as it is fierce, and when she is through she is dry of tears, more calm than tired. She unpacks her few things, folding her tee-shirt, setting her plane-sized cosmetics on the bathroom's marble counter. She hangs her dress and, wearing panties and bra, slides the score from the envelope Olivia gave her.

Suzanne has never been a savant who can hear music in her mind by reading a score—she has never been able to compose, beyond the basics, without an instrument in reach—but visual score study was part of her training, and she can analyze written music by sight. She can skim for structure. In her hands is a concerto for viola and symphony. The solo is complete, but much of the orchestration is merely sketched.

Preceding the concerto's three movements is the introduction Petra tapped out that first day, an opening whose ending upbeat is rhythmic. Perhaps it is a nod to Bartók's *Concerto for Orchestra* because throughout the first movement the main theme is prepared by a long crescendo that repeats the initial part of its motive over a subtonic rising through the orchestra—another move found in the Bartók. Suzanne sees it as the stretched curl of a wave, the kind of surf Charlie dreams of.

She senses as well the influence of Hindemith and nods to the nineteenth century in particular uses of sonata form. An interesting twist to Alex's fundamental conservatism? *Clever.* Toward the end of the first movement, there is space for an improvised cadenza. A direct challenge to the violist, perhaps.

The second movement is one of the strangest stretches of music she has ever read. It is traditional in its use of suspense-generating techniques, but it lacks the formal symmetry and stability suggested by the first movement, the symmetry and stability she would have expected from Alex. The articulation into sections is at best partial, due not only to open, even deceptive cadences but also to elision in the viola line itself. This elision denies respiration to the soloist as well as to the audience. Another challenge, this one as much physical as creative. *No catching your breath.* The movement is further destabilized and made unpredictable by the inclusion of significant new material, even in the stretches of recapitulation. Music that makes its own rules only to break them.

Merely seeing the music in black and white, Suzanne knows that it calls for incredible virtuosity. Alex was ever skeptical of the virtuosic, nearly disdainful. No Liszt fan, he. She stops breathing, as though she is in a real wave, and finally inhales sharply, a gasp. If Alex was writing for the viola, he was writing for her. She cannot guess whether this piece was supposed to be a challenge or a tribute, or whether it was written in sheer overestimation of her ability. Her hands tremble as she reads on, the movement animating the pages she holds.

As the final movement rises to its climax, it covers an increasingly wide register—again the Bartók influence—but it also raises harmonic tension. Yet the ending is false, and the piece moves on to a modified Beethoven scherzo, a small *pow*, followed by a diminishing line in which the orchestra slowly disappears, leaving the viola alone in a bizarre fall that halts before it fully fades away. *Piling it on,* Alex would say if someone else had written it.

Suzanne has never seen a piece of music like this. She understands now why Alex might have kept this work to himself, and she fears learning whether he was even more brilliant as a composer than as a conductor and arranger or whether he misguidedly assembled a clumsy bag of tricks. *For you.* She imagines a great poet, a formalist, writing his worst, most sentimental and sloppy poem out of love and then finding it published against his will because he is famous.

She will know whether the music works or fails absurdly only when she hears it, but already she knows that the piece is nearly unplayable. Perhaps, she thinks, he was taunting her, paying her back for defending Berio's circular-breathing excesses. Even at the basic physical and technical level, even with the emotional terror locked away, it will take her full skill.

She takes her viola from its case and stands over the score laid out on the high bed, the sheets of paper now looking almost harmless against the red bedspread. She plays through as best she can, straining to sustain the highest note her instrument is capable of, exhausting herself with the complicated fingerings and hand shifts, elbow pinching from the acrobatic bow work, patching through to the final eerie note.

An impossible piece of music, yes, but if she can ever play it well, then gorgeous, disturbing, harrowing genius.

Fifteen

Suzanne does not remember the dream, yet waking feels like escaping someone else's brain, as though she's been imprisoned in another head and is running down a foreign tongue, panicked to breathe fresh air before she is closed in forever.

After showering she dresses in jeans and tee-shirt, sandals and silver hoops. *Fuck Olivia.* She will go as herself, wear her regular uniform into battle; she doesn't have to pretend to be a better self, a put-together self, a composed woman. *Alex loved me.*

Downstairs she carries a paper cup of coffee across the lobby and down the hall to the business center, which is cramped in comparison to the otherwise extravagantly spacious hotel. In the breezeless room, she returns a short message from Adele: "I miss you, too!"

There is also an email from Daniel. "I'm in love, really in love. Don't worry, it's not with you this time, or even Petra. I know I just met her, but I'm going to marry her. You're a romantic still, right? So tell me you're happy for me."

"You know me," Suzanne writes back. "Sucker for a happy ending. Send me an invitation. p.s. Who the hell is she?" As she hits *send* she remembers seeing Daniel walking toward Linda at the party as she played with her daughter and Adele. *Ashes, ashes, we all fall down.* Maybe Daniel's proposing to her, to the only widow Suzanne knows, other than Olivia.

The next new email is from Petra. Suzanne scrapes her teeth over her bottom lip. Olivia asked what she'd told Ben, but the person Suzanne lied to about this trip was Petra. Her story was fabrication: she needed to lay filler to finish up some old studio tracks in order to be paid for work she'd done before the founding of the Princeton Quartet. So she not only lied to Petra but asked Petra to lie by not telling Anthony, who might not approve of her taking outside work at this point in their performance cycle. Her story was plausible enough, and certainly it wouldn't cost Petra much to withhold a small secret from Anthony. Petra agreed to do so if the lie was one of omission. "I hate saying things that aren't true," she said. Still Suzanne's stomach pinches at the idea, and she knows she will have to figure out a way to seem to have more money than she did, to cut some hidden corner and offer the savings to Petra for Adele's surgery. She lowers her head, realizing the worst of what she's done: she has used Adele, telling Petra they needed the time alone because Adele was becoming more attached to Suzanne than to Petra. She stares at her hands on the keyboard, hands that belong to someone who would manipulate the affections of other people. Perhaps this is how it happens: You slip along and have your reasons, and one day you wake up as a bad person.

She opens Petra's email, which holds news: Anthony has run the numbers. Princeton is against the war, or at least against war. "He wants to perform the *Black Angels Quartet*, with maximum publicity and a live recording." He's calculated that it's a risk but not much of one if they work very hard and play very well and look very good doing it. "He thinks there could be real money in it, that this could make us nationally," Petra concludes. "He's already asked for you and me to wear our hair down for the performance. Asshole!"

Relieved that Petra seems to be herself again, Suzanne writes, "You know me, slut like you. I'll play anything, and I'll have fabulous hair."

The next email, from Anthony himself, links to a list of ideas for increasing concert attendance. Developed by members of a children's orchestra in Texas, the list includes guerrilla performances in public places, door prizes, costumed events, and the participation of pop singers. "Just throwing it out there," Anthony's note says. "Keep an open mind, you guys."

Having squandered too much on yesterday's taxis, and because she is up early, Suzanne navigates Chicago's public transportation. After a ride in a crowded L-car that smells weirdly like sugar, a bus carries her from the urban to the suburban. Its belly is empty save for half-a-dozen young women who speak to each other in Spanish. They disperse at Suzanne's stop, which is the end of the bus line. Suzanne has about a mile farther to walk, but the day is pleasant and she wishes the walk would take forever. The idea of returning to Alex's house—Olivia's house—is as frightening as being trapped in the mind she awoke from.

The houses she passes proclaim upper-middle-class respectability. Though Suzanne knows that unhappiness can invade any home, seeping through its cracks as easily as the scent of honeysuckle or skunk, and that all people are deeply strange when you really know them, it's hard to imagine anything but perfectly browning apple pies, badminton games in the backyard, dinners eaten in the comfortable knowledge of growing stock portfolios.

Books romanticize the starving composer who survives on half a loaf of bread, but Suzanne suspects that comfort, or at least stability, are better friends to art than is squalor. Bach was poor, feeding all those mouths on an organist's take-home pay, but the income was regular, and feed the mouths he did. Suzanne thinks of George Crumb, composer of the antiwar music they will soon prepare for performance. He taught at Penn State for three decades before retiring to the comfortable home in which he and his wife of fifty years raised their children. A wonderfully ordinary life from which he wrote some of his century's most interesting music.

Despite Doug's biographical theories, Suzanne wonders if music doesn't exist outside its circumstances, standing alone across time, carried into the future by its score, its origins and motivations and even subject matter ultimately irrelevant. *Its composer's life irrelevant.* So why not a long, happy marriage? Why not a nice home with well-adjusted children, funded by a dependable salary? Ben always asks why happiness should be anyone's primary goal, but can't someone write great music and lead a normal, happy life? Crumb is not the only example, yet Suzanne has never expected to be happy. Even her relationship with Alex was more about compulsion than the pursuit of joy. And now—now she does not deserve to be happy.

Again Olivia seems perfectly ready for her. In a long, simple dress she looks even more elegant than she did yesterday, and the house smells of baking, of something yeasted and sweet. A guest bedroom has been prepared: tightly made bed with towel and washcloth folded on its corner, fresh irises, water pitcher, and magazines on the nightstand. Everything suggests a welcome visitor.

Suzanne sets her suitcase and viola on the taut bed, startled when she realizes that Olivia has reappeared behind her, in the doorway.

"I'll give you the tour before you get started."

As they walk through the house, Suzanne cannot hear her own footsteps. A ghost haunting Alex's house, she feels in long moments that he is the one alive, merely away on a short tour, about to phone home from Vienna.

Olivia leads her first to the music library, which comfortably holds a Bösendorfer baby grand at its center. In one corner is an armchair, a small stereo system, and, held upright by stands, two violins, a viola, and a cello. An inanimate quartet. In another is a cabinet, which Olivia opens to reveal smaller wind instruments, metronomes, wood blocks, papers, clips, pens. The room's side walls and most of the near wall, save for the doorway, are fully shelved, filled top to bottom with CDs, books, score binders. The far wall is split by French doors that open into the backyard. Suzanne sees the gazebo, Olivia's gardens, a sliver of Lake Michigan.

"This is where he worked and where you will work, in the conservatory."

The conservatory.

Alex always called it *the library* or *the music room*. His jump in class—a leap achieved partly through self-manufacture but also through marriage—was not singular and clean, though he said he sometimes felt more relaxed with the upper class than the middle. "So many eccentrics, and such good educations."

Despite his soft spot for Verdi, Alex mocked the composer's self-proclaimed anti-intellectualism. Verdi, born five months after Wagner, writing at the age of fifty-six: "There is hardly any music in my house. I have never gone to a music library, never to a publisher to examine a piece. I keep abreast of some of the better contemporary works not by studying them but through hearing them occasionally at the theater." He insisted, "I am the least erudite among past and present composers."

"Can you imagine admitting that, much less bragging about it?" Suzanne once asked, Alex's hand on the small of her back as she lay on a hotel bed.

146

Now she can remember the bed, what the room looked like, but not which city they were in.

"Sure," he answered, hand following the curve, "because he was lying through his teeth."

Olivia shows Suzanne every room except the son's closed bedroom. There are many, including three bathrooms. Each room is clean, airy, and decorated with both taste and real money. They reach the far end of the house. "Our bedroom."

Suzanne absorbs the high queen-sized bed, the matching nightstands, the reading chair and ottoman, the elaborate draperies—a cool green. *Alex and Olivia's bedroom.* Suzanne points to the head of the bed, to the pillow on left-handed Alex's preferred side.

"I suppose you've washed the sheets."

"What a peculiar thing to say." Olivia runs her hand over the bedspread, back and forth, the bed high enough that the action does not require her to bend. "Do you imagine that I'm not in the habit of washing the sheets every week?"

"His smell," Suzanne whispers. "I was hoping there would be something with his smell."

Olivia looks at her, her expression changing but unreadable. Her eyes don't exactly narrow, but they seem to pull long, as though she has control of facial muscles that other people cannot access. "I was about to wash his pajamas when I heard the news on the radio," she says, her gaze cast to her long-fingered hand. The nails are manicured but unpainted. "That's how I found out, you know, on the radio."

Suzanne feels no need to say, "Yes, I know what that's like; me, too." She is wondering if the radio is better or worse than any other way, if the form matters even a little.

"So I stopped. They were right over the machine, and I almost dropped them in the hot water, but I didn't."

"I want the shirt," Suzanne says. "You have everything else left of him. I want the shirt."

Olivia lifts her gaze, and now Suzanne can read her expression. *Hatred.* "I have everything because I was his wife. You have nothing because you were not."

"I want the shirt," Suzanne repeats.

"I'll let you have it after you finish the arrangement. A performance-night gift. No flowers for you."

"Performance night," Suzanne says, registering what Olivia is asking her to do, her dread swelling into something nearly unbearable.

Olivia's hand now sits still on the bed where she slept with Alex for more than twenty years. "You will be like Clara Schumann for Brahms, playing his music for the public."

Suzanne spends most of three days in the conservatory. She spends most of three days working through the viola part section by section, decipher-ing each movement phrase by phrase and then stringing them like beads. She spends most of three days in the music, most of three days trapped in Alex's mind. Unlike her nightmare, it is not damp, dark, and terrifying. But neither is it familiar or expected; it offers none of Alex's comfort.

Brahms, Olivia said, and Brahms is what Suzanne would have expected from Alex. Brahms, dismissed by many contemporaries as stodgy, a hold-over who would be flattened by the Wagnerian train to the future. Brahms, a brutal tongue and sour disposition hiding a deep generosity for those he respected. Brahms, brilliant but conservative in his use of counterpoint and sonata form, ever skeptical of program music, a man who never wrote an opera. Brahms, suspicious also of virtuosity, beloved by musicians instead of by fascists, whose music transcended its moment and outlasted its critics by centuries. Brahms, temperamental and emotionally difficult in life, elegant and restrained in his music. *Sublime Brahms.*

Yes, a reincarnation of Brahms would have made sense from Alex, but this difficult music is nothing like Brahms. In Alex's concerto, emotion is barely restrained, virtuosity is required, and a story seems to thread the movements. Almost always when Suzanne works with the score, her chest feels tight, constricted. She grows breathless quickly with the physical exertion required to play the piece and suffers mild tinnitus when trying to fall asleep at the end of each long day.

In this discomfort, painstakingly though sometimes with bright flashes of insight, Suzanne tries to decipher Alex's intentions in the black marks on paper. She tries to discern which sections are joyous and which written out of pain, which reflect desire and which satisfaction. If she can put them all together, she thinks—get each segment right and play the piece through—then she will have Alex's narrative of their love affair to twine with her own. Then maybe the story will become whole, the larger sum of her memory fragments, the parts of the story she failed to understand. Through Alex's music, she will know what happened to her.

Sixteen

On the second morning, Suzanne rises early and walks through the damp neighborhood, looking at the wide floral borders surrounding homes centered on their own half-acre or more. A man in a robe waves to her as he bends to pick up his paper. A woman runs past her, next a jogging couple, and Suzanne turns around.

Even at the front door she can hear the piano: Liszt's *Csárdás macabre*, its clashing harmonies, desolate sonority, bizarre parallel fifths. Written late in his life, a time when he began to fear death, which had already come to his son-in-law Wagner. A time when he told the last of the many women who befriended him, "I carry a deep sadness of the heart which must now and then break out in sound."

Suzanne guides the door gently closed behind her, treads softly through the foyer and down the hall. Holding back, nearly holding her breath, she watches Olivia play. Some people assume that Liszt's retreat from virtuosity makes his later music easier to play, but Suzanne knows well from piano-playing friends that this is true only superficially. Olivia's back and neck curve—regal posture gone—bringing her face close to the keys. Her hands are dramatic, lifting high and striking with surprising strength. A piece of hair sprung loose from her chignon stripes her face, stuck to her cheek with the sweat of her effort.

Suzanne waits after she finishes the seven-minute piece, waits to see if she will begin something else, but Olivia closes the piano, tucks back the errant strand of hair, straightens her spine, sets her hands lightly on her thighs, and turns to look out the window at the dewy yard, the morning sun glancing off her small piece of the huge lake.

"Your talent is exceptional."

Olivia doesn't startle but turns slowly, as though she already knew Suzanne has been standing behind her. "My talent isn't small, but it's certainly not exceptional. You know how much talent is out there, how little of it is truly special."

"Curtis also?"

Olivia stands. "Julliard."

"Of course you went to Julliard," Suzanne says, not hiding her smile.

"I suppose you needn't even have asked," Olivia says, "And now I will leave you to your work."

When she withdraws Suzanne is again alone in the room in which Alex composed the concerto that she fights to decipher. Today she concentrates on the strange second movement.

When evening comes Olivia makes a dinner of trout, new potatoes, roasted asparagus, sliced tomatoes with fresh basil. The meal is simple but perfectly prepared with good ingredients.

"She's a good cook, I'll give her that," Alex often said. Suzanne never, not once, cooked a meal for Alex.

The two women eat the food outside on the patio, encircled by border gardens of herbs and flowers. The lake smell is not stale and fishy, as Suzanne sometimes imagined it would be, but something fresh carried in on a cooling breeze. Strategically positioned citron candles and a ceiling fan attached to the overhanging roof keep away the mosquitoes. Again it hits Suzanne: this is a lovely home, a place someone would want to live. She reminds herself that it is kept by someone who does not have to work, but still it makes her feel inferior. It's no wonder that Alex never left Olivia and that Suzanne never quite believed him when he said he would leave her the day his son graduated from college.

Olivia draws a bottle of wine from an ice bucket and pours them each a glass. The wine tastes like grapefruit and minerals, expensive. They finish eating and together clear the table of Olivia's nice white plates and blue cloth napkins before returning to the patio.

As the sun recedes, Suzanne feels sponginess above the bridge of her nose, in the spot on her forehead where she always feels alcohol. She hears her voice: a little loud, some words indistinct, the occasional unfinished sentence. She tries to correct herself so she will sound as clear-headed as she still feels, but she cannot rid her speech of its slight slur. Her hostess drains the bottle into her glass, and Suzanne suspects that Olivia has not drunk her fair share.

"I tidied your room while you were working," Olivia says. "I couldn't help but notice that you are reading a book about cochlear implants. A deaf child? Do you have children?"

Suzanne fixes Olivia with her eyes, seeking to discern her intention, to understand the degree of pain she is capable of inflicting. Blurry with the wine and thrown by Alex's concerto, she does not trust her instincts. She mouths the words carefully: "A friend's child."

Olivia nods.

Suzanne decides to bare another weakness, to distract this woman from the fragile point she has laid her finger on. She says, "Alex's concerto is not what I expected."

"What did you expect?"

"To be Clara Schumann to Alex's Brahms," Suzanne says, hoping it will stand in for the more complicated thing she means.

"Brahms and Clara had a pure friendship," Olivia says.

"The analogy was yours, in the first place."

"You have to understand that I spent almost four years hating you, the woman stealing the man I loved. My *husband*. There were others; you know that?"

Suzanne nods, determined that she will not defend herself.

"Many others. But I do admit you were different, that he might really have left me for you." Olivia laughs, then shrugs—a rare spontaneous gesture. "Or maybe not. He did like it here."

"What's not to like?" Suzanne worries that Olivia can read her mind. She looks out at the lake, which shines like real silver, and breathes in the citron candles, the mint, rosemary, and sweet olive. Quietly she says, "So you loved him, then. Can I ask if that's why you married him, if you married for love?"

"Wouldn't you have married him?"

Suzanne massages her earlobe, something Petra taught her to do to relax. "You and I aren't a whole lot alike. I'm asking why you married him."

"He wasn't a conductor yet, you know, not when we met. He was a pianist. A handsome, charming pianist who couldn't quite hide his working-class accent and appalling table manners. I got the starter kit, and I made something of him. He was so very, very good on the piano, such expression and creativity in interpretation. He was wilder then, before the conductor's precision took over. You knew he was a piano talent, yes?"

"Yes," Suzanne repeats, her glass at her lips.

"So very good. But not quite good enough to take the world. I saw it if he didn't, though I think he knew, too, deep down. So I gave him something else to be, something better for him and longer lasting. I put the idea in his head, a baton in his hands, and all my money and friends at his disposal."

"Not that he needed much help."

Olivia's laugh is higher than her speaking voice. "Everyone needs help. Though I'll grant you all the talent and ambition were there when I found him. But plenty of talented people amount to nothing at all. Plenty of ambition goes unfulfilled. It wasn't even the money and the connections so much, though you need those to conduct. It was the direction."

"Behind every great man is a great woman?"

"There's truth to that, you know. It's not enough to be supportive. Anyone can be supportive."

Suzanne's ear is for music alone, so she cannot tell whether Olivia's accent is Connecticut or Massachusetts or Maryland. But it is certainly moneyed.

"Why did I marry him? He was irresistible, that magnetic pull. It's that simple, and the rest is extraneous." She leans back, sets her arms evenly on the arms of her chair. "If I decide to forgive you, that will be why—because I know he was irresistible, and all the more so after I made a success of him."

If I decide to forgive you. In this moment, for just a moment, they could be friends. Olivia could choose forgiveness over this—whatever this game she is playing amounts to. And Suzanne could forgive Olivia for being right, for marrying Alex, for having a child, for owning everything Suzanne now sees and touches. She seeks Olivia's eyes, trying to exchange something unspoken, the way she does with Petra when they lock gazes. But if they were ever accessible, already Olivia's beautiful eyes have gone opaque, and Suzanne cannot find her at all. Suzanne pushes back her chair to stand, and the difficulty of doing so tells her that, yes, she has indeed drunk too much of Olivia's fine wine.

Her sleep is light and fitful, sprinkled with dream fragments that feel only one beat from real life. In one she dreams she is watching a deaf bird fly into a wall, though she has just learned from her book that deaf birds do not exist.

The dream is followed by two hours of wakefulness and apprehension, in which Suzanne thinks about the new research on birds, whose ears naturally regenerate hair cells. But mostly she worries. She worries about the important things: the meaning of Alex's concerto, whether Olivia will destroy her marriage. She also frets over problems she knows daylight will make trivial: whether she watered her own scraggly herb border before she left, when Daniel's wedding will be if it happens, whether the purchase of a shed would allow the pantry to become a small office, what she will wear opening night of the *Black Angels*. Eventually she submerges, again just below the surface of sleep, and her eyes open early. She is exhausted but irrevocably awake and relieved to be rising rather than still suffering through the night.

In the absolute quiet she thinks Olivia is still sleeping, though she smells coffee. Perhaps Olivia set it up last night, or maybe she was up early and has gone out. Suzanne pads around the house, thinking she might sneak a look into Alex's closet or at the son's room but deciding that she wants to see neither. What she wants is to go home, so she showers and packs and practices until she hears Olivia return, calling out, "I'm ready if you are."

Ready or not, here I come.

In the conservatory, Suzanne rosins her bow and raises the music stand. Sections are impossible to play without bending at the waist and thus impossible to play seated. Olivia sits at the piano, her left hand on the Bösendorfer's keys but her body turned toward Suzanne. In navy-blue pants and a navy blouse, her hair smooth in its chignon, she looks like a silhouette of herself.

Suzanne strikes the opening and plays through all three movements as best she can. She's better at it now, able to interpret and not just sight-read, but still she lands at the concerto's end exhausted, humiliated as a performer. When her breathing returns to normal, she says, "It's ridiculously hard physically. It's like he was trying to kill me."

The rising sun has brightened the glass panes of the French doors, and the silhouette of Olivia looks dark against the glare, almost black. Suzanne cannot make out her features, only her shape. She cannot find even her eyes.

"Perhaps he was jealous of your talent," Olivia says.

"Alex was proud of me, not jealous, and you must have heard him rail against virtuosity. He could barely stand most concertos."

"But he was writing it for you. If he was proud of you, then maybe he wanted to show you off."

When Suzanne blinks, she holds her eyes closed a moment longer, which exaggerates the otherwise involuntary movement. "So many times," she says, "so many times Alex told me that the best concertos enact conflict and resolution. It's the reason to write them—the only reason, he said. The solo voice should have the larger part in the conversation because it is the weaker voice, the one playing against the many."

"Maybe he was challenging you to match that idea with this music. Try it again."

"Once more," Suzanne says, grateful that clouds have floated in to obscure the glare, finding it easier to concentrate on bow and strings.

Suzanne comes closer this time, but only by a degree. As soon as she finishes she says, "The pajama shirt—I want it."

Olivia's smile is wry.

Suzanne waits.

"I told you performance night."

"This was a performance, and I want the shirt now."

Olivia shrugs and smiles again—an expression that looks genuine. "The pajamas were already in the dryer when I heard the news."

Suzanne's hands shake visibly as she cases her viola, but she controls her voice. "Then why did you tell me you had them?"

Olivia answers quickly and with force: "I wanted you to be lied to."

Suzanne's hands feel suddenly weak, as though her bow might slip and fall to the floor. She places it in the lid, fastens her case's three latches. Leaning against the doorjamb, halfway in the hallway, she whispers, "Just because I'm doing what you want doesn't mean you can torment me."

"Perhaps what I want *is* to torment you."

Suzanne realizes that she was mistaken the night before. Olivia was never almost her friend, not even for that tiny shard of time. "You should have held on," she says. "You played your trump card. Now you have no way to make me arrange this music for orchestra."

Olivia has not stopped staring at her. "I expected you to be more intelligent, but maybe smart people tend to overlook the obvious."

Suzanne slides down the jamb, all the way to the floor, holding her viola case across her tucked legs. Something hard grows in her throat, and her swallow is painful.

"That's right. I can tell your husband whenever I want to."

"I'm not overlooking that," Suzanne says. She thinks of Ben the night before he left for Charleston, the way they looked directly at each other while making love. He saw her then, and they seemed in that time like two people who had chosen each other, who had found each other in the world and said, *That is what I want*. "Maybe I'll tell him first. Then you'll have nothing over me."

Olivia's face remains placid as she says, "I imagine that would be a good way to hurt all of us. Maybe what I wanted to do was torment you, but that's not what I want now. That sort of revenge can never be what one really wants, I suppose. What I want now is to have that music orchestrated, and you'll do it. You'll arrange the music because you don't really want to tell your husband, but mostly you'll arrange it because Alex wrote it and because it's good." After a pause she says, "Play it for me again—try it on his viola this time—and then I'll drive you to the airport."

Seventeen

Suzanne finds the porch light on—an unusual thoughtful detail from Petra—and Petra reading in the living room wearing underwear, tee-shirt, and slippers, her hair loose and her face clean. Suzanne registers the house's distinctive smell, a smell she notices only when she has been away for more than a day.

Petra stands and embraces her. "Thank god you're home. I'm not cut out to be a single mother."

Suzanne almost says, "But you are a single mother." Instead she says, "You're a great single mother. Adele feels lucky to have you."

"I'm trying, but I'm a disaster. I don't know what I'd do without you. And Adele missed you like crazy. It's like you're the mother and I'm the father."

"What does that make Ben?"

Petra shrugs and follows Suzanne to peek at Adele sleeping and then to the main bedroom. "So tell me everything about this mysterious session work."

Her back turned to her friend as she sorts through the suitcase on her bed, Suzanne says, "I kind of lied to you. There was another reason I went to Chicago."

Petra laughs. "Finally you're having an affair!"

Suzanne shudders, restraining tears, holding back her desire to tell Petra every single thing. She wants to tell her about the time Alex took her to hear the all-Argentinean program at Frank Gehry Hall, about holding his hand while Renee Fleming sang Strauss in a darkened Carnegie Hall, about watching the awkward left hands of aspiring conductors at a conductors institute in South Carolina until they were laughing so hard they had to leave. Most of all she wants to tell Petra about the night Alex made good on his promise of a private performance by the world's most celebrated violinist.

"I was just kidding, of course." Petra hops on the bed, her hair falling easily around her shoulders. She leans back on Ben's side of the bed.

Suzanne puts her dirty clothes in the small hamper in the corner, stows her earrings in the jewelry box in the top drawer of her nightstand. "Why 'of course'?"

"Oh, give me a break. I know you. But something's up. What?"

Instead of telling her the Felder story, Suzanne tells her the easier truth that Alex Elling's widow has commissioned her to complete and orchestrate a posthumous concerto. She says it in a plain voice, planning to attribute any quaver or false note to her travel fatigue.

Petra's response stings: "Why would she ask you?"

"Because it's for the viola, because I played under him once. Because . . . I don't know."

"But you don't have any composition credits to speak of. Of course you *should* have some, but it's really weird that she would pick you without them."

Now Suzanne shrugs. "Maybe she's crazy, I don't know. And maybe I'm crazy, too, because I told her I'd do it."

"Good for you." Petra's smile is fast and wide. "Good for you!"

Suzanne spins the empty suitcase onto the floor and lies down next to Petra. "Maybe it will be the start of something big. I need something new, something to change."

"Yeah, I feel like that a lot. I wish I knew what was going to happen with the quartet. Oh, oh, oh." Petra slaps the bed several times. "I need to warn you: Anthony is going crazy with the online promotion."

"Does he know he'll be rubbing elbows with the Neue Musik people?"

"He read an article about the conductor of the National Symphony Orchestra live-posting a performance."

Suzanne imagines Alex's reaction to that news. Her smile is stopped by the recurring thought she keeps pushing away: *I didn't really know him.* "Please tell me," she says, "that he's not planning that for *Black Angels.*"

"Not yet, thank god. But the rehearsal, promotion, stuff like that. He'll have to get people to notice him, of course, which I'm sure he plans to use you for."

Suzanne measures the information, the anxiety she feels in her throat. She has always been very careful not to self-promote, not directly, and she enjoys the conversations she has online. They make her feel in touch with some larger endeavor, part of a bigger music—a hint of the way she felt when she played with a traveling symphony and at receptions when Alex introduced her to people she never would have talked to otherwise. Yet Ben may be right that musicians have no business marketing themselves in words at all. Perhaps they should admit that they make something almost no one wants and that those few who do want it already know where to find it.

Not wanting to talk this kind of shop, she asks, "What about Adele? Have you decided?"

Petra turns to face her, head propped on one hand, tucking her hair behind her ear with the other. "I'm going ahead. I asked her, and she said she wants to hear us play."

"She's a little girl, though, honey. You're the grown-up."

Petra nods, her expression sad. "But she's smarter than I am, and she's old enough to know what she wants. And what she wants is what I want, too. I don't want to make her do it, but I want her to do it."

"You're doing the right thing. Inasmuch as there is a right thing, you're doing it."

Suzanne's eyes film with tears, and soon Petra is crying.

Through her crying Petra says, "When you're young you always think there's a right thing to do. You're obsessed with making the right choice, like your fate is going to go in one direction and you could jump on the wrong boat and get it all wrong."

The twin bedside lamps splash imperfect circles on the ceiling, casting the air straw yellow.

"But then you learn," Petra continues, "that there's no right answer. Just this thing or that, and the things you do and the things that happen to you add up to whatever they add up to, and you never know if whatever good or bad comes your way is because of some particular thing you did."

"I think I followed that," Suzanne says. "And I think the most valuable thing you forfeit when you make a choice is knowing what would have happened if you'd decided differently."

She holds her friend, lets her cry into her shoulder and neck, breathing in the clean smell of her shiny hair.

"I'm going to need even more help, though," Petra whispers. "It's going to take a lot of therapy and work. Driving to Philadelphia. Working with Adele every night. Eventually she'll have to change schools, and that's going to be hard. I can't do it without you. I'm sorry because I know it's not fair, but I really can't."

"You don't have to do it without me, and fair doesn't enter the equation anyway. What's fair? I love Adele."

"Things could change, though. Ben could want to move. Or the quartet could fail." She laughs through her crying, "Anthony could single-handedly ruin us with his 'online presence.'"

"There aren't many guarantees in life, Petra, but I promise that I'll always be your friend, and I'll always do anything I can for Adele."

Petra sits bolt upright. "No matter what?"

Suzanne nods and coaxes her back down. "No matter what."

"I don't deserve you," Petra whispers, and Suzanne hushes her.

When Suzanne awakes in the middle of the night, dressed and on top of the covers, the lamp on her side of the bed is on, but the other has been switched off. Petra huddles against her, shivering in her tee-shirt and underwear. Without waking her, Suzanne works them both under the covers and darkens the room.

Facing away from her friend, toward the wall she can no longer see, she replays the night in San Francisco, the story she wanted to tell Petra but did not.

Almost exactly one year after his prediction that Felder would become the world's most celebrated violin soloist, Alex made good on his promise for a private performance. He was guest-conducting the San Francisco Philharmonic, Felder as soloist, and Alex arranged an invitation for Suzanne to play with Symphony Silicon Valley the same week. Their last night, the night after they were both through with their musical responsibilities, Alex insisted that they leave the room to eat. "We'll get depressed if we stay in all night. We'll just be thinking about the airport."

Back at the room, Alex made her wait in the hall. When he opened the door to let her in, she heard music. A single violin, unmistakably live. Alex put his fingers to his lips, and she entered quietly. In front of the floor-to-ceiling windows sparkling with the city's lights sat Joshua Felder, blindfolded and bowing his elegant way through Bach's Sonata 3 in C major. Alex pulled her hand, leading her to the edge of the bed, perhaps four feet from Felder. Suzanne studied the line of the young man's jaw, the whiteness of his skin, the dark hair spilling over his blindfold. She gasped when he finished the piece and began the Bach-inspired violin sonatas from the humbly born Belgian composer Eugène Ysaÿe, perhaps her favorite violin music of any period. She felt Alex's breath in her ear: "He's going to play all six."

Alex pushed her back on the made bed and slowly, quietly unbuttoned her blouse, undid her skirt, disrobed her completely. Again he put his finger to her mouth and she nodded, yes, they would make love in silence, the only sound Felder's beautiful Stradivarius. She closed her eyes and listened to the long notes as Alex moved his hands and mouth down her body, slowly, taking time everywhere. She sealed her lips so she would not moan or cry out and felt that the entire world was touch and sound. She wanted time to pause, a permanent, exquisite caesura of pleasure.

When Felder finished the sixth Ysaÿe sonata, he set his bow on his knee for only a moment before lifting it and striking into Paganini's caprices. Alex lay on top of her, settling his full weight on her in his attempt to be quiet as he entered her and they made love, though certainly Felder knew what was happening. The only mystery could be her identity. They moved together until a few bars before what Alex must have known was the end of the evening's program, when he came violently, now making no attempt at silence.

Later, after Alex escorted the still blindfolded musician from the room, he said, "That's something I've always wanted to do. At my age I'm not willing to wait much longer to do things I've always wanted to do."

"But how did you convince him?"

"I have something he wants, and I have something on him." Alex smiled, looking ruthless.

"I like being with a man who can call in favors," Suzanne said. "Thank you."

"I wanted to give you something you would never forget. Years from now, when you're an old woman and I'm long dead, you can sit on the porch and tell your acolytes the story of the night you made love to the handsome conductor while Joshua Felder played the violin blindfolded."

Eighteen

Ben returns the following evening as Suzanne, Petra, and Adele are finishing a small meal of eggs and salad. He's tanned, just a bit, and perhaps thinner than when he left, a gauntness that shows in his neck and under his cheeks but nowhere else.

Adele jumps up when she sees him, and he hoists her into a large hug.

Suzanne registers his age in a way that she doesn't when she sees him every day. He looked mature to her that first day she saw him hunched over his cello, but of course he was barely a man then, and now he's one fully. There's a line across his forehead, slight shadows in the parentheses that curve down from his nose, more thickness to his long neck. Despite the evident fatigue and the pressures that seem to press down on his shoulders, he is a handsome man. She stands and hugs him when he sets down Adele. She is surprised to recognize that she is glad to see him.

"One big happy family," Petra says, a bit loud, patting them both on the back.

Suzanne makes more eggs and serves them to Ben with what's left of the salad. The three adults share a bottle of wine, clean the kitchen, listen to Ives's Second Symphony, and talk about music, politics, places they'd like to travel. It's almost like the old days, except the things that aren't said sit obvious and large between them.

Later Suzanne is half asleep when Ben emerges from the shower. Though she is tired, she feels his physical desire for her as such a strong presence in the room that she cannot pretend to sleep. She throws back the blanket and rolls into him, and he presses his mouth over hers so hard that it almost hurts. And she wants it to hurt, all of it, and to be something that she will never forget. And she wants to put everything back together again and make it all work and live happily ever after with Ben and Petra and Adele and a successful Princeton Quartet. In that moment, she wants her life exactly as it is but fully repaired and healed.

But she doesn't know whether the road there means telling the truth or hiding it.

Several days later, she still vacillates. While she was at first grateful that Ben doesn't ask her questions that would be hard to answer, she is surprised by how uninterested he is in her surprising new work.

"I'm glad you have something to work on that's not Bach for a change," he says.

If he pushed her, she thinks, she could do what she threatened on her last morning with Olivia: tell him everything. They would work through it, or they would divorce; either way it would be settled and Olivia would hold nothing over her and she could commence what would be the rest of her life. Maybe there would be happiness and children, maybe solitary important work, maybe nothing good at all. But she would know.

Sometimes she looks for opportunities to tell Ben, tries to drop a hint, pick a fight. "You're so preoccupied with your composing you haven't asked me about mine," she says one morning as Ben pours a cup from the pot of coffee she has made for them.

"Sorry," Ben says, looking up with surprise, as though her work simply hasn't occurred to him.

She is seated at the table over the score. She runs her fingertips in a half circle around the rectangles of white paper. Though she has polished the table recently, her fingers graze circular stains from goblets, glasses, her own mug. A knife of light pierces a white shape imprinted by a hot dish, and she runs her hand back and forth through the beam.

Ben moves behind her and rubs her neck. "Is it any good?"

Suzanne nods, pulling her hands back onto her lap, trying to relax into his touch, her drive to speak the truth dissolving. "I was just hurt you didn't ask." She feels his lips on her temple.

"I would like to hear about it, look at it. Soon. I'm just really pre- occupied. There's so much work with this one. It was a mistake to go Charleston."

While his music is almost ready, much of the business remains to be completed, from hiring additional musicians and technicians to designing and printing programs. Suzanne hopes Kazuo has more aptitude for the practicalities than Ben does. It is a distaste for this aspect of the composer's trade that accounts for Ben's lack of success after it seemed he was on the verge of a rare career.

Ben was not surprised when Suzanne said she would never live in Charleston. Neither was he surprised that she relented, easily, when, upon their graduation from Curtis, his mother offered them a spare house to use while Ben composed. They lived off the small trust fund from his father and Suzanne's tiny salary with the Charleston Symphony. Suzanne endured the social hierarchy of a city you aren't from unless your grandparents were born there, the politely delivered criticisms from Ben's mother, the feeling that she wasn't living the life marked out for her. It would be better, she told herself, for their children to be raised like Ben had been than like she had been. And then came the hints of inheritance. "Of course," his mother would say, "Ben will need to be better provided for in the will if he's to be a family man."

When she lost the baby—late, after a room had been cleared for a nursery and girls' names had been short-listed—the house mocked her. Ben's mother's comments about her ethnicity became more frequent. *Italian* and *Irish; how quaint. Did you go to mass every Sunday?* And then there was Ben himself, avoiding her tears, disappearing into his workroom, its heavy door closed. It was worse when he did try to talk about it. "Maybe it's for the best," he said one night while they ate at the dining room table—a huge piece of furniture that had come with the house. "Music requires sacrifice. You'd have to give up a lot, and we'd have to think about money." Suzanne's food stuck in her esophagus and she thought she might choke in silence, turning blue and cold, Ben never noticing.

Later he softened and said, "Maybe we can try again in a few years, after we've accomplished more."

When she auditioned for St. Louis, she told herself it was for the practice. She wanted to test herself, to see if she'd make the first cut past the blind performance and through the finger workouts of the grueling week of semifinals and finals. She didn't think she had any real chance, not at first, but as the week moved along she could hear herself playing well—very well—reading along without hesitation, her tone the best it had ever been. And she could tell that people liked her. "Most viola players are so goddamn moody," the music director told her, "but you're a normal person."

He laughed at her wisecracks, introduced her to people, showed her the neighborhoods where a musician could afford to live. And so she won the job and went from third chair of the Charleston Symphony to principal violist of one of the country's best orchestras, where she was happy. But Ben was not.

When she was offered the job, she knew she would take it. Ben asked her if it was ego, and she admitted that was part of it. To his credit, he never believed they wouldn't move. When he saw her salary—more than triple her poverty-line wages in Charleston, where so many of the musicians were the talented offspring of serious old money or part-timers with day jobs—he merely nodded and said he would tell his mother. Since the Minnesota premiere of his first symphony, he'd burned all of his completed compositions except one full-length work and a few short pieces, none of them performed save a partita at a college student's recital. They had watched the numbers in their checkbook register tick down like an odometer running in reverse.

"You're making a mistake," was all Ben's mother said, and Suzanne wanted to prove her wrong. Suzanne had overheard her telling Ben's sister, Emily, that she was a heavy chain, making Ben follow her to a crime-ridden city so she could fulfill the ambitions of a girl who'd grown up on the wrong side of the tracks. *The wrong side of every line: city, religion, immigration year.* Suzanne pushed into the room where they chatted over coffee, saying, "Find Ben a job he'll take, and we'll stay." *Or*, she thought but did not say, *make good on that other offer.* "I would never interfere," his mother answered, her back straight and her voice modulated. Good breeding, the Charlestonians said of her, someone whose grandparents' grandparents had been born in their city.

After the move Ben was miserable, though he was kind enough to pretend they were happy when his mother phoned every other Sunday at three. Suzanne saw him shrivel, his sullenness giving way to something more self-destructive, living across the river in an Illinois suburb, despising all things Midwestern and hating her for taking him there. Her work was more intense than it had been in Charleston, of course, with a longer season, some travel, and frequent rehearsals.

Sometimes, looking back, she thinks they could have made it work. Ben could have tried harder to make friends and contacts in St. Louis. They could have moved across the river into the city after they realized the suburb was a mistake, after they realized they were not the kind of people who could live comfortably next door to people who do not listen to music. But when the symphony announced an ambitious tour schedule, Suzanne imagined Ben alone in their house, dying. A melodramatic vision, but she believed in it. Also, she told herself, the life they were making there would never accommodate children. So when Petra called, she figured it was for the best. Perhaps Ben's mother was right about her: she'd always had a smart poor girl's desperate desire to succeed and have the world notice.

Over time Suzanne heard in Ben's remarks a disdain for the work that paid most of their bills. And she wondered if he heard in her sentences conformity, utilitarianism, a lack of the kind of imagination he equated with intelligence. Always she was too tired to debate the subjects that really interested him, the theories that sparked his fire. Once she started to tell him that she still thought about those ideas, but she didn't get around to saying it. If she had, would their life have unfolded in a different, better shape? Or would he have heard only the accusation? Over time they talked of music less and less; like other couples they knew, they spoke of other people, of household lists and chores, of money in and money out.

Now, about twice a year Suzanne tries to bring up the future, to discuss what they will do when his trust fund runs out, if the quartet doesn't make it, when her performance days are waning, at what point it will be too late to have a child. Even if the quartet succeeds, they aren't many years away from using only soft-light photos on their CD covers—if CDs survive or classical musicians figure out a way to profit from downloads. And if they make it more than a few years, then there will be no photos at all. What will happen the day Anthony tells Suzanne and Petra to pin their hair up?

Suzanne hopes that Kazuo will be able to help Ben into a teaching position more permanent than the occasional course he teaches at the Westminster Choir College. She considers it for herself sometimes as well. She could be happy teaching at Curtis; she knows this. She might even be willing to teach children for supplemental income, in order to have children of her own. She'd been willing to give up on children to lead an extraordinary life, but since Alex's death, the pull has returned. It feels impossible, though, even without Olivia's long shadow. When Suzanne wakes in the middle of the night, as she does every night, the fear that gnaws at her after she sorts through her quotidian worries is that her life will be a paltry version of ordinary. It will be unremarkable yet lacking the common rewards of living like everyone else.

And then comes the deeper, colder fear, the one that stops her from telling the truth and starting over clean: that she will wind up alone, her only solace being able to play, rather well, music written by people who are dead.

Nineteen

As his premiere nears, Ben rises even earlier, and Suzanne stays up late. Unable to practice in a sleeping household, she uses the late caffeinated hours to study Alex's score. Using an electronic keyboard and earphones, she begins to sketch ideas for its arrangement. But the concerto is an unfinished composition, and she knows that she cannot finish the work without coming to a deeper understanding of its nature—an understanding profound enough to complete it on its own terms. At moments she feels as though she is inhabiting Alex's very soul, and it is a place more foreign than any country she has ever stood in.

Her days go to practice, both alone and with the quartet as they prepare the *Black Angels* for performance. There are key problems to solve, most pertaining to amplification. All four musicians listen to what the music tells them to do, and their answers are remarkably similar. Perhaps this is why, despite their personality differences, they formed an ensemble.

They will not use an electric violin. They will amplify more than was possible when Crumb wrote the music but not as loud as is possible now. They will use bold physical gesture in addition to sound to create the necessary triple fortissimo. They will rosin heavily to play the ponticello right on their bridges without falling off. They hire a mixer—a young man Kazuo recommends—to ride the levels so that the nuances they have discovered while taking the music apart bar by bar will not be lost. They will highlight Crumb's superstitious numerology: the trinity of three, the holiness of seven, the devil of thirteen. When it is suggested that Daniel be the one to cue, he says, "I don't cue. That's why I picked the cello." But he is joking; he will cue the opening.

All four musicians agree that the *Black Angels* will be the concert centerpiece and will follow intermission. Everyone but Anthony wants to begin the program with the only quartet Ravel ever wrote. Rejected by the Prix de Rome and the Conservatoire de Paris, the music was criticized by none other than Gabriel Fauré, the man to whom it was dedicated. Fauré declared the final movement to be stunted, poorly balanced, a failure. Ravel himself viewed it as imperfectly realized but a great step forward. Frustrated, he left the Conservatoire in what proved to be a good move. The listening public soon embraced him, and Debussy wrote to him, "In the name of the gods of music and in my own, do not touch a single note you have written in your Quartet."

"Debussy was right," Petra declares. "It's imperfectly perfect."

They sit on the green outside Richardson Auditorium, each cross-legged except for Anthony, who sits with his legs in front of him, knees just a little bent. There are clouds, moving slowly, obscuring and then revealing the sun. Suzanne likes the warmth on her face but is relieved when a cloud takes it away and again pleased when it is returned.

Anthony argues for Haydn's String Quartet in G major. "It does contain some real surprises, particularly that ending. It's a good setup."

Suzanne looks around at the other three. "Maybe Anthony is right. We could pitch it as a history bookends kind of thing—an early quartet and a late one."

A black squirrel chases a gray one as she speaks.

Daniel's expression is muddy. "That's strange, isn't it? I thought places were supposed to have either black squirrels or gray ones, not both."

Petra cocks her head. "Let me get this straight. Suzanne is advocating that we play Haydn? You've got your eye on the checkbook, too? Counting people in seats?"

"Let's just say I've been reconsidering a few things. Anyway, it's not like Ravel is some risky statement. Who doesn't like Ravel?"

Petra shakes her head. "People say they like Ravel. Really they like Haydn and Vivaldi. People should like Ravel, and we should make them."

"People," Suzanne whispers. "Who is that, anyway? And how can you make them like something they don't just by playing it? They either won't come, or they'll come and won't like it, though they may, as you say, say they do."

"As long as musicians have required food, money has played a role in music," Daniel says, a sarcastic imitation of one of their teachers at Curtis.

"Perhaps," says Suzanne, looking directly at Petra, "we should be like Meyerbeer and pay off some critics and hire our own *corps de claque*."

She is thinking of the worst night of her musical life: downtown Charleston, beautiful warm weather, swaying palmetto trees, the orchestra's back to the bay, streets filled with tourists and Spoleto festivalgoers. Between pieces the conductor broke off to raffle off a Jaguar, assuring the audience members that they could understand classical music. He brayed like a donkey—the memory still reddens her cheeks—as he introduced the worst piece of classical music she ever had to perform. "Hee-haw!" he cried, shaking his intentionally stereotypical white mane. "Hee-haw!" And then Suzanne and her new colleagues sawed away at Ferde Grofé's *Grand Canyon Suite*, the music swaying ugly to suggest the covered wagons, the musicians' humiliation complete.

The next day Ben told her he'd turned down a paying stint at a conductors institute in Maine—a chance coveted by composers better known than he. He said, "I don't want student conductors butchering my music, me having to scream at them not to speed up the crescendos and sitting around while professional conductors tell them how they look from the back, calling out, 'Your hands are going to run into each other! Put your left hand down! No, not in your pocket!'"

When he told her how much it paid and who would have heard the piece, she couldn't speak to him for a day and a half. Then her anger shrank into something cool and hard and she vowed to put her career ahead of his.

"Now I know you're kidding," says Petra.

"There's nothing wrong with starting with Haydn," Suzanne says. "He invented the goddamn string quartet, so who are we to be too good for him?"

Petra leans back on straight arms, stretching her long legs out in front of her. "Okay, okay, I don't care. This is the question I have for you: How is a viola like a premature ejaculation?"

Suzanne knows the punch line but lets Petra have her fun.

Petra shakes her legs and says, "Even if you see it coming you can't stop it."

Suzanne watches the gray squirrel chase the black one around and up a young ash tree. She turns and sees Daniel watching the same scene, and then he turns, his eyes meeting hers, sharing this small seen secret.

"So you're really going to break our hearts and marry someone else?" she asks him.

He tilts his head, the lids of his eyes lowering, giving him a sleepy look. "Somehow I think you'll get over me."

"I'm happy for you, you know."

He nods slowly. "I know you are."

Suzanne lies on her back when the sun emerges from another cloud, her face absorbing the warmth, her ears softening to the rustling leaves of the trees surrounding the green, her mind retuning to Alex's confounding concerto. It is time to begin the hard work in earnest.

Twenty

While the *Black Angels* rehearsals are going well, Suzanne's work on Alex's score is an ongoing failure. The second movement of the concerto in particular feels beyond her ability, beyond even her powers to understand. She can play it now, without the score in front of her, but this is more a matter of memorization and counting than interpretation, and she cannot imagine an arrangement. The music simply doesn't add up—angry crescendos alternating with slower mournful sections, the odd additions during the longest section of recapitulation.

For a while she works under the theory that the movement is about sex. She never deluded herself about that: her relationship with Alex started because of her looks and was always saturated with sex. It wasn't only sex—neither of them ever thought that—but every aspect of their friendship was colored by physical attraction, by the warmth that spread in their chests upon sight, by the things they tried in bedrooms in dozens of cities, by the fact that those acts were stolen from their real lives and always wrapped in music.

So for a time she thinks she has found the key to the movement in sex, even placing the night Felder played while they made love. She believes this will allow her to fit the pieces together, to produce a whole that coheres and has broader meaning. She lets it guide her tentative decisions about instrumentation. More brass, she thinks, than she would have considered otherwise. It alters, too, the way she thinks about dynamics as she considers the ways that love is loud and soft, remembers how it felt when Alex made love to her noisily when he was angry, the intensity of her silent orgasm the night Felder played in the room.

But her theory breaks down halfway through the movement. Besides, she tells herself, Alex disliked not only program music but any music guided by extramusical ideas. He was like Ben in that, saying, "Music is its own language. It should not take its grammar from any other."

So she starts over, taking the movement apart again, measure by measure, even slower. Once she and Alex attended a concert in which the pianist added a full ten minutes to the usual length of Beethoven's third sonata. It was at the cathedral in San Juan, and afterward Alex and Suzanne sat across the street in a small park made strange by a statue of a penguin sailing a boat, the balmy tropical air soft on their skin. A man with a parrot on his arm rode up on a bicycle and offered to take their picture with his bird for five dollars. *"Hola!"* Suzanne greeted the bird, who answered "What a pretty lady."

After Alex paid the man to leave them alone, Suzanne said, "I thought parrots could only repeat a line, not converse."

"He was repeating a line, just not yours. I think they even imitate punctuation and speed. Unlike that pianist. It took him forty-one minutes to get through the thing." Alex tapped his watch. "I guess he thinks he can find something in Beethoven that no one else has ever noticed if he just plays it slow enough."

Now she finds that slowing down doesn't help her any more than did learning to play the concerto faster. Over and over the work whispers, *You never really knew me; you never understood.*

She determines to do what forlorn and failing women often do; she decides to consult a psychic.

"I've got to see Doug about a bow issue," she tells Ben, thinking that between this partial lie and the Chicago trip she is lying as much as she did when she was having an affair with a living man.

When he opens the door to his Hell's Kitchen shop, Doug greets her with his full bass voice. "Don't tell me there's a problem with the bow. My work is always perfect."

"It's kind of embarrassing, but I'm here for your other talent. I need you to look into your crystal ball, or whatever it is you do."

He puts a hand on her shoulder, looking down to make direct eye contact. "That's not nice, my dear. It's not quackery, and it's not magic. I guess you could call it emotion theory, but really it's about music. Go on back. I'm going to step out for a quick smoke while you tune."

Alone in the crowded repair room, Suzanne strokes her viola, tightens the E string, rosins her bow. She notes the soreness under the calluses of her finger pads from playing more than usual. She needs to take a couple of light days before the *Black Angels* performance.

When Doug returns smelling of fresh cigarette, he takes a seat on a stool, crosses his long legs, places his hands palm up in his lap, closes his eyes, nods his readiness.

Suzanne almost laughs and tells him he's taking his new vocation too seriously, but she stops before she speaks. She wants him to take it seriously. This is her life: the concerto is the story of her past, the reality she lives in now, the possible ruin of her future. There's nothing at all funny about being here. Being here may save her life, which, when she closes her eyes, she envisions as ancient ruins crumbling in a stony Irish field. She inhales as deeply as her lungs allow and plays the solo voice all the way through, pausing in silence between the first and second movement and again between the second and third. After she plays the last falling note, she smiles because she has never played the composition better. The concerto almost comes together, the answer to its riddle on the tip of her tongue.

"I'll save you a little trouble," she says to break the silence. "He's contemporary. Trained in performance more than in composition. Favorite composers Bach and Brahms, though with wide-ranging tastes, except not a fan of serial music."

"I could have told you all that." Doug grins, but his mouth falls back into the downward tug of the rest of his face, and the corner of one eye twitches. "But this is a tough one. Really tough. Shostakovich's last work was his Sonata for Viola, and everyone always says that's fitting because of the viola's timbre, because it's so melancholic. But this, wow, no simple melancholia."

Suzanne paces along the back wall, examining the instruments and bows set out for repair. The light coming through the barred windows is striped, giving the room an oddly modern look. It is like looking at a new photograph of an old place.

"Many contradictory impulses. A lot of emotion, that's for certain." Doug rubs his forearm as he looks at her. "A lot of negative emotion mixed in, but not simply sadness."

Suzanne's rib cage contracts, an internal wince that she fears shows on her face. *Sadness at my absence*, her mind's voice insists.

"The composer was confused. There's passion but also a lot of anger. A serious wound there, but there's control, too, a kind of patience. Brilliant but a bit of the overestimation of the autodidact. You said he wasn't trained in composition?"

Suzanne nods. "But he was trained in music."

"So many broken rules. I'm not sure this is someone I would ever want to meet."

His reading stings as Suzanne hears its truth. The childhood cuts that Alex's ascendancy sealed off but didn't heal. His love sometimes mixing with an anger that turned him cold. His self-assurance bleeding into sheer narcissism at his most manic. His vast musical learning telling him that he could compose without specialized theoretical training.

Fonder memories of Alex rise in her, drowning out the difficult man Doug has described. Alex with his hands in her hair and a smile beginning to curl his lips. Alex walking down Sixth Avenue eating an unlikely ice-cream cone in midwinter, the prop turning the serious, distinguished man into someone playful. Alex leaning back into a stack of pillows, reading a book in silence but still tapping his foot. Alex weeping openly over a wasted half hour of a weekend in Seattle, now irretrievable. Alex with his baton, about to set loose a perfectly prepared orchestra on an audience.

"No," she says.

"I could be wrong. I don't often say that, you know, but this really is a tough one. Very hard to decipher, not a straightforward person at all. It's not another collaboration, is it?"

She shakes her head, rueful.

"So who is it? You know?"

It surprises her to realize there is no reason to lie. "Alexander Elling," she says, starting to add, "the conductor" and "Chicago" and "who died."

"I know who the hell he is," Doug interrupts her, his goofy grin winning out again. "I didn't know he composed."

Suzanne returns her viola and bow to their case, fastening the locks with a close attention unwarranted by a manual task she has completed thousands of times. "No one did except his wife, apparently. There's only this piece, and she's asked me to arrange it. He started to orchestrate it, but there's some stuff left to be written. For the life of me, I can't quite get a hold of it."

"So you came to me as a last resort?"

"Something like that. I thought you could give me some insight into him, or at least the part of him that he put into the composition. Please don't be mad at me. I really couldn't take it right now."

"Don't take this the wrong way, okay?" His deep voice pauses, and he waits for her to answer by meeting his kind eyes and nodding. "Don't take this the wrong way because I think you are as beautiful as ever—maybe more so because I've always gone in for the anemic look. Remember that girl Helen, the one I went loopy for? But you look tired to the bone. I thought you were going to fall down while you were playing." He stands behind her, hands pressing down into her shoulders. "I'm going to buy you a sandwich, fries and milkshake not optional, and then I'm going to put you on the train, and you're going to go straight home and sleep all the way through until tomorrow."

She nods her compliance, her relief. Since Alex died and Petra regressed, no one has taken care of her. Once, early in their courtship, she asked Ben if he took her for granted, and he said he did. "Isn't it a good thing to be counted on?" he asked, waiting for her to say yes.

Exhausted, she tries to sleep through the trip home, but she is bombarded by cell-phone talkers, by music she doesn't like seeping around cheap earphones, by the intercom announcements of train cars and stops. For a moment she envies Adele; in the next she castigates herself for the thought. Better to hear everything than nothing—just ask Beethoven, Fauré, Boyce, Vaughan Williams.

On the walk home from the Dinky, Suzanne takes the slightly longer route down Witherspoon, stopping at the little market, ducking in under the "Wire money to Mexico" banner to splurge on a tamarind soda for Adele.

Twenty-one

On Sunday Suzanne and Petra help Adele get ready for Ben's concert. Adele turns from her closet holding a dress in each hand, eyebrows raised. Petra points to the lavender dress, Suzanne to the dark blue one. Adele looks uncertain—a child who likes to please others caught in a bind. With her hands occupied, language is only in her facial expression.

"Actually," Suzanne signs, "the lavender one is perfect."

Adele smiles her relief and dresses. She sits on the bed between Suzanne's knees. Suzanne brushes and gathers her hair, cupping it in her left hand in a loose ponytail as she brushes with her right, releasing the honey smell of baby shampoo. Suzanne is looking not at the silky hair but at the swell of bone behind Adele's left ear—the place the surgeon will puncture with a loud drill, boring a hole straight through, a procedure during which a small error would be devastating. Suzanne's stomach retracts to a tight pit. No wonder Petra took so long to decide.

Suzanne tips her head to kiss the precise spot where the drill will enter Adele's lovely egg-shaped skull. After she secures the ponytail, she spins

Adele by the shoulders and signs, "You'll look absolutely beautiful as soon as you brush your teeth!"

"That's the part I always forget." Petra leans into Suzanne and waits until Adele leaves the room to say, "Tell me again that it's going to be all right."

"It's going to be all right," Suzanne says steadily, though the tight circle of her stomach quivers as it releases with her breath.

"And you'll be there for Adele no matter what I do."

"You sound like you have a one-way ticket somewhere."

Petra looks up, alarmed. "I would never leave her, not that. I don't ever even think that, not even for a second."

Suzanne runs her hand down Petra's hair, a thicker, lighter version of Adele's, just as silky.

"But I'm not a nice person. I could do something awful that would make you hate me, and that would be terrible for Adele."

"Petra, you've done lots of awful things, and I never hate you."

Petra's laugh is a small snort. "True. But promise me you'll always love Adele."

"I've already promised you that. The promise is still good."

Once Adele is ready, they walk down Leigh Avenue and turn up Witherspoon, walking in their dresses in front of Princeton's most run-down rentals and then the little market. A man standing in the doorway says, "*Que bella!*" as they walk by, and Suzanne nods at him. Across from the new library, they stop at the bakery for brioche. Petra chooses a chocolate-walnut stick. Adele points to a round brioche with a peach half as its center. Suzanne serves herself a cup of coffee from one of the large thermoses. The sound of the coffee flowing into the cup is reassuring, a reminder that the laws of physics are still in place. She breathes its rich-smelling steam before securing the lid.

Twenty minutes later they enter Richardson Auditorium holding hands, Adele between Suzanne and Petra, and take their seats near the back of the main floor. Suzanne is surprised: more seats are occupied than empty, even in the balcony. Scanning the audience, she recognizes a few of Ben's associates and some friends from Elizabeth's parties, Daniel with Linda, Anthony with Jennifer. Mostly, though, the crowd is the anonymous audience a musician desires: people who have come to listen to the music.

A few more arrive. Ben and Kazuo take their center seats. The musicians file onstage—an orchestrated entrance—stand in place, then sit *en masse*. The lights dim. Hush spreads.

Suzanne watches Adele as the music begins. A deaf child at a concert many adults couldn't sit through, she looks not bored but rapt. Her chest rises and falls slowly with her deep breathing, and her eyes open fully to take in the darkened scene. Since she was a baby Adele has been a serious watcher of people—so serious that her only lapse in etiquette, seemingly ever, is this tendency to stare.

Suzanne presses her small hand between her own, but she distances herself by closing her eyes and giving herself over to the auditory world that is shut to Adele. Something Alex often said when she called him at an unexpected time and asked if it was okay: *I am all ears.*

Suzanne listens. She has heard Ben discuss the composition, and she has heard individual lines and pieces, but she has not attended a rehearsal and has never heard the music as a whole. Now its surprising beauty saturates her. There is no experiment for experiment's sake any longer, no exclusion of the audience, yet Ben and Kazuo have invented something. They have not abandoned history, nor have they simply reclaimed it; they have extended music's long, fascinating past into the new.

As she listens to the fugue, she remembers what Doug guessed about the composer of the music: emotionally restrained but not without effort. Someone who uses intellect to translate emotion. Fair-minded but stubborn and sometimes blinded by it. A deep point of pain. Someone not unhappy with how his life has turned out, though maybe only because he expected no more.

Maybe, she thinks, but what she mostly hears is the thing she values most in the world: perfect music. She sees colors with her eyes closed, mostly blue and purple but also orange, red, green, white. The music sounds beautiful, looks beautiful, is beautiful. It holds her, and when it comes to its end, she doesn't understand why she was deaf to it before. All of Ben's promise and talent are still there. For a moment she understands that it is worth everything to have this music in the world, whether the world wants it or not.

Deaf to. She opens her eyes, kisses Adele's temple. Adele is smiling and indeed looks to Suzanne as though she, too, is suffused by the music she cannot hear, as though she, too, has rediscovered the meaning of what they do, the reason they live and work and live lives that others think are strange.

Adele wriggles her hand, and Suzanne realizes she has been holding it too tight. She remembers Evelyn Glennie, deaf since the age of twelve, playing percussion barefoot in order to feel the music. And those case studies, those deaf people whose brain waves when listening to music mimic the patterns of the hearing, perhaps because they sense a percentage of the sound through their skin. Adele and Suzanne raise their hands to clap simultaneously. Suzanne leans back to tell Petra, again and this time sure of it, that everything is going to be all right, that Adele has the ability to hear music at least in her mind.

But she halts her voice when she sees Petra staring ahead stone-like, tears jagging her face. She is looking not at Adele but still at the stage, her expression illegible save for the tears, which Suzanne cannot interpret.

The applause in the auditorium is heavy, even ecstatic, but Petra's hands remain in her lap.

The reception on campus is Kazuo's doing, but Ben has agreed to go. He seems even to be enjoying the attention, at least a little. He seems lighter, a weight lifted like a stone from atop his head, and his smile comes more readily. From across the room, Suzanne sees him shake hands, nod in response to passing comments, make conversation with Anthony, with Daniel, with people from the music department. He accepts Petra's quick hug. Suzanne holds her distance, supervising Adele as she scours the refreshments, getting her to eat a sandwich half and some fruit before she raids the selection of petits fours.

"Congratulations," she says to Daniel and Linda as they approach.

"I know it's fast," Linda says, "but we're in love, and I'm getting too old to wait."

"You're not anything old," Daniel says, putting his arm around Linda's slim shoulders.

Anthony joins them, saying, "So that was very good, and very well-received." He's surveying the room, nodding approval, comforted by success.

Suzanne discovers that she is smiling, perhaps over their shared surprise that the music was obviously appreciated.

It is late in the day when Suzanne finally tells Ben what she thinks. She leaves out the fact that she was surprised, saying, "Don't be insulted by this because I don't mean beautiful in any kind of simple or stupid way, but it was absolutely beautiful."

"Or beautifully absolute?" He is smiling, playing with his words, staring at her breasts as he parts her blouse. "Did you really think I'd be insulted if you called my music beautiful?"

"You never know."

He grabs her wrist as she reaches for the light switch, tells her he wants to see her standing naked. He strips her and walks around her in a circle before lifting her, completely, and carrying her to the bed. He kisses her mouth, stomach, legs, back, arms. When he pauses, just for a moment, he lingers at her ear and whispers, "It's beautiful because I composed it for you. I don't care what those other people think. It's you I wanted to like it."

She tries to make her sobbing silent. She does not want him to ask her why she is crying because she could not explain it. Ben kisses the tears on her face, her crying mouth, but he asks nothing, says nothing, and when they are done they fall asleep hard.

It is just dawn when they are awakened by a ringing phone. Suzanne bolts up, thinking, *Olivia*, grabbing a robe so she can hurry down the hall to answer first. But Petra has already risen to answer it and is calling, "It's for you, Ben. Some woman."

Suzanne throws down the robe and puts on jeans and a tee-shirt. She uses the bathroom, brushes her hair and teeth. If this is it, she does not want to be undressed. She feels each step as she walks to the living room, which is suffused in dawn's pinkish gray light as the streetlight in front of the house clicks itself off. She hears the phone receiver set down in its cradle, the sound of her husband crying.

This is the first time she has heard him cry, ever.

She sits next to him on the sofa, lightly places her hand on the back of his head, trying to fashion words to explain, if indeed it was Olivia who triggered his tears. "Ben," she whispers.

He turns into her, wetting her shirt with his tears. She waits, stroking and holding his head. "Ben," she says again with her breath.

"It's Charlie," he says when he lifts away from her.

Her loud and involuntary response brings Petra back to the room. "Are you—" she begins, but she backs away when she sees them.

Twenty-two

While Petra takes Adele to school, Ben and Suzanne sit at the table with their coffee, Suzanne with a bowl of cereal. She has given Ben a plate with sliced banana and red globe grapes, figuring maybe he can eat fruit, but he pushes even that aside. He tells her she doesn't have to go to the funeral.

"I want to," she says, meaning it, "but my contract is pretty unforgiving, and performance night is almost here. I'm going to talk to Anthony. I want to come."

Today the quartet breaks from preparing the *Black Angels* and works on the Haydn quartet it will play during the concert's first half. Sometimes Suzanne regrets advocating for the piece; at other times it feels right. Today it feels like shelter, a building she knows and needs, a place to be.

The quartet plays well, each of them and the four together. It is one of those days on which years of practice distill into a clean energy and the work seems easier than it is. When the last notes are played, rehearsal disbanded, and her viola back in its case, the shock and sadness of Charlie's death return, streaming into the whirlpool of Suzanne's other emotions—her grief for Alex, her fear of Olivia, her delight at Ben's successful premiere, her sorrow that his moment of triumph was undercut so immediately by his brother's death.

When Suzanne talks to Anthony, he proves surprisingly human: he tells her she should go to Charleston, practice schedule be damned.

"If I missed a family funeral," he says, moving their stands to the wall, leaving the room in the condition they promised, "Jennifer would have me bullwhipped in Palmer Square."

Suzanne picks up the water bottle Petra has left by her chair and sets it by her purse. "So you know that about her?"

"More than anyone, believe me." He brushes his trousers with the palms of his hands, wiping off chalk and rosin dust. "Which isn't to say that I'm unhappily married. We all have our arrangements—give up this to get that. I know you guys don't like her, but Jennifer helps make me who I am, and I love her for it."

"Thank you, Anthony."

"Don't tell anyone I'm going soft. I wouldn't send you off if we weren't ready for the performance, and I don't want Petra and Daniel thinking they have a license to sleep all day."

Petra is lurking outside and startles Suzanne as she emerges from the subterranean practice room. The day is overcast but weirdly bright, and the buildings and trees are gray outlines against a metallic sky.

"Is he all right?" she asks.

"Yeah, he's being great, actually. Told me to go to the funeral."

"No, Ben. Is Ben all right?"

Suzanne shrugs. "I suppose. Inasmuch as he's ever all right." She is thinking that he cried in front of her for the first time, wondering if it will be the only time. It has made her want to protect him, even from Petra's curiosity.

"Tell him I'm sorry." Petra hugs her suddenly.

Suzanne steps back and hands Petra her discarded water bottle. "You can tell him."

"Sorry for you, too. I know you liked Charlie a lot."

When they get home, she tells Petra she's going to lie down for a few minutes and then pack a bag for Charleston, but instead she searches for the shell that Charlie gave her at Folly Beach. She is surprised when she remembers that she put it in her box of Alex mementos. Her box of souvenirs has become a coffin, containing reminders of only the dead.

She holds the shell in her hand as they enter Charleston, Ben pressing their car slowly into a downtown clotted with summer tourists. Their route takes them past the location of one of her worst professional memories: the night she played the *Grand Canyon Suite* as a Jaguar was raffled. But it also takes her through more pleasant memory terrain, including the theater where she played in the small orchestra for a theatrical event at another year's Spoleto festival. They'd had fun, the group seated behind thick black netting, visible only partially to the audience, only to the first few rows, playing music that was easy yet not uninteresting, music that was fun. Before and after, they'd sit outside in the warm breeze, listening to the stage performers speak Chinese, watching them warm up for their contortions, legs behind their heads, cigarettes hanging from their dry lips.

She unfolds her hand, uses one palm to press the shell into the flesh of the other until it hurts, and then examines the temporary imprint.

As much as she wishes they could stay at a hotel—guesses, even, that Ben's mother would prefer it—it is not possible to suggest. And Ben's sister now occupies the house she and Ben once lived in, the one intended to be a home for their child. Morbidly—she knows this—she wonders what happened to the mattress she stained with blood, the only physical evidence that her child existed.

She speaks kindly but minimally to her mother-in-law, who has put herself together with clothes and makeup but whose face reveals something broken inside. Sometimes, when she closes her mouth, her upper and lower lips don't quite line up, and she does not rearrange them. Her stare has gone sideways, too, but still she manages to look at Suzanne with disapproval.

Suzanne determines to fold herself into something small and quiet, to be helpful but not fully there. She keeps their belongings neatly stored in the guest bedroom, tidies the gardens outside when Ben's mother is inside and the kitchen when Ben's mother steps into the yard. *Blameless*, she thinks; she wants to be blameless.

The days after her mother's death were a span of too much food, of neighbors and friends and distant cousins she'd never heard of bearing casseroles and pies and muffins and fruit salads—far more than one grieving person could eat, dishes that spoiled, leaving Suzanne later to thaw and eat the posthumous food her mother had cooked for the freezer. At Ben's house, it is different. Despite his mother's standing in local society, her membership in a church, her many clubs, there are few visitors. Flowers arrive in florists' delivery vans, filling both the house and the funeral home with expensive arrangements, but people do not arrive with them, and no one brings food except Ben's sister, who has stopped by a bakery. Suzanne cooks some simple dishes to have on hand and slips out to a sandwich shop for a platter in case people do show up.

Ben moves about his childhood home, seeking empty rooms and not eating at all.

At night Suzanne stares at the floral wallpaper, the matching bedspread, the beads hanging from the reading lamp. Ben stares at the ceiling.

"Are you okay?" she asks.

"What's okay?"

She turns to him. "I have no idea. Stupid question."

"I'm okay." He turns off the lamp, and the room turns powdery with only the pale summer-night light that slides through a gap in the heavy brocade curtains.

The funeral is efficient. That's how Suzanne thinks of the short service at the Episcopal church—family and parental friends in the front few pews, Charlie's beach pals in the back. Suzanne touches the closed casket, which is shiny enough to return her own image, stained burgundy and perfected as if airbrushed.

She remembers the time she complained about the *Grand Canyon Suite* and the raffle. Ben's mother said musicians shouldn't gripe about efforts to enlarge their audience. "You'll never make a living if no one comes. Maybe playing music people want to hear is a good thing." Charlie smirked and said, "And what about your church, Mother? Should the priest tell people what they want to hear, soften its stance on adultery to increase its audience?" Her face tightened as she told him it wasn't the same thing at all. "To them it might be the same thing, a kind of infidelity," Charlie answered, and Suzanne didn't even bother to mask her smile.

Now she sees tears in her reflection and pulls back her hand from the casket's cool, hard surface, wishing she had been as good a friend to Charlie as he had been to her, wishing she had been more alert. Her sin, she thinks, is not adultery but self-absorption, of cutting herself apart from the people she is supposed to love, the people she does love. It's what Petra was trying to tell her.

The service is followed by a scattering of ashes from a small rented yacht.

"He would want to be in the ocean," Suzanne whispers to Ben, holding his arm, trying to say and do the right thing.

Overhearing, Ben's sister says, "He would want to be with our father. This is where our father is."

"Of course." Suzanne mutes her voice. "That's part of what I meant."

Ben's mother joins them at the prow on the way back to shore. With her regal stature, she reminds Suzanne, just a little, of Olivia. Or, more accurate: she reminds her of Olivia come unhinged. Though her lipstick is perfectly applied, the mouth underneath still sits crooked, makes her frightening.

"Such a terrible, terrible accident," she says. "I know he would have found the right kind of woman if this hadn't happened. Then he would have been all right. He still could have done so much in life. He would have had children and a business, everything a man's supposed to have."

Suzanne is still not certain of the surrounding details—she has not wanted to pressure Ben—but she knows that Charlie took his head off with a shotgun and that his mother has not cried in front of anyone.

Ben walks away from them and stands alone at the back of the boat, looking out to the sea that holds the remains of the only other men in his family. Suzanne faces the curvature of the shoreline, the wind off the ocean buffeting her back, her hair lashing her face in irritating strands. The sounds of wind and wave and fluttering sail meld into a single wail, its tone at first cello-like and then giving way to a plaintive bassoon and finally the sound of sea from a shell. In that moment, Suzanne hears the very sound of grief.

Twenty-three

Charlie's letter arrives two days after Ben and Suzanne return home. The sense of strangeness is immediate because the envelope is addressed to Suzanne and because Charlie never sent letters. He'd call occasionally and talk to whomever answered. Sometimes he would forward an email with a surfing joke—once even a viola joke that not even Petra knew—but he never mailed paper.

Suzanne sits on the porch stairs. She waves at the neighbor across the street, who tends her yard guarded by her dogs, and watches a couple of cars pass. She hears them slow briefly at the stop sign at the end of the street, then turn onto the 206. Finally she opens the envelope, conscious that it is one of the last things that Charlie may have handled: folding the sheet, licking the seal and the stamp, writing her name and address in blue ballpoint.

The letter begins with a sweet salutation, followed by an apology for pain inflicted on her and on Ben. It is a suicide note, because it was written by a suicide, but it lacks the explanation for the act that such letters are supposed to provide. "I'm going to blow off my head so there can be no revision of the cause of death. I am sending you this so that my mother cannot destroy it and make everyone pretend it was not suicide, which is what she did when my father killed himself. She denied us his last words. Now you have mine. I have lived. I have loved saltwater. Warm or cold, sunny or overcast or raining, I love surfing. In the ocean I feel at home. On land I do not. Soon I will be in the ocean forever."

Suzanne inhales and exhales to slow her speeding heartbeat. She hears light footsteps coming from the kitchen and folds the letter, flipping the envelope to make it anonymous.

"What are you looking at?" Adele signs.

For maybe the first time Suzanne feels compassion for Ben's mother, a woman who tried to protect her children from an ugly truth. "More junk mail," she signs, forcing a smile with the lie. "Will you help me make dinner if your mom doesn't need you? I missed you while we were gone. Meet me in the kitchen. I'll be right there."

In her room Suzanne hides Charlie's letter in her box of secrets, setting it on top, next to the shell he gave her at Folly Beach. She feels shame because she is both hiding the letter and making sure it's the first thing Ben will see should he open the box. She winces at what this tells her about herself, wonders how she became a person she does not even like.

The kitchen is noticeably bright with the lengthening days of midsummer. Dust motes are visible in the streams of light that slink through the blinds over the sink. Suzanne soaks in the warmth, trying to fix the simple pleasure in her mind.

Under her direction, Adele washes and spins the lettuce, peels the shrimp, measures and mixes the dressing ingredients. Because Adele cannot easily sign while she cooks, their work is mostly wordless.

Once Adele pauses to say, "Next summer I'll be able to hear."

Suzanne smiles at her, and the worry must be evident on her face because Adele adds, "Not really hear, I understand, but I like to say that."

Suzanne returns to slicing the red onion, then looks at Adele straight on. "Are you scared?"

Adele shrugs, makes the signs for *yes* and *no*. She opens a can of mandarin oranges and drains the syrup into the sink. Due to the cut of her tank top, her wing-like shoulder blades are visible, and Suzanne can think only of a bird—delicate but strong enough to survive—though she knows it is wrong to reduce Adele to anything other than who she is.

"That seems right," she says. "It's normal to be scared before an operation, but you're right there's nothing to be afraid of. It's something you have to go through once to get where you want to be."

An hour later they are eating the supper with Ben and Petra. Petra opens a bottle of white wine and grows chatty with her second glass.

"Okay, okay," she said. "A violist was crying and screaming at the oboe player sitting behind him. I'm making it a *him*, Suzanne, just for you. Okay, so this violist was crying and screaming at the oboe player. Finally the conductor asked him why he was so upset, and the violist said, 'The oboist reached over and turned one of my pegs, and now my viola is out of tune.' The conductor nods and asks him doesn't he think he's overreacting, and the violist screams, 'I am not overreacting! He won't tell me which peg he turned!'"

Suzanne smiles and nods her recognition; of course she has heard it before.

"Absolutely hilarious," Ben says softly, staring stonily at Petra.

"Here's one," Suzanne says. "A viola player is finally tired of being so unappreciated, and she's tired of all the stupid viola jokes, so she decides it's time for a change and walks into a shop and says, 'I'd like to buy a violin.'

And the shopkeeper says, 'You must be a violist.' So the viola player says, 'How can you tell?'"

"Because it's an ice-cream shop!" Petra exclaims.

Adele looks around to gauge everyone's reactions, to see if she is supposed to laugh now. Her expectant face collapses when she sees Ben push away his plate and stand. "Excuse me."

A minute later Suzanne hears the front door fall shut. She continues to eat, encouraging Adele to do the same.

"What's with him?" Petra asks.

Suzanne looks at her while Adele is looking at her plate and whispers, "His brother just died, in case you forgot."

Petra's voice has no tone that Suzanne can interpret as sarcasm, but it's hard to accept at face value when she says, "I'm sorry. I did forget."

Suzanne watches Petra drain her glass and refill. "I'll clear the table."

Ben is gone for hours. After Petra and Adele go to bed, Suzanne waits for him out front, the porch light off but the living room behind her still lit. When he returns, she waits for him to go inside and come back out before she asks him about his father. The humidity slows their already careful words.

It is as Suzanne suspected: Ben has always known his father's death was a suicide.

"I knew but I didn't always know, if that makes sense." He looks at her when he talks, and this, in its unfamiliarity, is as disarming as anything. "Sometimes I let myself believe my mother's version of events, though of course I always really knew."

"Why didn't you tell me?" She cannot stop herself from asking.

He shrugs, then holds his head in his hands, elbows propped on his knees as they sit side by side on the porch steps. "I didn't want you to think I was genetically predisposed to be weak or crazy. I thought you'd be afraid of the Schumann biography and run from me. I thought you might be afraid to have children with me."

"You're the one who stopped that."

He sits quiet for a moment. "Maybe my wanting to wait did have something to do with my father. I don't know."

Suzanne pauses, biting into her lip, crying now. "I'm really sorry about your father. And Charlie. I loved Charlie. And I know I should be better than this, but I don't understand why you let me believe I wasn't good enough for your family. And why you didn't tell me."

This is, she thinks, the most honest conversation they've ever had.

"Suzanne," he says, disbelief shading his voice, "I have never thought I was better than you, ever. I've admired you from the beginning. I've always felt like you saved me by marrying me. I would be lost without you; don't you know that?"

She shakes her head, her mind yelling, *No, no, no*. She has no idea whether he is lying now or misinterpreting the week's emotion, or whether she's misunderstood all along.

Finally they lean into each other, shoulder to shoulder, still in the thick summer air, in a neighborhood quiet with night except for the orchestra of insect life, the occasional car sweeping down the 206, the electric buzz of the streetlight as it struggles to life.

After a long time Ben puts his arm around her shoulders, pulls her weight into him. "I always wanted to tell you about my father. It was never that I didn't trust you. I just—I just could never say it."

Suzanne has been supporting some of her own weight; now she lets the tension holding her spine drain and collapses into Ben, breathing in his smell.

They can start over, she thinks. They can still have everything, get everything right, even if they cannot undo what they've already done. In this moment she wants to wind back all the world's clocks, send its calendars fluttering in reverse. Where she would stop them, she isn't sure, but it might be that first day she saw Ben, who was wrapped over his cello and looked at her with mournful eyes, all his sadness there for her to see if only she'd really looked.

III. Appassionato

Twenty-four

Intermission is over, and they are playing the *Black Angels Quartet*. All four musicians know it: they are playing extremely well, so well that the music holds them and not the other way around. The nearly full auditorium belongs to them, to the piece. They possess the audience. The air itself vibrates, electric with the loud music.

Anthony and Petra make their violins scream, sawing away during the section that represents insects swarming the Vietnamese jungle. Daniel plays with his eyes closed, his outsized score but a stage prop. His gestures are large and loud—music on high volume even for the hard of hearing. Suzanne's heart beats wild and hard in her chest, and sweat drizzles down the back of her neck, between her breasts, along her slick waist. But her hands are steady even as the veins running down her forearms buzz. At the end she gasps audibly; they all do.

The applause falls hard, breaks into the exuberant. Suzanne sets her bow on her lap and pulls sweat-matted hair back from her forehead and temples. She is grinning. Petra is grinning, and Daniel, too. Anthony stands, bows, extends his right forearm for them to follow suit, which they do. Before she takes her bow, Suzanne looks up to the facets of the concave ceiling, the design that allows their music to find its ears at just the right angles. The manic pride and relief she feels remind her of that night in St. Louis, the night she played *Harold in Italy*, and Alex's absence stabs her.

She wishes he had heard her play tonight, that he was watching now, that his hands contributed to the applause that continues. She closes her eyes and listens to that clapping, trying to discern particular people from the group of mostly strangers. Friends pepper the audience, and surely other people she sees around town. Ben is out there, she knows, with Adele and maybe, just possibly, her father. No, not her father. *And not Alex.* Suzanne opens her eyes and the applause again becomes communal, an audience clapping in unison. She searches for Ben and spies him in an aisle seat half-way back, looking right at her, his hands clasped but now still.

Jennifer has planned an extraordinary party at her parents' stately Nassau Drive home. The sign-in sheet will be a glorified order form designed to secure advance sales of the CD before enthusiasm wanes and forgetting begins. It's not long after the final curtain call that Anthony assures them the recording was a technical success and tells them about the guest book.

But that's the only tacky aspect of the party. Everything else speaks class, from the good chocolates to the excellent pianist sliding lightly across Debussy and Chopin. Suzanne and Petra enter together, still in their black dresses, though Suzanne has brushed her sweaty hair and spun it into a chignon.

"Nice house," Petra says, "but the people are going to be really annoying, aren't they? Anthony told me I have to be on my best behavior, no fun at all."

"Who was that pianist?" Suzanne asks. "He was hired to play at a party for the Vanderbilts or some family like that? And Mrs. Vanderbilt offered him a thousand dollars and told him that he was not, under any circumstance, to mingle with the guests."

"Yeah." Petra nods. "So did he tell her to go to hell?"

"He told her, 'In that case, madam, you only have to pay me five hundred.'"

"That's actually funny," Petra says, dropping her arm around Suzanne's shoulders as they move in and around the large downstairs rooms, which have been cleared of their usual furniture and set up for the party.

After she and Petra separate, Suzanne drinks a glass of champagne. She eats crab puffs and strawberries dipped in chocolate. She talks to small groups of people: Elizabeth and some of her friends, Jennifer's parents, Anthony and a man who teaches at the Institute for Advanced Studies, people she does not know, Daniel and Linda.

"It's soda water," Daniel says, lifting his drink. "Proof positive that love changes people."

"You guys are sickeningly sweet, and you look irritatingly good together," Suzanne says. "I'm very happy for you."

Linda continues looking up at Daniel's face as she speaks to Suzanne. "I can't believe I found him. What are the chances?"

It is just beginning to feel late when Suzanne steps into a conversation boiling over between Petra and Jennifer, who beckons her to join something she would prefer to avoid.

Jennifer wears what Petra calls "a big black dress" with a double strand of pearls. As Suzanne steps close enough to make the conversation a triangle, Jennifer is saying, "When someone cheats, they're not just cheating on their spouse. They're cheating on their children."

"You're so American." Petra's voice is sloppy and sharp all at once.

"If by 'American' you mean I know the different between right and wrong, then yes. Guilty as charged."

"By 'American' I mean that sex is too important to you, so you have less of it. It just doesn't mean as much to me, for instance. It's not a big deal, just two bodies for a little while. No big deal."

"If it's not a big deal, then why do people bother to promise fidelity? Isn't it a big deal for a man to know his children are actually *his* children? If it's not a big deal, then why do so many couples break up over it?" Jennifer's face glows with her certainty.

"Because they're American!" Petra's words are loud enough to attract attention from nearby conversations.

As if sensing trouble, the pianist launches into a suddenly louder piece: a Liszt transcription from Gounod. Suzanne remembers reading once, in a biography of Liszt, that at each performance he would toss his glove to his choice for that night's pleasure, a different recipient every night.

"You and Liszt have similar appetites," Suzanne says, losing patience with having to secure Petra when she drinks too much.

Petra strides away.

Suzanne shrugs at Jennifer. "Sorry about her. I think maybe she's had a little too much champagne."

"Nothing new, I suppose, but so vehement. If I didn't know better, I'd think she was seducing Anthony." Jennifer laughs now, fingering the beads of her pearl strands, adding, "It's not that I don't trust him, necessarily—he is a man—just that I keep his leash very short. I read that the number-one predictor of infidelity is opportunity."

Suzanne looks anew at Jennifer, seeing in her broad face a woman more self-aware than she'd noticed before. Jennifer is one more person, Suzanne thinks, whom she has misjudged or at least misunderstood.

"I'd better find Petra and get her out of here before she talks to a potential donor."

Jennifer's hair swings at her shoulders as she nods. She touches Suzanne's shoulder. "Thank you for coming, and thank you for getting her out of here before she does any damage."

Getting Petra into the car is easier than Suzanne expected. Petra has gone docile with a turn in mood, though now she is crying and her tears are fierce.

"Honey," Suzanne whispers, "if it's not such a big deal, why are you so upset?"

"She's a stupid woman. Stupid and fat," Petra exclaims before going submissive again. "I'm sorry. I just drank too much on an empty stomach. The performance and all. We were really good, weren't we?"

"Yeah." Suzanne grins. "We were really good. Really, really good."

"We rocked!" Petra high-fives her. "We were awesome!" The American slang or the champagne exaggerates her ordinarily slight accent.

After Suzanne maneuvers the car through the narrow driveway and into its space, moving the gear to *park*, Petra slides herself out of the car and totters toward the back door. She points to her shoes. "I'm not actually drunk. I'm just tall."

"You are definitely too far from the ground." Suzanne slams shut both car doors and then follows her friend inside, where she assumes not only Adele but Ben is deep in sleep.

Twenty-five

The quartet's performance now part of her past, Suzanne returns to work on the concerto. She works the way she used to, the way she worked when she still believed the world was hers for the taking if she just tried hard enough.

But still it is not enough. Working with Alex's score, her hands and mind in his measures of music, was supposed to keep him close to her, in her. But the harder she seeks him, the more remote he becomes. She cannot find herself in his work, not even herself as violist. *Maybe he knew you as little as you knew him.* As she works, grief reverberates in her ears, an inaudible sound felt rather than heard. Grief not that she has lost him but that she is losing him always, over and over. It is the sensation of abandonment, of being left alone and not knowing in what form you will survive it.

She tries every theoretical approach she learned at Curtis and through her own studies, and she tries the more personal, remembering Alex's reactions to other concertos. Once, in Seattle, they heard Vassily Primakov play Chopin's first piano concerto. Flawed and brilliant, the work has been criticized since its premiere for its elementary orchestration. "But the piano itself!" Alex said, eyes lit with excitement.

But that does not apply to his viola concerto—the solo line is not enough.

The best concertos are relational; their very subject matter *is* the relationship between the soloist and the rest of the orchestra. She doesn't want to write a second-rate piece of music, and she doesn't want Alex to have conceived of one. There has to be a key, she thinks, to open the door between the brilliant and difficult viola score and the rest of the instruments.

Again and again she wants to throw down the work. Yet she continues, clinging to the belief that she will restore Alex to herself, that if she follows him around enough corners, she will reach the end of the maze and find something of him to grab. Then she will understand—the music, the person Alex was, the person she was with him, what she is without him.

She also knows, when she lets herself think about it, that she works because she fears Olivia. Suzanne does not want her life undone. She does not want Ben hurt more, and she does not want to lose him. Her life may not be the life she wanted, but it could be much worse.

Or perhaps it is the challenge that keeps her working: the old ambition, the deep desire to compose and now, at last, a chance to start that part of her life, to be alone and see in what form she will survive it. So she comes back to the work every morning and most nights.

It is midmorning on a very hot Tuesday when she breaks through. It is the most mundane of moments. She is sitting in her living room, cross-legged in shorts and a tank top, her hairline and back damp with sweat because they cannot afford to run the air conditioner all the time. She is eating grapes, slowly because they have seeds.

Understanding doesn't come in a single flash, but it does develop quickly, building like a strong wave. She stares at the score and in her mind hears what is missing from the concerto: an elegiac echo against the viola line. Alex left space for it but left it unwritten, almost as though he foresaw his own death. Holding the dead and the missing in her mind—her mother, Charlie, her baby, Robert Schumann, the Adele born with hearing ears, but mostly Alex—she writes for the orchestra an elegiac line, a subdued but emotion-saturated voice to accompany and answer the viola. Less than an equal conversation but a clear voice that she allows to snake among the double reeds and the cello. Mostly it will be carried by the bassoon, that comic tragedy of a tone, an instrument like a man with the face of a clown and a heart aching with unrequited love.

There is more than one solution to every musical conundrum, yet Suzanne believes she has found Alex's true intention, or something very close. It solves for her the mystery of a concerto written by a man who found most concertos distasteful. The viola does not perform a virtuosic solo, though virtuosity is required, but is the stronger half of a duet before the crowd of the orchestra. The central voice is witnessed, and it is answered. She spits out a grape seed and nods.

Twenty-six

After Suzanne completes her work on the concerto and sends it off to Olivia, she returns to full-time practice. When playing alone, she finds a new lightness and pleasure in her instrument, its look and feel, smell and sound. She plays whatever she feels like, including some frothier baroque tunes, some Roma dance music, Debussy, moving from one thing to the next according to mood or whim.

With the quartet she practices portions of the regular repertoire, and the members discuss their next moves. Anthony is working on the marketing of the *Black Angels* CD and has accepted some invitations that suggest the quartet's swelling reputation. They agree to a performance in Montreal and to appear at festivals in Salt Lake City and Austin. As they consider their future programs, Petra continues to advocate for the Ravel quartet and Anthony shows signs of softening on the point. Domestic bliss has made Daniel unusually easygoing. "Sounds good," he says a lot, regardless of who is proposing what. One day Petra suggests a Christmas CD, just to see if he's listening, but he catches on and grins, giving Petra what can only be called a bear hug. "I'm not quite that far gone. Linda has made me happy but not stupid."

The news arrives by certified letter when Suzanne is home alone, practicing. She is playing Hindemith and eyeing the angle of her elbow crook when the doorbell rings. Her arrangement of Alexander Elling's Viola Concerto, Op. 1, has been accepted into the Minnesota Orchestra Composer Institute. If she accepts the invitation—and they hope she will—there will be breakouts and rehearsals, analysis and feedback, instruction in the business of composing, dinners with other aspiring composers. At the end of the grueling week will be a full public performance of "the work." Compliments of Olivia's industriousness and cunning, Suzanne will hear the composition, fully orchestrated.

She rereads the letter, her body tingling. It is the sort of letter she fantasized about receiving when she was younger, when she still thought she might make her way as a composer as well as a performer. It is Alex's piece that has been accepted, she understands, and the weight of his name is heavy. But the concerto is her work. too, in its interpretation and execution. Suzanne wrote the second line, did much of the orchestration.

Yet when her excitement slides away, soon, the emotion gripping her is cold, quaking fear. Not insecurity or stage jitters but true fright—the terror of free fall. Olivia may be trying to destroy her, beginning with her marriage, but only beginning there and ending in something even larger and darker. That night Suzanne wakes over and over, each time in a sweat, seeing every hour the clock passes at least once: eleven fifty-eight, twelve sixteen, one forty, two ten, two fifty-six, three twenty, four o'clock. She rises for the day shortly after five, exhausted but relieved to be out of bed, away from the twisted sheets, away from the sound of Ben's even breathing as he sleeps through the hot night.

Her eyes and skin are scrubbed raw by the insomnia; her logic is untrustworthy. Fortunately there is no practice scheduled. Not good for much else, she decides to make breakfast for the others. She'll need to tell them about Minnesota, but not today. She'll think about it more and make the announcement when her mind is working more swiftly. Now she concentrates on the simple work in the kitchen. She brews coffee, relieved by its smell as it begins to drip. She cuts into a pineapple, slowly, rendering it into matching cubes. She slices apple, squeezing lemon over the slices so they do not brown. She washes blueberries and blackberries, cuts up a kiwi. Next she mixes pancake batter, stirring in cinnamon and walnuts to make the recipe her own.

An hour or so later she is eating the food with Ben, Petra, and Adele. Suzanne smiles at everyone, foists seconds, pushes fruit, but only Adele seems happy with the breakfast. Ben's aloofness is at its most marked. He and Petra do not look at each other and only occasionally look at her. Petra and Adele sign a little but not much. Petra looks haggard, as she often does these days. Her eyes are shallow on her face but shadowed by dark spots where they meet her nose. Underneath are bruised circles. Her normally straight back slumps as she sits. Suzanne feels fatigue pull on her own spine so lifts her posture and pulls back her shoulders, refusing to curl into the deep tiredness she feels.

When Petra returns from taking Adele to the summer camp at her school, she suggests a long walk. Suzanne begs off to practice a little and then nap, but her friend presses. "*Please.*"

They cut down the 206, keeping tight to the left side of the road until they can peel off into the woods surrounding Mountain Lake. The day is hot but not so humid as it has been, and walking feels good.

Suzanne quickens her step. "Let's make it feel like exercise," she says. "Maybe we'll outpace the mosquitoes."

They find the path that circles the lake. It's a workday for most people, and they pass almost no one. A middle-aged woman jogging, two young guys fishing the lake with simple line poles, a man running a border collie.

Suzanne waits for Petra to talk—there must be something behind her uncommon invitation—but Petra just walks on. They cross the mucky section on the lake's far side, near where an icehouse sat until it was taken down last summer.

"This lake was put here for ice; did you know that?"

Petra shakes her head. "I should come here more. It's nice."

"Back when I was trying to run, I came here a lot. Petra," Suzanne starts, thinking she should talk to Petra about her drinking, which is beginning to take an obvious toll on her physically as well as emotionally. But she is so tired herself she is afraid she will get it wrong, and she is in no position to give anyone advice about how to live their lives. Maybe Daniel can say something to Petra, can talk to her about how he stopped and how he feels.

"I was up all night," Petra whispers.

"Me, too. Full moon?"

Petra shakes her head. "New moon, totally dark."

The path takes them away from the lake and then back around, up a long hill. The path widens considerably, though the foliage is thick on either side and in places obscures the lake below. Suzanne feels the climb in her hamstrings, her gluteal muscles, her expanding lungs. Maybe she will start running again, when she gets back from Minnesota. It feels good to be moving, to be breathing a little hard, to be outside.

As the path narrows near its end, where it will drop them back near the 206, Petra asks, "Have you talked to Ben much lately?"

"Every day, Petra. I talk to him every day."

"I mean really talk to him. Mr. Aloof."

Suzanne stops and turns to face her, but Petra keeps walking, saying over her shoulder, "You need to talk to him."

Suzanne opens her mouth to ask Petra what she's talking about, but Petra is already across the road and walking fast toward home. Despite the day's heat, despite her physical exertion, Suzanne's skin goes cold and she shivers, her stomach a core of ice.

Twenty-seven

It should even the score, what Ben confesses to Suzanne. She should forgive him the second he speaks, given her more extended offense. But human emotions are not balanced equations, and there is the wild variable: Petra is her best friend. *Was* her best friend.

Outrage chokes her, yet there's a cooling relief in knowing that she is not a worse person than everyone else, that what she's done isn't off the charts. She sits on the very edge of their bed, not wanting to ask if it happened there and not wanting to sit further back in case the answer to that unasked question is yes. She imagines Ben and Petra here while Adele slept on the other side of the house, all alone. She feels the blood pulsing through her carotid arteries so hard it feels visible, and her vision fills with small black dots, as though she is about to lose consciousness.

"It just happened," Ben is saying. "I don't know, really, it just happened."

She blinks, and the visual static clears. Staring at the small squares of her knees, she thinks that this is something she can understand, that she should understand. Still she says, "You just happened to take your clothes off with my best friend?"

Ben surprises her by saying, "More or less."

"How many times?"

"I'm not sure." He shrugs, looking helpless, looking like he wants to run from the room. He breathes a few audible breaths, settles into himself a little. "About five, I guess."

"Each time that memorable?" She hears the ugliness in her voice, the predictability, the easiness and wrongness of the hypocritical path she is starting down.

"They kind of blur; they're part of one thing."

Suzanne swallows, tries to soften her voice. "Would you tell me when the first time was? Maybe it doesn't matter, but I would like to know."

"About a year ago, maybe. It wasn't any particular day or event. You were out of town, and we were drinking—we were pretty drunk—and it just happened. It wasn't a big deal, and we promised that it was just a fluke and we wouldn't be weird about it. The next day or so we avoided each other, and then you came home, and it actually felt like it never even hap-pened. Like it was a movie I saw once."

"Until it happened again."

"Not for a long time, not until a few days before that party at Elizabeth's, a day you went into the city for some reason. I don't remember exactly."

"Is that why she was drunk and belligerent at the party?"

"It was different the second time, maybe because it was the second time, and she wanted to tell you right away and beg forgiveness." Ben rubs his forearms, which are clenched, their veins three-dimensional and blue. "I told her not to, that I didn't want you to know, not ever."

"When was the next time?"

His voice is faded, not so much a whisper as his full voice eroded and made rough. "Don't do this. To yourself, don't do it."

Suzanne stands, leans her forehead into the door of her closet, rests her weight there even though it hurts a little. "So why tell me now if you didn't want to tell me ever?"

"I did want to tell you the truth, but I didn't want to hurt you. And then Charlie died and I told Petra never again and she agreed and so I decided not to tell you. I didn't want to hurt you, and I didn't want you to leave. I was afraid you were going to leave when you found out I lied about my dad, and I figured you'd definitely leave me if you found out I was lying about something less . . . less sympathetic." He shakes his head the way he does when he steps out of the shower and gulps a large breath.

She repeats her question when she realizes he hasn't answered it. "So why tell me now?"

"It was killing Petra—she was really cracking up, drunk all the time, going crazy. You know she doesn't lie, and I'm starting to think it's because she can't, not without making herself sick."

"So you're telling me for her sake?"

Ben shakes his head. "I wouldn't do that. I'm telling you because she's making me. I'm telling you because she was going to tell you if I didn't." He runs his fingers through his hair, smoothing it down and then messing it up, taking a long time to speak again. "I don't know what to say except that I'm really, really sorry. I kept trying to make things better between you and me and it never worked and then, I don't know. It didn't mean that much, you know."

"It means all kinds of things."

Suzanne imagines Ben at home, black pen making notes across page after page while she is at a concert with Alex in Chicago, Los Angeles, Pittsburgh, Baltimore, Cleveland, London. She should tell Ben; she knows this. She should let him off the hook, relieve his guilt and herself from her lying.

She always figured he must know, at least generally—but if he did, wouldn't he bring it up now? Wouldn't he fling it in her face, defend himself, blame her infidelity for his? She flips it over and back, but still she doesn't know the answer because Ben isn't like other people, and even if he was it's increasingly plain that Suzanne doesn't understand anyone at all, that she has misjudged everyone who matters to her.

"But not that much," he says, his voice insistent. "It doesn't mean that much."

She turns, looks down to where he sits, now slumped, and into his eyes. "Do you think we'll be able to find a way to start over?"

Ben shakes his head, and again she shivers. This is not what she wanted, not really, not now.

"No, Suzanne. People don't get to start over. And even if we could, I don't think I would want to undo everything just to undo a couple of the worst things. I don't want to start over; I want to just keep going."

"Keep going with me?"

Ben nods. "I want us to keep going."

She steps toward him and shoves his shoulders back as hard as she can, pushing him off balance, wishing she had the nerve to punch him in the face. "I am really, really pissed off, so pissed off I can't see straight." She squints to release her tears.

"I know," he answers, righting himself. "I can tell."

She leans back against the wall and slides down halfway into a squat, her feet pressing down and her back flat on the wall. Her thighs, parallel to the floor, burn with the effort. For just a moment she feels something opening between her and Ben. And for a moment their whole predicament seems funny. She laughs. "That's progress, right? You being able to tell what I'm feeling?"

"Yeah." Ben nods, finds her eyes and holds them. "That and you telling me straight out."

He is not laughing, and now she isn't either.

She braces herself tighter, concentrating on the strength of her legs, the muscular pain. "I'm going to think while I'm away. I'm going to Minneapolis."

"You're running away from me."

He stands and holds out his hands to help her up, but she uses her legs to slide up the wall without his assistance. She folds her arms and looks past him, across the bed at his nightstand, noting with part of her attention that it's covered with a fine layer of dust except for the circle where his water glass sits at night and the rectangular shape indicating a book's phantom presence.

"I'm not running away Ben. I actually have to go to Minneapolis, and then I'm coming back. I will come back, and we can see then. I can't do anything now anyway."

"You shouldn't leave. It's a mistake."

"It has nothing to do with this, or you. It's about the music. Of all the people in the world, you should be able to understand that."

"How long will you be gone?"

"I don't know. A week. And you need to keep Petra away from me until I get back. Tell her not to call me because I won't be answering." She opens her closet to pull out her suitcase. "And when I get home I want to run the goddamn air conditioning at night. I can't sleep when it's hot, and I don't think our marriage can survive another night of me listening to you sleep while I can't." She doesn't speak her other thought, which is that Petra should stay away not just from her but from him.

224

Ben sits back down, watching her pack. "If it means we can keep going, we can run the air conditioner more."

Suddenly calm and focused on what she is about to do, she says, "I'm not promising that, and neither can you. We've let things go pretty far."

"But maybe not too far. We're not like other people."

"No," she admits, "we're not much like most other people."

"I feel like I've always been waiting for you, so what's another week?"

She peers back into her closet, wondering what a person is supposed to wear at a composers' institute. She grabs jeans, shirts, and black dress and drops them on the bed next to the suitcase. "You'll work while I'm gone?"

"Of course," he says. "It's what I do."

Twenty-eight

The composers are housed in a large hotel. They are six, if Suzanne counts herself and Alex as one. She feels dwarfed by the huge lobby but even more so by the other aspirants. One of the young men wears a Hawaiian shirt and an eagerness for friendship, but most are reserved. Two—one man and one woman—seem frankly hostile. Suzanne remembers the competitiveness from Curtis and from her summer at Marlboro, but it was friendlier there. Even Anthony knocked off with only a comment or two, not actually wanting others to fail but only himself to succeed.

Or maybe it only seemed friendlier, given her naïveté and the more youthful stakes. Maybe she just didn't know enough to feel threatened or to wield her own knife. Occasionally Ben was accused of a cutthroat attitude, but she understood immediately that this was a misreading. There was a confidence there, verging on arrogance, and a disdain for laziness and shortcuts of any kind. And aloofness always. But no malice. He could be fairly accused of ignoring other people, of failing to notice them, of frowning openly at their musical tastes, but not of wishing anyone else failure or harm. Even before she knew much about him, she could feel that there was no aggression. He never schemed. And even now, when she has learned that so much about him is not what she thought, she knows she was right about that. He is not a mean person.

What she does know now that she didn't know when she was a student is that some people are indeed mean, with no compassion. Perhaps they are the least dangerous of all people, the least likely to hurt you, because you know they would if they could. That's what she thinks when she meets Lisa-Natasha and Eric. Though she doesn't think they are a romantic pair, and maybe not even allies, they are sticking together for now, and Suzanne thinks of them as joined, as male and female halves of the same taut ambition. They even look alike in their dark skinny jeans, black shirts, and streaky hair, with their fast-moving eyes, with their speedy assessments and dismissals of the people they introduce themselves to, never shaking hands or asking much.

"Not Lisa. Not Natasha. Lisa-Natasha," the female one says, and Suzanne whispers, "Got it."

But other composers' attitudes aren't at issue, not really. Suzanne is not here to make friends, if she could even remember how to go about it or figure out whom to trust. She is here to finish whatever it is that Olivia started. She has come for the learning and the work. Perhaps she is here to become, at last, a composer. Mostly, though, she has come to Minneapolis to have the concerto worked on and performed. She has come to hear what it sounds like and to have her farewell from Alex.

Her relationship with Alex was an education in how to compartmentalize her emotions, her thoughts, parts of herself. Even so, she is surprised at how easily she sets aside Ben and Petra. For the first time she understands Ben's ability to work in the days after she lost the baby. She wasn't able to play, not even a little, for several weeks, and his capacity to overlook her pain and write music made him seem monstrous and her feel weak. *And to overlook his own pain*, she realizes for the first time. Now maybe she sees: he wasn't ready to think about it, and he knew it wasn't going away. Why not work?

She studies her itinerary in her large room, and for a moment she feels as though Alex is in the bathroom or has run down to the lobby for aspirin or a newspaper—as though he will be right back. No, she reminds herself sternly, but then she thinks, *He is here in the music.* There is comfort in this thinking, but it's not mere comfort. She believes it.

The itinerary names the work: Viola Concerto, composed by Alexander Elling and Suzanne Sullivan. They are united on the page even if they are divided by life. Her hands shake, and she lowers the paper to the bed to read the five-day schedule of meetings, panels, critique sessions, lectures, readings, rehearsals, and, finally, the Friday-night public performance of the six works.

It is late when she turns her lights off, and she sleeps the deep sleep available to her only when she is both alone and very tired. If she dreams, she does not remember her dreams, and so upon waking she thinks instead of the Chicago dream of being trapped inside the moist head of another person, attempting an escape that may be futile. She comforts herself again, telling herself that it is Alex's head she has been inside, inside his music and his mind, and so no escape is necessary. She feels oddly confident about the concerto itself: she has solved it, and the result is both daring and beautiful.

Showered and dressed, Suzanne finds her way to the continental breakfast set out in one of the hotel's conference rooms. As she serves herself coffee, weak orange juice, and an oblong wheat roll, she greets the other five composers. Again Lisa-Natasha and Eric respond icily, turning their heads slightly away as they speak to her and saying something mildly clever.

She wants to assure them that she is no threat at all. The friendliest of the bunch wears another Hawaiian shirt, this one even brighter than yesterday's. "Bruce," he says, shaking left hands with her as his right balances a plate holding his breakfast and a steaming mug.

"I know," she says. "I've had the pleasure of seeing you play."

She overhears Lisa-Natasha say to Eric, "It's easy for him not to care. He's already concertmaster in Baltimore. This is a second career for him, and he doesn't need to succeed. That one, yes, her, she's also a performer." Suzanne smiles at Lisa-Natasha, almost impressed that she didn't whisper.

She also exchanges names with a slightly ghoulish-looking young man with a British accent—Paul—and a haler, tall guy who introduces himself as Greg. She has read the short biographies provided by each, but Greg Michael Simon is someone she has heard of before. She cannot remember if Ben mentioned him with admiration or disdain; she will know for sure when she hears his composition, which the program bills simply as a short symphony for small orchestra.

Given the unusual provenance of the concerto—"the tragic circumstances of its collaborative nature" is how Olivia phrased it—special permission has been granted for Olivia to shadow Suzanne.

Making the emotional literal. Olivia is at her side by the time she sits to eat. In black pants and a tee-shirt-styled sweater, Olivia looks slightly more casual than she did in Chicago, though she is as collected as ever with her hair smoothed back and her earlobes dotted with silver knots. The sweater that looks easy on first glance is, on a closer look, make of good thin wool.

The composers sip their beverages and eat their breakfasts at the large round table, and soon a second table fills with the week's instructors and lead musicians, some of whom nod to them and some of whom ignore them altogether and instead catch up with each other. The conductor stands at a lectern and taps the microphone. He holds himself tall and speaks with confidence, as did Alex, as do most conductors, who have sought front and center and are accustomed to being watched. He's younger, though, and takes up more space. Alex was already trim when Suzanne met him, and his response to aging was to lose more weight, not realizing that it made him seem not younger but rather a tad more frail—something she never told him.

"Your week will be a microcosm of the real orchestral world," this conductor tells them. "It just gets worse from here." He holds open his palm and sweeps his arm to indicate the outside world.

Only Suzanne and Bruce, the two participants who have played in professional orchestras, do not laugh.

The lovely red-haired Minneapolis concertmaster stands next at the podium. She will be the one to go over all the violin parts in all six scores. "Remember, we want to play what you want us to play, but musicians also care about sounding good. Most of us are cooperative, but we want to sound good, and we get tired. Remember that if you find a musician difficult, it's either because he's tired or because you're not making him sound good."

Their workdays are to last twelve hours. The most important part of Suzanne's first day will be her afternoon meeting with the principal viola player. She has also asked for another breakout session with the violist together with the cellist and double-reed section that will make a fugue of the solo, but that will not happen until day three. Today is only the viola.

First are the morning meetings, which Olivia tells Suzanne she will skip. "I've had enough of the business of music to last my life. You have no idea what it means to be a conductor's wife." It's such an obvious dig to take, and delivered so smugly, that Suzanne wonders if she has overestimated Olivia, if her revenge can be that pedestrian.

Suzanne's first meeting is with one of the orchestra librarians to discuss any errata. She doesn't have many, just a few accidentals carrying over octaves, but they need to be made on fifty parts. The librarian takes the news easily. "Not even close to bad," he tells her. "You're careful in your work, clearly."

She has never thought of herself this way, yet nods. "I suppose I am."

Following that meeting is a grant-writing workshop for the whole group. Suzanne takes notes, thinking that the person who should be attending is Ben, who works intensely hard on his music but has never been interested enough in the business to give himself a real chance. "We're not filmmakers; we can write music without money," he sometimes says, as though music is something that can live on paper when it is not played, performed, recorded in forms that others listen to.

Olivia finds Suzanne at lunch, which is held in a private room of the hotel's restaurant. They eat to the sounds of a live saxophone player who plays not classical music but jazz standards with a few popular songs tossed in.

"Someone's idea of texture," Eric says.

"I think the change of tone is a good idea," says Greg.

Bruce nods his agreement. "I'm actually studying jazz more and more. It was completely missing from my training."

"That's because you're a violinist," Lisa-Natasha says with salad in her mouth.

"As opposed to brass?" Bruce asks, looking genuinely confused.

Lisa-Natasha swallows the salad, then waits another moment. "As opposed to a composer."

Greg glares at her. Bruce simply whispers, "Ouch."

"We have a session," Olivia says, scooting back her chair. "Suzanne?"

Suzanne rises and follows her to the lobby, where they are greeted by the driver who will take them to the university music school. On the way Olivia says, "We're required to use the orchestra musicians, but at the real premiere you will be the soloist, of course." It had crossed Suzanne's mind to request to play, not because she wants to but simply because she *can* play the piece, which is not something that will come readily to anyone who gets less time with the music. Or cares less about it. But her *not* wanting to won out, as did her desire to participate as a composer, to hear her music played rather than to be heard playing.

The practice room looks like every practice room Suzanne has ever known, with the superficial exceptions of the black-and-white-striped floor and one wall painted red behind the large green chalkboard. The viola player is a young man who is immensely talented and has worked on the music in advance. Still he stumbles on the technical difficulty, particularly during the second movement's most difficult passages.

Suzanne says what she can say: "I understand." She adds, "If we need to, we can amend the music in a few places to make it more natural for you. But give it one more try as is, okay?"

He looks lovely when he plays. His dark, longish hair is mostly straight, but a few locks curl over his forehead, a flourish over his wire-framed glasses. Though he is thin, he owns a wiry strength, and there is a great smoothness to the movements of his bow arm. Nothing flashy, just pure competence and an obvious love for the viola.

It hits her, watching him, that the solo isn't merely a part but a role, and one intended for a female player. It's not a thought she likes—that music can be male or female. It took anonymous auditions behind opaque screens before the musical powers would accept that women have the lung capacity to play brass, and, still, after so much time, the hiring of female conductors is protested by whole orchestras, including the female musicians.

But the truth of the matter here is not self-loathing but something simple: Alex wrote the music for a woman to play. He wrote it for her to play. She looks back at Olivia, who sits behind her, eyes closed as she listens. It doesn't matter, Suzanne decides; the piece has to stand on its own. Whatever Alex's late conversion to program music was about, the music has to work without the story.

At the end of the day she is so tired that she skips the dinner and sinks into another night of sleep with no dreams, waking sprawled diagonally on the huge bed. In her prewaking moments she imagines a warmth next to her before she shakes off the sleep.

Day two is more business. At breakfast the conductor tells them, "I know all you can probably think about is your music. We put this stuff first so you can move on to that but also because it's in many ways the most important thing you will take away from this week. I cannot emphasize that enough."

Today *business* means a seminar with one of the orchestra's artistic planners, a good-looking woman, perhaps in her early thirties, groomed and dressed for the corporate world. "My title says *artistic*, but it's really about the planning, and the planning is about the money. In many ways I have the best job of all because I get to make the ideas and dreams of the conductor, the music director, the concertmaster, and so on, a reality." She dims the light and uses PowerPoint to tell them about working with unions, about the relative virtues of renting versus owning everything from a building to flower vases, about production costs and the least painful ways to slim down orchestration if your budget won't stretch to match your vision, about new marketing. Suzanne is surprised by the small nuts and bolts:

from the risks of cost-tiered seating to labor costs on different days of the week, at different times of day.

They move to a larger room for the seminar on copyrights, to which the public is admitted provided they are orchestra donors or members of the American Composers' Guild. Suzanne spies some of the usual types—guys with briefcases carrying pages of their unpublished and quite likely unfinished scores who will ask detailed questions about protecting their copyright to music no one wants to steal.

Yet she listens as closely as she can, jotting notes when an intellectual property rights attorney and someone from the American Music Center advise the young composers on commissioning fees, managing risk, payment considerations when considering hard and soft deadlines, and responding to plagiarism accusations or suspected plagiarism of your own work.

When Suzanne steps out, she scans the lobby. Relieved that Olivia is nowhere in sight, that Olivia's presence is only the invisible mantle always heavy on her shoulders, Suzanne pushes through the revolving door. For four years travel to a new city almost always meant Alex—concerts, paintings, restaurants, long walks—and she feels her solitary stroll sharply. Her senses have returned, and the air feels like hands on her face. The shifting smells of evergreens, car exhaust, hot-dog stand, and newsprint alter her breathing, making it deeper or more shallow, more or less pleasant. She walks a loop of a few blocks, perhaps twenty minutes, before returning to the hotel, walking through the taxi circle, nodding to the young doorman, pushing back through the revolving door, feeling as though it did indeed spin her out and back in.

Standing in the center of the lobby, back to Suzanne, blond hair shiny, is Petra. Petra spins, tucks her hair behind one ear, and stares directly at Suzanne, as though she saw her coming in a mirror that Suzanne cannot see.

"It's about time. I'm buying you a drink." Petra laughs and adds, "I promise mine will be cranberry juice."

"Why, are you pregnant?" Suzanne asks, her voice more bitter than she feels.

Petra shakes her head, and Suzanne follows her into the hotel bar, to a table in a dark far corner, a table perfect for secret assignations. True to her word, Petra orders juice. "But you should have a real drink," she says and tells their waiter to bring Suzanne a whiskey.

They wait for the drinks to arrive and the server to leave before they start their conversation. Petra starts with a joke: "Why don't viola players play hide and seek?"

Suzanne sips her drink and says nothing.

"Well?"

"You're really going to make me answer a joke so old?"

Petra nods.

"Fine. Viola players don't play hide and seek because they know no one will look for them."

Petra reaches across the table and squeezes Suzanne's forearm. "Except we did look for you. That's what we were mostly doing, you know, looking for you."

Suzanne decides to hold her own words until she hears more. "We were lonely. We were lonely for you. That's mostly why we did it." Petra tips her head to the side and smiles. "That and the fact that I'm a slut."

"The girlish charm isn't going to work on this, Petra. And it's not likely that I'm going to buy into the explanation that you and my husband slept together to be closer to me." Suzanne pauses. "That's kind of a question."

Her answer is simple: "Yes. We did."

"That's bullshit."

"Since when do you swear?"

Suzanne takes three large gulps of the whiskey, burning her tongue, palate, the left side of her throat. "Since you screwed my husband."

Petra is shaking her head. "Maybe he wants the part of you I have, and I want the part of you he has."

Suzanne waits, but Petra offers no more, so finally she says, "So you slept with my husband because you wanted to sleep with me." Forgetting for a moment everything but that Petra is her best friend, who has always told her the worst about herself, she laughs.

"And if I asked you to, what would you say?" Petra returns her grip to Suzanne's forearm.

Suzanne leaves her arm still, consciously, but ignores the question, and ultimately it is Petra who retreats from the physical contact.

"What I know and Ben doesn't understand," Petra says, unwrapping and removing the scarf around her neck, "is that those parts aren't even half of you. You checked out on us a while ago, Suzanne. You left us alone, and we took comfort in each other."

With nothing to say, no words coming at all, Suzanne feels the hollow in her neck, that ache that can be filled only with chin rest and wood. She wants Petra to leave so she can go upstairs and play music and think about nothing.

"I always figured that part of you died when you lost the baby, or maybe you saved a little of that and poured it into Adele. But it's been gone from me and I'm pretty sure gone from Ben, and even he's not so emotionally thick that he wouldn't notice, even if he can't name it."

Suzanne begins shaking her head vehemently. "No," she says. "You don't get to do that. You don't get to make this my fault. You don't get to use Adele like that, and you don't get to talk about my baby, not ever. If you ever say that again, if you ever even mention it in passing, you will never see me again."

"Does that mean I will if I don't?" Petra's lips are stained a sheer bright pink from her juice.

What Suzanne wants, more than anything, is for her marriage to be happy and Petra to be her best friend. She wants Alex alive and perfect and unharmed—someone she admires but has never met. She says, "I would like you to leave."

Petra is not stricken, as once she would have been. Or maybe she is stricken in some unseen way, because her transparency has clouded and Suzanne cannot read her. She merely nods, drains her juice, and shoulders the straps of her purse. "Call me if you change your mind. I have a room here. I can't help but think you're here because of me, because of me and Ben, and I'm not having you here alone."

Suzanne drinks the rest of her whiskey in a few short sips. "It doesn't have anything to do with you, or with that. Not the way you think. I really would like you to leave. Leave all the way."

"I already paid for my room." Petra shrugs and starts to leave, but she turns around and steps close to the table, bending over, making Suzanne look at her. "You know I've always liked you more than him, even during."

Petra's words make her physical presence stronger, and Suzanne looks at the thin white pipe that is her neck, the collarbones revealed by the scoop-necked shirt, the shape of her shoulders underneath. It is now that she imagines Ben and Petra actually together. She has seen each of them naked many times, and now she fits them together. His hand tracing the line where Petra's small, perfect breasts become her armpits, the V-shaped lines of her thin stomach, the scant hair between her legs, the slight inward curve where her long thighs join her body. Ben, just a little taller, lining up chest

237

to chest, hips to hips, feet to feet. *Eyes to eyes.* She blinks and sees them other ways, the ways she has been with him: Petra straddling him on a chair, pinned by his weight against the wall, on her tiptoes in the shower, on top of him but facing backward. She pictures Petra under him, over him, in front of him. *Stop.*

Petra tries to smile, but it doesn't hold. "Anyway, I hope you'll call me."

Suzanne closes and opens her eyes, slower than blinking. "I'm not going to change my mind, but we'll talk when I get home."

She watches Petra as she walks up to the bar and signs for the bill. The server asks her something and she stays for a moment, talking to him, and Suzanne sees something new in Petra's body language, in the angle at which she stands, in the position of her shoulder—a slight reserve. It's not just that Suzanne hasn't noticed it before; it is utterly new. Suzanne looks down and is surprised by her own forearm, unmoved from the place it rested when Petra held it tight, sitting on the table as though it doesn't belong to her at all but is just something someone left lying there.

Twenty-nine

The third day of the institute marks the serious turn to the compositions. After a score seminar with a master copyist, the day will be spent in reading sessions with various sections of the orchestra, beginning for Suzanne with percussion and ending with the full strings. Throughout the day Olivia watches and writes copiously with a blue pen on a yellow legal pad, but she says little, leaving it to Suzanne to listen, guide, negotiate. Suzanne tries to ignore her, to forget her as much as that is possible, but Olivia's silence makes her presence louder. If the concerto is the story of Alex's love with Suzanne, then Olivia is entirely the wrong audience.

The most challenging reading of the day is the requested special section with the principal cellist and double reeds. This is the music that Suzanne has not merely filled in, arranged, or embellished. This is the music that she herself created from scratch, summoned into existence from whatever void holds music that is unwritten.

It is nearly impossible to notate music completely. Marks on a page are but an elaborate shorthand, an approximation of the language the composer imagines hearing, desires to hear. There is always room for interpretation and so misinterpretation, but Suzanne finds that the young oboist with dark circles under her eyes understands her intentions, using dynamics to represent various states of sadness and agitation, following the tempo Suzanne wants. The bassoon player, despite his obvious talent, has less feel for the piece. His changes in dynamics are overstated, almost clumsy, making Suzanne's compositional moves sound hackneyed and amateurish.

She recalls the concertmaster's advice: "We want to play what you wrote, but we want to sound good." She needs to make the music make sense to the bassoonist, to help him find the best tonal color, to help him feel the timbre. She tries to describe it in words, remembering a children's book she used to sign to Adele that described sadness as a single petal fallen from a flower, a seal stranded on a beach while his family rode the current back out to sea, a marble that rolled under a sofa and was forgotten.

Olivia looks up from her pad, speaking softly but with audible, crisp words. "To give a less childish example, perhaps it would help to imagine a woman home alone while her husband goes to hear her favorite tenor with another, younger woman."

Suzanne remembers that concert. She didn't like the program at all, and she and Alex left early and went instead to a blues bar, where they drank gin and smoked cigarettes—two things she hasn't done since—and watched people dance, their bodies close and sweaty, taking the dark room's permission to move lewdly.

Suzanne tells herself that it isn't due to Olivia's analogy, but nevertheless the bassoon player's reading of his part improves. She is relieved because she feels too exhausted to make it through more than once after that. "One final go at it," she says, and she puts up her feet to listen.

Before she goes up to her room to rest before dinner, Olivia taps her shoulder. "Who was that woman—the blond—you were with yesterday at the bar? She's not one of the composers."

Suzanne wants to tell her it's none of her business, but it seems easier to answer, and she's no longer sure what belongs to whom, whose business is whose. She looks directly at Olivia and says, "I guess you could say that she is to me what I am to you."

For once Olivia looks confused instead of like the person in charge. Suzanne walks away at a pace Olivia would have trouble matching without obvious effort, without denting her armor of composure.

In her room Suzanne pulls open the thick curtains and sits in the gauzy light permitted by the thin inner curtain. She rests her feet on the ottoman and closes her eyes. Even as she is thinking how nice it is to be alone—to have no one looking to her or even at her—the impulse to call Petra tugs. She can imagine them sitting cross-legged on her bed, her telling Petra what Olivia is doing to her and Petra reassuring her that Olivia is indeed diabolical but won't eat her alive. Even the imagining gives Suzanne a sliver of relief, but as soon as she feels it she closes herself to the idea. Everything that has happened is too huge to be treated as though it were small, too difficult to make easy.

Instead she rouses herself to wash her face, change clothes, primp as though she cares how she looks when she goes down to the lobby to be ferried with the others, in small groups, to the Greek restaurant where they will dine.

An hour later she is sitting, in a dark blue dress and silver jewelry, at a large table as a waiter and waitress who could be brother and sister bring bottles of retsina, baskets of bread, olives, sauces in small white bowls. They splash skillets of kasseri cheese with ouzo, set them on fire with disposable

241

lighters, and douse the flames with lemon juice. It is the same start to a meal Suzanne shared with Alex in Detroit. He'd made an excuse to come hear her play in a university auditorium, and after her recital the two of them braved streets so empty that deer mingled on the yellow center lines, searching for what the pianist had told her was the only decent restaurant in walking distance. Now she watches Alex's wife as she feels Alex soak into her with every sip of the resin-flavored wine, every bite of the lemony cheese, the warm bread, the salty olives, the garlicky *tzatziki*.

Fuck Olivia, she thinks yet again, and then she is pierced by the thought of Petra, alone in her large room, maybe thinking the same thing about her.

The young composers talk business at first, debating the pros and cons of university sinecures, wishing aloud that there were more organizations like the Minnesota Commissioning Club—the group of ordinary people who pool their money to commission contemporary music.

Red wine follows the retsina, and they toast Minnesota as heavy plates of food arrive. The talk begins to bridge business and music.

"I'm just not sure what the future of the orchestra is," says Lisa-Natasha. "Find me one where half the audience doesn't have gray hair and a walker and I'll say we have a fighting chance."

The quietest of the group, Paul, now speaks, his accent so strong that he seems to be speaking in a second language, although he is English. "Of concern to me is the future of the orchestra in the compositional landscape. In a world where composing is more and more private, and more and more about recording and not performance, why should we bother arranging for seventy parts?"

Bruce smiles at Suzanne. They know the thrill of being one of those seventy.

The others' responses are equally predictable according to each person's stance toward music and place in the world. Suzanne thinks back to Curtis, when these conversations excited them to stay up late, drinking and arguing. She wishes she was still capable of that. But she is hardly paying attention until she hears Alex's name. It comes from Greg.

His voice is beautiful, with a complex texture to the tone, the sound of beads being pulled across a stiff fabric. "How was he trained?"

Olivia fields his questions, and those of the others, about Alex's early days on the piano, his first job as a conductor, his rise. But mostly she shares his stories of musicians, particularly of the difficult or downright insane. She tells the story about the principal flutist who chose to be demoted rather than sit next to her ex-boyfriend, the orchestra's second flutist; the soloist who demanded all red candies; the famous pianist who played with tobacco tucked into his lip; the pubescent violin prodigy with a drinking problem; another who would eat only organic food; a beautiful cellist who always slept with someone seated on the first row of the balcony. "Never mind if she got a more attractive offer. Had to be someone from the first row of the balcony."

They are stories Suzanne has heard before, told better. It seems that it is now Olivia's turn to be the one who has drunk too much, whose composure has frazzled.

Her mouth moving like a hinge, the shape of her skull evident under her skin, Olivia asks, "You played under him, didn't you, Suzanne? I don't recall him having any stories about you. I guess you were easy." She smiles. "To work with, I mean."

Greg looks at Suzanne, a gaze she interprets as sympathy. Lisa-Natasha stares at her, forgetting to either eat or put down her fork.

"You know me," Suzanne says, "always aiming to please the conductor *and* the composer. May we be so lucky tomorrow." She raises her glass to the table, hoping this is enough to turn the attention away from her, away from Alex, to move the conversation along to something else.

"Here's one for you," Olivia says. "A conductor and a violist are standing in the middle of the road. Which one do you run over first?"

This is not one of Petra's jokes, and Suzanne does not know the punch line. No one else answers, either.

"The conductor," Olivia says, her voice now low and controlled.

"Okay," Bruce says. "Why the conductor?"

Olivia's smile widens greedily. "Easy. The conductor first because you always take care of business before pleasure."

Eric laughs hard, and Bruce laughs politely. Greg stares at Olivia. Lisa-Natasha stares at Suzanne, who looks over her shoulder. She's not looking for any concrete reason, but it catches the waiter's attention. Suzanne realizes that she is still thirty minutes and a piece of baklava away from escape, and then she realizes that there's no safe ground to hide from anything that's happening. Her eyes follow the jumpy light of the twin candles at the center of their table, and she wishes she could will herself out of time altogether.

Thirty

Olivia is late to the fourth day's rehearsals, which are held in the orchestra's broad, spare, absolutely beautiful performance auditorium. Despite the cavernous ceiling spaces and open wings, the hall is made warm with color and the textures of wood, concrete, fabric. The effect is not emptiness but simplicity. Suzanne loves it immediately and wishes Alex could have conducted here instead of in the dilapidated glory of Chicago's red-and-white auditorium, suggesting a heyday decades gone.

Despite her jitters, despite everything, Suzanne feels strong, or at least at ease in her own body, with her own face. Today is the first time the full orchestra will work through each of the six compositions, and Suzanne is glad to be free of Olivia for now. Established composers and other guest faculty listen in, give broad impressions, occasionally make specific suggestions. There won't be much time to fix anything beyond the most horrible wrong moments—the public performance is one night away—but still this is meant to be an educational experience.

"Not ideal circumstances, but not unique," the conductor tells them. His Finnish accent, all but untraceable on the institute's first day, comes heavier now. Fatigue, Suzanne assumes, based on her experience with Alex and with Petra, though she hears Lisa-Natasha whisper "Faker" to Eric.

"Don't get caught up in the thrill—or in the agony—of hearing your work. Listen as dispassionately as you can to what you are actually hearing, not what you think you are going to hear or want to hear or what you are afraid of hearing. What you are actually hearing—that's its own skill—and be open to alterations as needed. This part is as important as the original setting down of notes on the page or whatever you thought you heard in your mind that day inspiration hit you while you were eating your oatmeal or—" he pauses and finds the spot where Greg is sitting. "Or while you were drinking your third scotch."

Suzanne sits through the compositions of the other composers, assuming the weight of Alex's name is the reason they are scheduled last. Eric and Lisa-Natasha are up first, and Eric leaves immediately afterward, as though there is nothing to learn from the others. Their two pieces have some similarities, including evidence of mathematics-based training, reliance on percussion and bass to drive rhythm, and certain uses of atonality and line fracture that have become stock in any music wanting to proclaim itself postmodern. There are differences, too, mostly in mood, with Lisa-Natasha's piece having a bit more fun than Eric's, which is almost uniformly dark and, Suzanne guesses, self-pitying. Wishing Doug were at her side, if only for entertainment value, she jots down a few personality notes for him.

Bruce's piece is also unsurprising given what she knows about him. It shows his classical training, his lifetime of experience in full orchestration, dependence on the violin roles, a pleasing if safe sense of symmetry, and a bright, exuberant sensibility. Paul's work is more complicated and interesting. The ubiquitous note-counter tabulated his piece as having the fewest notes of all the compositions, and he draws many of them out, letting them reverberate in the hall's still, cool air, reverberate in the listener's ear. The composition is titled "Water," and in it Suzanne feels water in a multitude of its forms. The music trickles, babbles, bubbles, sinks, gathers, roars, moves tidally in and out. Yet there's nothing obvious or easy about how he's done it. There is a bit of cleverness, but depth, too. Mostly it is lovely, nearly everyone agrees, and Suzanne looks at Paul with more respect, nodding when she catches his eye, glad that he seems pleased by his audience's enjoyment.

Suzanne appreciates the institute's willingness to produce such disparate works of music, its understanding that style is so often temporary in young composers, its desire to look beyond that for a more fundamental talent. All four pieces have been quite good, and she suspects the best is yet to come after the break, with Greg's short symphony.

The music proves her right. Greg's piece jumps in quality above everything else they've heard, and so she is surprised when two of the guest faculty voice sharp criticisms—not merely suggestions for the performance but actual dismissals of the work as a whole, words that cannot possibly help anyone a single day before a public performance. An older man leaps up to defend the piece, saying, "You can't criticize it just because it's a hundred times better than anything you ever wrote."

Greg, who sits two rows in front of her, spins around and puts his hand alongside his mouth. "Oh, good, we get to hear a battle of the Old Schools. I don't know whether it's worse to be attacked or championed."

"Your piece," Suzanne says as the speaking men continue to argue. "Your piece is really great."

His answer is simple—no puffing up but no false modesty, just an honest confidence. "Thank you."

247

Maybe she's so suggestible that Greg's turning to talk to her prompts her to imitate the move, or maybe she can feel the gaze on the back of her head. She turns, and there is Olivia. Suzanne does not know how long she has been there, presumably since the end of the break, throughout Greg's symphony and the discussion afterward.

There is something off about Olivia, or maybe on, some natural wildness she usually sleeks back, places under control. Maybe it's just her hair, which now sprays loose about her shoulders. But there's also again a strange set to her mouth. Though it's not crooked, it reminds Suzanne of Ben's mother on the boat at the scattering of Charlie's ashes. Someone with a plan gone astray, someone letting something out of herself that she's carefully hidden before.

"We're up next," Suzanne says just loudly enough to carry two rows. She spins back to face the orchestra, taking the deep inhalation that she has taken before every performance since her first recital in a church in South Philadelphia, wearing a dress her mother found at a consignment store, playing the Beethoven-for-kiddies piece well enough that everyone in the room knew she was different, knew she had something the rest of them didn't.

The violist barely keeps up with the technical difficulty, but he gets through, and the double reeds play beautifully—better than she's hoped or, more true, exactly as she's hoped. She closes her eyes and tries to hear the relationships between the solo line, her moving line, and the full orchestra.

One of the guest faculty members halts the peculiar second movement and suggests a stronger entrance by the brass. "Also," he says, "the strings are trying to rush the crescendos. Is that what you want?" he asks, turning to Suzanne. "It's your job to speak up."

From behind her she hears Olivia call out to the orchestra. "Let the conductor hold you, even slow down the crescendo at D. Too slow is better than too fast."

Suzanne's throat constricts, and she feels a twitch in a small muscle on the right side of her face. For that brief moment she thinks she is having a stroke. Her recovery is immediate, but still she remains silent, listening to the orchestra play out the Viola Concerto by Alexander Elling and Suzanne Sullivan. With full orchestration and herself in the audience instead of with bow in hand, she hears it for the first time. The concerto was written not to show her off but to ruin her. It was written not out of love but out of hatred.

Again her face twitches, followed by a crushing weight on her chest, and this time it feels not like a small stroke but like the end of everything. She *has* been wrong all along, spectacularly, humiliatingly, unbearably wrong. And now she has been undone.

As the conductor and concertmaster discuss strategies to prevent the audience from being fully duped and so angered by the false ending. Suzanne stands to leave.

She sees concern on Greg's face and on Bruce's, but only fascination on Lisa-Natasha's as she tries to back away but instead leans over and vomits all over the empty seat in front of her.

Thirty-one

Alone in her room, her stomach empty and her arms weak, Suzanne raises her viola and plays the viola line as if for the first time. Just to be sure, she tells herself, though she already knows. She digs her bow hard into her strings, makes every crazy turn, every rise and fall, twisting at the waist so she will not miss a note. Her breath fails her more than once, her right arm aches, and her neck pinches. No matter how much she wants to distrust her instincts, the music is now obvious to her. The concerto is an act of retribution.

Suzanne feels stripped even of profound grief, and the emotion she is left with is shallow and pale, thin as gauze, its color washed away. *Doloroso.* But nothing more.

She can think of only two ways to stop the farce that Olivia has cast her in: she can call the music director or she can call Olivia. She spins out each scenario. The first one unfolds predictably: there is anger, a scratched program, upset musicians, public exposure, humiliation. The second she imagines in several alternatives, but the truth is that she cannot imagine what will happen if she confronts Olivia because she cannot imagine what

Olivia will do. She has overestimated Olivia's humanity and underestimated her brilliance. She does not know if Olivia cares if her whole plan is exposed—maybe the publicity is even what she wants. Almost certainly she will threaten to talk to Ben. She will tell Ben, and Suzanne will lose him, too.

She thinks of her musical reputation, of the quartet, of Anthony's aspirations for them all. If the false Wikipedia entry about Alex calling music "a healing force" made headlines and ripped through the online world, how large a scandal might this be? What will its salacious headline be? Will people remember and care? Will they forgive Suzanne because she is the dupe, or is that the least sympathetic role of all to play? And she isn't just the victim, of course; she is the *other woman*, the one who set into motion the whole sordid sequence.

It is two in the morning when she calls Petra, and so she is surprised by her quick answer. "Thank god," Petra says. "I was starting to think you really wouldn't call me."

"It's not good news," Suzanne says and gives Petra her room number.

Petra arrives fast and wearing street clothes, as though she's just come in from a night out. Suzanne asks her how much she's had to drink.

"None. I quit." She meets Suzanne's look. "Not quite, but really I haven't had anything to drink tonight. I'm trying to quit. I talked to Daniel about it. I figure there's a chance I'm going to be a real single mom soon, and I need to learn how to do it."

Suzanne takes the armchair, propping up her feet, insisting upon that distance between them.

"Where is Adele? You didn't leave her with Ben, did you?"

Petra takes the bed, stretching out on her side, head propped up by her bent arm. "I asked him. Because he really is good with her, but he said no because he didn't think I should come here. He told me to stay away from you."

"So where is she?"

"This is how much I love you: I left her with Jennifer. She's probably charting her progress day and night, turning her into some color of cat." Petra rolls onto her back, then resumes her sideways position. "Suzanne, do you think we can start over?"

Suzanne laughs, a small sound. "That's what I asked Ben."

"And what did he say?"

"He said we can't undo what is done. We can just keep going. He wants that, I think, to keep going."

"And what's your answer? What do you want?"

Suzanne cannot see a simple reconciliation with Petra, but neither can she imagine that they won't be lifelong friends. Adele will need Suzanne, more than ever, even if Petra does shape up, grow up. After the terrifying surgery, she will need months of training, years of understanding. Her life will always be shaped by the simple, hard facts that she was born deaf and has no father she knows.

"I need you," Suzanne whispers.

Petra springs up, starts to approach Suzanne but holds back a few feet. "I need you too, honey, more than you can guess."

"No, I mean I need you right now."

Petra looks confused, then hurt. "Taking me up on my offer? Maybe I deserve it, but please don't do that to me."

"Not everything's about sex, Petra. There are other ways to connect people. Always going for the genitals is not a permanent strategy."

"Maybe it's the only way I'm good at."

"I have a lot to tell you. If you love me, really love me, you're going to promise me that you'll never tell any of this to anyone, no matter how tempting, no matter how mad you get at me. Or how mad you get at Ben. Or how drunk and gossipy you ever feel. Can you say that?"

Petra sits down, leaning back on her hyperextended arms, feet hanging off the side of the bed. "It's the least I can do. Tell me the whole thing of it."

Suzanne starts at the beginning, with *Harold in Italy*, and the telling of her story takes a full hour as she tries to reconstruct the geographical order of her love affair with Alex. She tells Petra about the music, about her early jealousy, about his dark moods, about the night they made love while Felder played, about how lonely she always felt with Ben, about her guilt, about wanting money and fame or just to be special, about every performance she and Alex ever sat through together. She tries to remember details as she tells, so that Petra can understand what her story really is. Maybe her friend can tell her how she has felt, how she feels. Finally she tells Petra about the plane crash, about Olivia's machinations and how fully deceived she has been, which brings her to this moment.

"My god. I always think I'm the shocking one, but look how boring I am."

Suzanne smiles, a genuine gesture.

"How did you hide all that? From Ben. From me."

"Maybe that's the part of me that was missing."

Petra lies down. After a stretch of silence, Suzanne wonders if she has fallen asleep, but she listens closely and hears the pattern of Petra's normal, waking breath.

Finally Petra sits up. "I think you just have to play things out."

"Do what she wants? Go on with it all?"

Petra nods. "Unless you want to explode your whole life, that's what you should do."

"It might explode anyway."

Petra nods. "But it will definitely explode any other way."

Suzanne nods short and fast, for a long time, settling into the idea, the plan that is no plan at all. "I'll be at her mercy."

"I think you already are, sweetie. If you defy her you'll be exploding your own life, but still it won't really be on your terms."

Petra and Suzanne sleep fully clothed, side by side, all morning. They order room service, Suzanne adding a ridiculously generous tip to the already steep bill. "It might be my last meal. Besides, empty stomach."

"I'm glad you can laugh about throwing up in front of a room full of music people."

"The alternative is too depressing," Suzanne answers, biting into a strawberry, trying to decide which sandwich she wants.

"I'm flying home a day later than you. I thought it was the right thing to do, to give you and Ben the house to yourself at first."

"You know we can't live together anymore."

"I figured that out by myself. I was just talking about right away."

"I promised I would always be there for Adele, and I will. We'll work it out so that it's good for her, so that it's okay for everyone. It doesn't have to happen tomorrow, so we can figure it out. We can't live together, but I will be there for her."

"Will you be there for me?"

Suzanne shrugs. "We're going to have to play that by ear."

Petra smiles, rueful. "Rotten pun."

"The best I can do, but I promise I'll be there at the surgery, and after. She's going to be able to hear, to hear music."

"Okay." Petra looks away, biting her lower lip, obviously close to crying. She repeats herself in a whisper, "Okay."

Thirty-two

Suzanne cannot stop the farce. She cannot even skip it. So when the time comes she dresses as if for performance, does her hair, puts on makeup, and packs her suitcase so she'll be ready to leave for the airport first thing in the morning.

She sits beside Olivia, not looking at her, among the other composers in the beautiful and full concert hall. She applauds for Eric's piece and Lisa-Natasha's, for Bruce and for Paul. She offers her loudest applause for Greg's symphony, because it is a work of art, a thing so smart and perfect that it throws off cool sparks.

Though the biographies of the great composers offer plenty of evidence to disprove it, Suzanne wonders if basic decency somehow makes a person a better composer, natural talent being equal, which of course it isn't. A question for Doug when she gets home.

When the orchestra retakes the stage in the configuration she designed, Suzanne's heart beats so fast that again she thinks she may die. The viola player stands, the director's baton falls, and the concerto is being played by a full orchestra, at full volume, for a full auditorium. An inverted fantasy, a nightmare.

It is also being played well. She may have stayed up all night, but however the viola player spent the night has done him good. He has her full admiration. Few players could even get through the torturous piece, and it's almost impossible for her to imagine pulling it off before an audience. Nevertheless, the compositional flaws in the piece as a whole are evident. They were inevitable, really, given the circumstances of the involuntary collaboration, one of the collaborators so fully in the dark. The piece is not without real merit, though, and Suzanne is proud to hear that the double-reed and cello parts are among its finer aspects.

There is some tittering and coughing during the second movement—though perhaps only because the evening's program has been so long and variegated—but the applause that follows the final of the twin endings thunders. Suzanne feels it in every bone. It seems that even her seat shakes. The standing ovation is hesitant at first, perhaps even reluctant, but when it comes it builds to mass release.

Olivia leans into her, squeezes her shoulder, and kisses her cheek with wet lips. Suzanne shifts her shoulder away, the movement more subtle than a jerk but with the same effect. She wipes the moisture on her cheek with the sleeve of her black crepe dress. Olivia tilts her head, her eyes wider than normal, then shifts to shake someone's hand.

The young composers turn to each other left and right, to the rows in front of them and behind, as people do when offering the sign of peace during Mass. Even Lisa-Natasha and Eric wear generous smiles. Bruce hugs Suzanne warmly, patting her on the back as he does. Paul shakes her hand with surprising strength. She and Greg simply make eye contact. *Sublime,*

Suzanne mouths to him. "What you did with that piece was really smart," he says, "I can tell it wasn't easy."

The rows of people disperse into the aisles, some heading toward the exits. Others move toward her with congratulations, which she accepts as quickly as possible without being rude and which Olivia accepts with clear pleasure. The heads coming and going, the lights, now on—all of it feels like moving through a carnival crowd, and Suzanne is relieved by the audience's eventual retreat, the fading noise. Some of the hangers-on, together with the other composers, depart for the reception with the musicians and orchestra donors—the institute's final event, one last chance to schmooze, the one chance to let loose. Suzanne doesn't feel like doing either, but she goes along, looking around for Petra's periwinkle dress.

As they enter the reception space, a quartet is playing Ravel. Coming up behind Suzanne, Petra says, "Everyone loves Ravel."

At first the composers hold together as a group, but eventually they are individually lured by the bar, the tables of food, people seeking conversation. Bruce lingers, probably for Petra. When the quartet moves from Ravel to Haydn, the energy of the crowd seems to lift slightly, and there is more noise from plates and glasses. Suzanne winks at Petra and says, "What they really like is Haydn."

Petra answers, "He's just easier to talk over."

An older man comes up to Suzanne and tells her he saw her play in Buenos Aires. "You were fabulous," he says. "I still remember it. Bach."

She thanks him, though she remembers vividly that she did not play Bach. Alex had managed to get them both invited to the festival, which had an all-Mozart program that year. Felder was there, on his rise, as were a lot of musicians. It was perhaps a year after St. Louis. Maybe because they were in another country, Alex and Suzanne were reckless, walking down the street arm in arm, holding hands at performances. They found breakfast one morning in an outdoor market, going stall to stall for fruit and bread and cheese. Alex surprised her with his fluent Spanish. "And you thought I only knew English, German, and the language of love," he said. People stared at them everywhere they went; she remembers that, too. At first she thought it was her imagination, but Alex noticed it, too, and said it was because they were so visibly in love.

They ate in a small park, listening to a *bandoneón* player—an old man with his hat out. When they finished, Alex gave him a twenty-dollar bill.

"A success!" Olivia says, approaching.

Petra watches her, saying nothing.

Olivia ignores her and fixes on Suzanne. "So I'll take it back to Chicago. If they say no, which I don't think they will, I'll move on to Philadelphia. And of course you will be the star next time. The music was written for you."

Olivia and Petra say nothing to each other, not even to exchange names or some pleasantry about the music or the food, until Petra says, "Do you know the story of Tomaso Albinoni?"

"Excuse me," Olivia says and leaves as though Petra has said nothing at all.

Petra maneuvers Suzanne to a corner of the room. "I was wrong."

For a moment Suzanne thinks she is talking about Ben, but she quickly understands that she means Olivia. "You can't let her take the concerto to a major symphony. When I told you to do what she said, I thought it was ending here."

"What about exploding my life, being at her mercy?"

"Bad advice. I underestimated her. I hadn't seen her yet. She's . . . she's . . . I don't know, maybe just really, really angry. More than I thought.

Now I think you have to stop this all and get away from her. Whatever happens, enough is enough. You can't take that to a symphony and say that Alex Elling wrote it, and you should never play it again." Petra's eyes are wider than normal, and she continues to nod as though she will nod until Suzanne agrees, however long it requires.

Suzanne looks into Petra's sea-blue eyes, looks at her soft mouth, her sharp curve of cheekbone, her neck, her shoulders. Her best friend. She wants to believe in her, in Ben, in herself, to choose to trust, to believe the words of the people who love her and not the people who wish her harm. The person who wishes her harm. She begins to nod with Petra.

After scanning the room, Suzanne makes her way to the corner where Olivia is talking to Lisa-Natasha.

"Please leave," Suzanne says, and her glare shuts down whatever half-clever remark Lisa-Natasha was about to zing her with.

Suzanne turns her back to the room, facing Olivia, who moves her glass of champagne from one hand to the other. Her composure seems to have returned, and the sequined jacket that looked gaudy in the hall when the lights went up looks more understated, sophisticated in soft light.

"Which quartet is that?" Olivia asks as the quartet starts a piece by Beethoven.

"A late one." Suzanne says, refusing to have her line of thought pulled away. "About Chicago. It's true that they might be interested in Alexander Elling's only work, but they won't be interested in the concerto. You'll soil his name, and yours, not just mine."

Olivia straightens herself to her full height and looks at Suzanne by casting down her eyes. "Do you think it isn't good enough? Did you fail to notice the standing ovation?"

Everything behind Suzanne softens, even the sound of the strings. "That was a generous audience clapping for a respected dead man after being warmed up by student compositions."

"That's not a very nice thing to say to me." Olivia's eyelids are half lowered, giving the effect of disdain but also of boredom—an inability to concentrate on words that are not admiring.

Suzanne does not know whether Olivia is feigning denseness or whether she has been genuinely blinded by her obsession and twisted success. "You never answered my friend's question about Tomaso Albinoni," Suzanne says, "Do you know the story? His most famous composition, the only one in anyone's repertoire, is the Adagio in G minor."

Olivia sips her champagne, now opening her eyes fully.

"And do you know when it was written?" Suzanne asks.

Olivia waits, never breaking eye contact.

"It was written in 1958," Suzanne says. "Albinoni died in 1751. Seventeen fifty-one."

Olivia still does not speak, so Suzanne continues. "It was written by Remo Giazotti, who after he was found out claimed the piece was based on Albinoni fragments. Maybe it really was, or maybe not at all, but Albinoni didn't write that adagio."

At last Olivia speaks, and vehemently. "It's not the same at all. All you did was some of the orchestration. Yes, you wrote some bits, the bassoon line, of course, and those stretches of cello. Brilliant, actually, but don't delude yourself that you wrote this."

Now Suzanne knows that Olivia's dimness is theatrical, a desperate performance depending on the slivered chance that Suzanne doesn't really know. Suzanne says, "I know I didn't write the concerto, Olivia. And neither did Alex."

Olivia watches her, her stare fierce and wild, the look in her eyes that of an animal deciding whether to attack or take flight.

"Did he ever write any music at all?" Suzanne asks.

Olivia exhales, and her mouth goes slack. "You were right in the first place. He was never fond of concertos, and he would have told you if he was writing music. He would have shown you. You should have trusted your instinct. You should have trusted *him*."

Suzanne changes the angle of her stance and steps back until she finds the wall. She leans her head back, resting it so that she can look up into ornate rafters striping the ceiling. "Months," she says. "For months I thought I was in his mind, that I was getting closer and closer to him, learning more about him. That I was playing what he wrote for me. That I was *with* him again."

She glances at Olivia, who faces her, arms crossed and chin lifted—a gesture not of defeat but of triumph.

Olivia's voice is at once deep and hissing, a tone Suzanne has never heard and does not want to ever hear again. "That's right, and all that time you were in *my* mind, playing my part, feeling how you made me feel. From now on, when you think of him you will also think of me."

The several hundred people in the room seem distant, separated from them by an ocean of air, their voices blending into a faraway hum. Suzanne shudders as she closes her eyes, lets the remaining image of low lights spin. Everything Olivia claims is true.

"Yes," Suzanne says, her eyes still closed, her head depending on the wall for support. "I thought I was in his mind, but I was in yours." She pauses before adding, "I promise you, it's a terrifying place."

Olivia's voice is right in her ear, moist. "If you met him tomorrow, would you do it all over again?"

Suzanne breathes in the question and turns it slowly, wishing she could give a true answer to herself. She pushes out from the wall, standing straight, a small but quick movement that startles Olivia.

When she recomposes herself, Olivia says, "I *would* do it all over again. I don't have to think about it for a second."

Suzanne feels stripped down to something simpler than emotion, in a place where honesty is all that is possible yet has little value. As she walks away, she hears Olivia say, "I took something away from you, but I gave you something, too."

The noise of the party blends, the individual sounds of quartet, voices, cutlery, feet melting into a homogeneous buzz, farther and farther away.

As Suzanne sits outside, in front of a hotel that could be in any of the cities she shared with Alex but instead is in one she barely knows, she pictures herself at home, in command of keyboard and paper, composing her first serious piece. It will be something modest in its ambitions, perhaps, but whole and hers from first measure to last. She imagines completing that last bar and bringing the score to Doug so he can tell her who she is.

Tomorrow she will fly home, and when she crosses the threshold of their house, she will find Ben, hunched over a cello, as though it is a child he is protecting from breaking waves. While the instrument stays silent, his long fingers will move along the strings and his foot will tap time. When he looks up, Suzanne will be unnerved by the dark eyes staring straight at her from under lashes so fair they are nearly white. She will take a seat across from him and say, "Really play it, full volume," and he will close his eyes and play a sonata—delicately layered, low and graceful, lovely and sad. In the music she will find the desire to tell him as much as he wants to hear, and, if he is willing, they will not start over but continue, a better variation on what they are.

Coda

The talcum light is just enough to guide Suzanne across the bridge to the place she seeks: a ramp near Notre Dame that slopes down into the Seine, a ramp that will soak her feet if she follows it to its end. She stops shy of the water.

Paris still sleeps, but the avian world awakens. Gulls shriek—one or two at first and then more—and ducks glide on the river, occasionally diving, their elegant silhouettes tipping to reveal their functional webbed feet.

From below the city looks very nearly as it has for centuries, as it has since the rebuilding of its first church, where Abelard taught and Dante prayed and where Suzanne once played on a cold January night.

It was the next morning that Suzanne stood here, watching these same ducks, or their forebears, glide atop the river's teal surface. Up early, though not quite this early, she stood shivering with Alex until they were interrupted by a man walking a tiny dog, which lifted a hind leg to wet the ancient rock.

Standing here, as Paris still sleeps, it feels possible that this is that morning. It feels possible that this is the morning Chopin arrived in the city or the morning Berlioz died here or any morning at all.

Paris still sleeps as Suzanne walks back through an uncannily empty Latin Quarter, toward the small hotel that houses the quartet's other members. Toward Ben, who has accompanied them as composer of one of the pieces they are performing. Toward Adele, who has traveled to hear the music.

Acknowledgments

I am deeply fortunate to be edited by Fred Ramey, represented by Terra Chalberg, and published by Unbridled Books—intelligent and generous people committed to the text entire.

Though I alone am responsible for any factual or musical errors contained in this work of fiction, two books informed my work: *The Lives of the Great Composers* by Harold C. Schonberg and *What to Listen for in Music* by Aaron Copeland. I also gleaned information browsing such music composition websites as *Music Theory Online: A Journal of Criticism, Commentary, Research, and Scholarship* and *The Harmonic Wheel*. Sitting in on a master class given by the St. Lawrence String Quartet was invaluable to my research, as was observing sessions of the Conductors Institute of South Carolina.

My greatest debts are to the composers and performers of the many recordings and concerts that fueled my writing—and to David Bajo and Esme Bajo for their companionship and saving humor.